HOME TO THE OUTER BANKS

By

DIANN DUCHARME

ISBN 13: 9780578373089
Kill Devil Hills Publishing, Kill Devil Hills, NC

For Sean, who loved the house at the beach too

Other books by Diann Ducharme

The Outer Banks House

Chasing Eternity

Return to the Outer Banks House

CHAPTER ONE

Abigail Whimble
January 1, 1881
Nashville, Tennessee

The stillness, the solemnity that brooded in the woods, and the sense of loneliness began to tell upon the spirits of the boys. They fell to thinking. A sort of undefined longing crept upon them. This took dim shape, presently—it was budding homesickness. Even Finn the Red-Handed was dreaming of his doorsteps and empty hogsheads. But they were all ashamed of their weakness, and none was brave enough to speak his thought.

—The Adventures of Tom Sawyer

I was never skilled at art, but I was tolerably capable of drawing straight lines using a ruler and a pencil. Now the paper was covered with both short and long lines in the dubious shape of a schoolhouse.

I'd been drawing the same schoolhouse almost every day, with minor variations, for many months. It was a simple, wooden structure, with three windows on each side and a small room in the back.

My own schoolhouse.

But first, I needed the money and assistance to build it.

I rubbed my icy hands together and looked out one of the second-story windows of College Hall, where I'd taught future teachers for the past four and a half years. Wind whipped the young branches of the elm trees that Mr. Stearns had planted five years earlier; they'd grown slowly, as had the Peabody Normal School, now officially called the State Normal College.

Though I rotated the classrooms in which I taught, the building was the only place in Nashville that seemed to offer solace, and I fled to it as often as I could. And with today being the start of a new year, I was filled with inspiration, so that I'd covered several pieces of paper with possible lesson plans well before noon.

A brief knocking came at the door, startling me. The building was dark and empty, the students and other faculty having gone home for the holidays two weeks before.

"It's me," came a man's voice.

"Come in, Mr. Wharton," I called, hurriedly pushing the pile of sketches and plans to the corner of my desk.

Yet his exuberant opening of the door flipped the papers, so I awkwardly bent sideways on my bustle to slap both hands atop them. Before I could turn, he was standing over me, smelling of starched cloth and coming snow.

"Teaching art next semester?" he asked, bending over the papers.

I flicked my hand, dismissing them, and stood to greet him.

"Happy New Year to you too," I said.

"Happy New Year, Abigail."

He kissed the back of my cold hand, his graying auburn beard pricking like pine needles. My eyes found the window again, avoiding his gaze.

"How did you know I was here?"

"In fact, I didn't. I was visiting with Eben earlier, and on my way back across the grounds, I saw the light of a lamp in the window. As usual."

He was to fetch me at the nearby house I shared with Emma Cutter, another female faculty member, in half an hour, to have a special New Year's meal with him at his home. To save time, I'd already donned one of the fine dresses he'd purchased for me, for the purpose of giving proper teaching demonstrations and conveying a sense of albeit uncomfortable professionalism. Provided as well were gloves and hats and, most recently, hair combs and perfume.

"We may as well depart, if you're quite finished with your sketching there. Wyatt is waiting with the carriage."

Yet instead of readying to leave, he reached for my drawings. "May I?"

I shook my head, but the papers were already in his hands.

"It's just...some scribbling. Nothing more."

Mr. Wharton perused the papers, more and more slowly.

"A schoolhouse, I see."

I strove for nonchalance, though my cheeks flared. "I'm pleased you were able to make it out."

"Oh, it's plain to see. You've devoted some careful effort to its rendering. Hardly scribbling, I'd say."

I watched him helplessly as he continued to stare at the drawings.

"What's all this?"

He pointed to the hills surrounding the schoolhouse, which were comprised of hundreds of tiny dots.

"Sand," I choked.

"Ah."

His eyes flicked to mine. He knew me as well as a father knew a daughter. Or a husband knew a wife, as some would surmise.

"And where would this schoolhouse on sand be constructed?"

"Nags Head."

The two words of which I was so fond came out as nothing more than a whisper. But the vision of my island schoolhouse shouted from my heart.

He slowly squared the papers on the desk before him, but instead of leaving them there, he rolled them up and held them tightly in his gloved hand.

Mr. Wharton's longtime employee, Wyatt Hayes, waited atop the carriage; both he and the horse were hunched against the cold. Yet he grinned when he saw me, fumbling with the blowing ribbons of my hat with my gloved hands.

"Afternoon, Miz Whimble," said Wyatt, jumping down from the carriage. "He found you working on your day off again? New Year's Day too."

"I'm busier than ever. Did Mr. Wharton tell you that as well? I'm teaching grammar, English literature, geography and even physiology, though I know nothing about it. That's why I can never leave College Hall."

"He don't tell me none of that," he said. "But he did say he's tired of paying your rent at the house yonder."

"Did he?" I asked, over Mr. Wharton's playful objections. "I do go home to sleep, you know."

"If you say so," he chuckled, opening the carriage door for me. "How's that Miss Cutter faring these days?"

My housemate Emma was a lively and intelligent woman who

sandy soil. Close enough to hear the lullaby of the sea. A heartbeat, deep in the ground.

She would have been twelve years old now. And if she hadn't passed on, I would never have left Nags Head. We'd be a family. I'd be a part of life there, one of the hardy people who lived on the shifting islands, keenly aware that every day brought a new challenge, a new risk. And, often times, simple joy.

Not living in this city, with the constancy of shouting trains and sprawling construction and crowded streets. The emboldened thrust of white superiority. The whiskered faces of the curious men lacking the sun-warmed affection of Ben's.

Day by day, the schoolhouse had taken shape in my mind.

The next afternoon, Mr. Wharton appeared at my snowy doorstep, his cheeks red from the cold. Wyatt waved from his seat atop the carriage, his breath encircling his thick wool hat.

"Good afternoon, Abigail," he said, a business-like clip to his voice. "Have you a few moments to spare?"

"Of course. Come in," I said, trying to read his blinking eyes for a sign of his intention. "Tea?"

He stamped the snow from his boots. "That would be welcome."

I heard him stoking the fire in the small parlor while I boiled water on the tiny kitchen stove. It was never hard for him to make himself at home here, in the house where he paid my rent.

"Is Miss Cutter at home perchance?" he called.

"No, she's visiting her beau's family home in Kentucky," I reluctantly called back. He didn't like for me to be here by myself, and would without fail offer me the guest quarters in his home if he ever learned of Emma's absence.

I prepared a tray and carried it to the table, then seated myself in the chair opposite him and poured the tea. The fire struggled on its grate, and we stared at it for too long in the heavy cold.

Finally, he spoke. "I suppose I shouldn't delay in telling you. *I* will finance your school."

"What?" My rising hope overrode the dismay filling my belly. "No, Mr. Wharton. I couldn't let you fund it yourself. That was never my intention."

"Ease your mind, Abigail. I've thought it over quite carefully, and I must say, I'm looking forward to the venture. Something we can take on *together*. A fitting tribute to our longtime, mutual interest in education."

"I don't know what to say," I stammered.

He would own the schoolhouse, I thought. But that didn't matter, I reasoned quickly, as long as I could teach there.

"Your passion for the downtrodden and disadvantaged has always inspired me. It's why I came to the Freedmen's School in the first place, you know."

"Thank you," I said simply. "Thank you very much."

He nodded, his eyes cast to the tea tray. "Will you write to Benjamin of your plans?"

"Of course." And yet putting more words in another stifled letter filled me with dread.

He seemed to be leaning closer to me across the table, his mouth struggling to connect thoughts into words.

"Since Anna passed, you've grown to mean so much to me. More than I ..."

"Yes," I interrupted. "You've always looked out for me. And I am in your debt, Mr. Wharton, for your guidance and wisdom."

"I've asked you to call me Graham."

Repulsed, I shook my head, yet smiled to ease the blow. "I could never do that."

A ripple of irritation darted across his face as he reached for the teacup.

"You should publish articles for the education journals, so be sure to take note of each step of the process. A daily journal."

"I always do."

He was quiet for a long moment, sipping his tea. At last he reached into his case and pulled out some papers.

"You may think this a strange coincidence," he said, placing the papers on the table. "But a while ago, I came upon some quality research regarding so-called word blindness. For your former student at the Elijah Africa School."

"Luella," I said softly.

I'd thought of her often, her determined eyes beaming from her beautiful face. She'd struggled with the way words broke down according to sound, which had made reading and writing almost impossible.

Asha had written that she'd stopped coming to the schoolhouse not long after I left the Outer Banks. Then, at the age of fifteen, she'd married a sharecropper from the mainland, and she and her mother Ruth had moved to live with him. Asha had received no mailing address.

From what Mr. Wharton had discovered in his line of work, their departures were part of a growing trend on the island; we'd learned that there were hardly any Negroes remaining in the once-thriving freedmen's colony.

15

Even Asha had left for a teaching post in Bertie County, because despite the surplus from the Peabody Education Fund, the schoolhouse where we'd taught had stood empty most days of the week. At last, it had closed, its supplies cleared out and sent to the school where Asha now taught.

Mr. Wharton launched into a discussion about the findings of the word-blindness research, but my mind had traveled to North Carolina and would not easily come back. The shape of the schoolhouse I would bring to Nags Head no longer seemed dreamlike; it appeared in my mind as if drawn with a master hand, strong and sure and full of promise.

I'm coming, Ben. I'm coming home.

I pulled one from my bag and handed it to him. He touched it gentle. "Where did you find them?"

"Down south a-ways. Just washed up on a sandbar during low tide, I'd wager. I'll show you, if you want."

He picked up his shovel and one of his glass jars and walked alongside me down the shore. The sanderlings gave chase to the backing water, peckin' away for food and payin' us no mind.

"I've been on these shoals for over a month, and you're the first man I've seen," I said.

"You'll see more of us, now that we've all begun our collecting," he said. "You're a shad fisherman?"

"Sometimes I am."

"Most of the shad fishermen are set up at the mouth of the North River."

"Yessir, I hear 'em day and night. But shad aren't what I'm after, right now. You see, I'm on a holiday of sorts. A bit like Robinson Crusoe, excepting the fact I can leave on my skiff any time I want."

"Indeed," he said, looking askance at me. "Have you read *Crusoe*, then?"

"Oh, sure. First book I ever read. And just about the last, truth be told."

"The first book? You must have had a very good teacher," he said, shiftin' his glass jar into the crook of his other arm and holdin' out his hand. "I'm Wilson Baptist."

"Benjamin Whimble," I said. "From Nags Head, up yonder on the Banks a-ways. Never been this far south afore. But I've lived on barrier islands my whole life, so it wasn't too hard to pick up and plant myself here for a time. Though I don't have a notion what these collections of sand are called."

"Where we stand is called Carrot Island."

"Carrot, huh? Nary a carrot to be seen here, and I've looked all over."

"That bit there is called Town Marsh, then Bird Shoal, and Horse Island. I've heard Bird Shoal is the most fruitful collecting grounds. A considerable proportion of living shells, and tubiculous worms of several species. Echini, starfishes, and jellyfishes too. That's likely where you found the sea biscuits."

When we reached the sandbar, Wilson waded out into the shallows and started diggin' about. I lay down in the sand, hands behind my head.

He called over to me, "You don't have to supervise me, Benjamin."

"Oh, I don't give a darn about your diggin'. I'm just enjoyin' the human company. Like good old Robinson and Friday, you know."

But every now and then I snuck a look over to him, back hunched over and draggin' his shovel about, where the sea cookies were likely burrowed. A grist of time passed, and he still hadn't found a single one. I started to diggin' with my hands right where the water met the sand and soon found two of them, purple and spiny and wigglin' in my hand.

"Jackpot, Wilson."

"Where did you find them?"

"You can just see the shapes of their shells, right under the sand. Like little ghosts."

He hurried to fill up his jar with salt water and sand.

"May I?" He took the sea cookies from me and placed them gentle into the jar. We watched them float around and settle onto the sand.

"You seem to have a knack for this," he said, with a fair amount of jealousy. "I suppose you could say I'm more of the *academic* variety of scientists. Fieldwork has always been challenging for me."

But instead of offerin' to buy the lot, he said, "I'm impressed with your innate ability and knowledge of the area. Are you interested in working for us as a collector, Mr. Whimble?"

"Workin'? As in, for money?"

"Indeed. You can live on Carrot Island and collect specimens for us all over the coasts here, for the summer season. That is, if you're not otherwise engaged in bird-watching."

I'd never thought a man could be paid for collecting the ocean's cast-offs. I looked about once more at the books, the jars, the living creatures all around me, and a queer feeling came upon me, a feeling I hadn't felt in a long time.

"How about we cut a deal where I collect your specimens, and in return, I can come in here to this laboratory now and then and learn from you?"

Both men looked at me, then at each other, then back at me. "You say you want to *learn* from us? In exchange for your work?" asked Dr. Brooks. "No payment?"

"Yessir. I believe that's what I mean. I like the looks of this place."

Dr. Brooks shook his head. "I will have to insist on paying you for the work you do."

"Well, if you *insist*, I reckon I can't say no."

He clapped his hands together. "You happen to be in luck, Mr. Whimble. I'm teaching a six-week elementary course in zoology, starting next week. Daily lectures will be given to a selection of collegiate students and professors. Right here in the laboratory. You are welcome to attend."

"A class? For college folks? I don't know if that's... I was hopin' to just peek in now and then. I might not be able to...you know, keep up. I don't have a notion what all those fancy names mean, for starters."

"No matter. It's an elementary class of instruction, as I said. We will go out dredging and collecting, in an effort to show them what can be done in their own classrooms. As our professional collector, you'll be right at home. It's nowhere near as challenging as one of my university classes at Johns Hopkins."

"I reckon that's alright then."

Dr. Brooks reached out a hand for me to shake. "So we have a bargain. We'll see you on the morning of June the sixth. Bearing more of your valuable specimens, I hope. Oh, and have Mr. Bishop here find you a new set of clothes for the classroom instruction. Yours are...well, rather worn."

Wilson and I sailed back to Carrot Island with a heavier load than what we'd left with. I no longer had my collection, havin' left it all with the scientists, but I did have a grist of supplies I'd picked up in town for my summer stay on the island. Coffee, hardtack, cans of peas and beans and sardines, a bag of apples. And a set of new clothes Wilson had given me from his own wardrobe.

The night came upon me soon after, and I was so tuckered I couldn't hardly think about warming up a supper. I headed for my hut to sleep, but my mind would not be settled.

Me, Ben Whimble. Learnin' from somebody who wasn't his wife. Learnin' about animals in the zoo of the world. Zoology, he called it. Just the notion of it seemed to light a fire in me, deep in my chest, that warmed my blood and thawed my limbs.

A new feelin', to be sure, for these days I saw nothin' but wood on water. Felt to be one and the same with that wood, dried and darkened by sun and salt. *Tessa*'s every creak brought on an ache in my bones. Every lap of the water on the hull was like time passin' me by, year by year by year.

Not learnin' much except how to get old.

There was a time when loggerheads and hammerheads and cow-nosed rays came to me in dreams, messengers of plenty. But those golden dreams had gone rusty. The truth had been set before me, not much more savory than a bucket of chum: *Tessa*'s days as a fishin' boat were done.

And as for my marriage—well, Abby was long gone. I figured it had come time to let her go, from my heart and my mind both.

But there wasn't any accountin' for what the heart's learned and reckons it still knows.

CHAPTER THREE

Abigail Whimble
June 30, 1881
Nags Head, North Carolina

*He had discovered a great law of human action, without
knowing it—namely, that in order to make a man or a
boy covet a thing, it is only necessary to make the thing
difficult to obtain.*

—The Adventures of Tom Sawyer

I stood like a figurehead at the bow of the steamboat, the first to
sniff out the salt on the breeze, the first to feel the marshy air lifting
from the Roanoke Sound.

What once had seemed impossible—laying my eyes on this fragile,
lonely land—now grew real before me. Some days, awash in the foul
air of Nashville, the Outer Banks had seemed nothing but a dream.

But now, the tallest of sand hills, and the trees and houses they
embraced, spread before me like old friends in a receiving line.

Witchcraft, how the view would have me believe that no time
had passed at all.

Was Ben one of the many fishermen already out in the sound, his skiff cutting through the waters so close to us? I tried to search their faces but couldn't make them out in the shadows of their sails.

My fingers curled tightly about the railing, even as my fellow passengers crowded about me at the bow, full of excitement, the long day and night of travel from Elizabeth City on a crowded steamboat now just a bad memory. The summer season was in full swing, and everyone, children and adults both, jabbered loudly about the giant sand hills, the crashing waves, the fish and foxes that awaited them. I had been one of them, thirteen years ago.

I tried to partake of their excitement, yet it washed over me, dripping wasted to my feet.

"Abigail?" Mr. Wharton had positioned himself beside me once again. I'd spent a good portion of our long journey from Nashville evading his proprietary presence.

"Are you feeling unwell?"

I shook my head. My years of seasickness had long ago left me, thanks to Ben.

"Are you hungry, perhaps? The cook has prepared bacon and eggs. I can fetch you a plate, if you wish."

"No, thank you. I'm not hungry."

"Perhaps some coffee?"

I ground my teeth. "No. Nothing, thank you."

The steamboat trawled toward the shoreline, but the hotel hadn't shown itself. I still recalled the way that it had looked when it was new. It had grown over the years, I'd discovered, and apparently stood three stories tall and boasted one hundred rooms, a ten-pin bowling alley and nightly square dancing in the dining room. There was even a wooden railway to the oceanfront, with a mule and tram making trips back and forth from the hotel.

Mr. Wharton had acquired two rooms for the duration of the summer, as we hoped to have the schoolhouse up and running by the fall.

In my heart, I imagined spending most of my nights at the house with Ben, but I would never say such a thing to Mr. Wharton, who I could feel watching me from under the brim of his top hat.

"Does it seem like home?" he asked, rather impertinently.

Was home where my husband lived? Where the sandy earth held the remains of my lost child? Was home where I wanted to spend the rest of my days? I refused to answer him.

"I'd forgotten how barren it is," he said, moving even closer to me. "Except for Nags Head Woods, of course."

The deep green of Nags Head Woods, the site of our wedding, thirteen years ago, stretched for five miles along the coast, hugged on both sides by the large, white sand hills.

"Ben told me that long ago, the whole of the Outer Banks was lush and green with all manner of trees, threaded with grapevines. But once the English arrived, they cut down the trees and grazed livestock, eventually leaving nothing but sand."

"How unfortunate. Now it seems the sand hills are taller than the trees!"

"The hills grew so tall that they acted as a barrier. The forest has thrived in the shadows, protected from the salt spray and wind," I said. "Some of the trees are hundreds of years old. But when the northeast winds blow, it moves the sand steadily southwest, covering the trees and leaving stumps in its wake."

He chuckled. "The sand has appeared to devour the hotel as well."

As we watched, the roof of the big hotel slowly came into view, surrounded on all sides by the encroaching dunes. Oblivious to the towering sand, guests milled about the property and stood outside their rooms, enjoying the morning.

"That structure can't be long for this world," said Mr. Wharton. "One big storm could cover it completely."

I shrugged. "I've learned not to predict anything where sand and water are concerned."

"How wise," he said, a touch of sadness in his voice. "You must sound a true Banker, Abigail."

Soon, the long wharf grew out of the water before us, and the steamboat anchored. Little scows were at the ready to load our cases and other belongings to transport the half mile to the hotel. With our baggage safely stowed, Mr. Wharton and I made our way down a narrow staging of plank, soon becoming one with a crowd of people on the land near the hotel.

A few locals milled around the nearby market, watching the new visitors with wary eyes. I searched every face, ready for a reunion, but recognized no one.

Settled in my simple room, my mind stalled, more concerned with the sand piled halfway up the window, blocking the morning light, than I was with my impending reunion with Ben. He'd never answered my letter, so I wasn't even sure where he was living.

At once, I was faced with my own folly, and I had the most twisted notion of returning to Nashville on the next steamer. Perhaps I was tired from the journey, a jumble of trains, coaches and inns, but I was no longer spellbound by Nags Head.

I lay back on the rough bed coverlet and stared at the unpainted, unplastered ceiling boards, listening to the commotion of voices and banging doors of my fellow guests. My room smelled of pipe smoke and chamber pot, yet opening the window would risk the pile of sand crashing straight onto the hotel room floor.

A rap on my door startled me from my malaise.

"Mr. Wells is here," Mr. Wharton said through the door. "I suggest we take our luncheon with him and discuss preliminary plans."

My nerves fired with irritation; Mr. Wharton well knew that I wanted to seek out Ben before I'd done anything else. But since he'd taken on the financing and the construction, as well as the travel accommodations, I'd become a shadow of a presence on my own project. And now the builder from Elizabeth City whom Mr. Wharton had hired was already here, waiting.

"Yes, of course," I bleated, despising myself.

The humid restaurant puffed with the scent of fried fish and spices. Mr. Wells was already seated at a table, large papers before him, but he stood when we entered the room. He was a clean-shaven, trim-bodied man in a tie and brown suit coat.

Not wasting any time, he turned his papers toward Mr. Wharton.

"See here now, sir. I've kept the general look of your school. Added windows to the room in back, all with storm blinds. You'll need those for certain. And here's the door, with the woodstove in the middle," he said. "And the big difference is this—I've put her on pilings, just over the sound. Access is important. If the school is on the water, folks from all over can come right up and tie their boats."

"I should've thought of that myself," I marveled, sifting through the architectural drawings.

But he barely spared me a glance as he explained even more of the intricacies, including the strategic locations of the well pump and the outhouse.

"I'll hire a local crew once we settle on a location. I've got a couple places in mind I'd like to show you," he said, taking the papers from my hands.

"Now?" I asked, endeavoring to quell the frustration in my voice.

"Unless you want to eat first? It's not quite the dinner hour, is it? The locations aren't too far from here, and my buggy is waiting just outside."

I still wasn't remotely hungry; my stomach clenched with nerves, with thoughts of Ben, possibly waiting for me in the house he'd built for us, sitting like a stone in my core.

Mr. Wharton clapped his hands. "I say we get started. Bring along some ham biscuits from the kitchen and a jug of iced tea. Abigail often forgets to feed herself, she immerses herself so deeply in her work."

On the bench of a horse-drawn buggy, we began to carve our way along the road of Nags Head Woods, which was more of a sandy pathway than a paved avenue. There were few farms this far south; most of the homes here housed fishermen and were perched on pilings over the sound. From my seat on the buggy I could see laundry lines full of clothing, linens and fishing nets, and skiffs tied to the pilings below their homes.

Mr. Wells and Mr. Wharton discussed the history of land ownership on the island, but I was left to dwell on my thoughts, my opinions and observations not required. I fought the gurgling urge to tell Mr. Wells to stop the horse—that seeking out Ben was my priority.

But the men wouldn't understand. They would question my ability—a maudlin, oversensitive woman—to be a part of this project in any way, other than as its future teacher.

After a few slogging minutes, the buggy stopped, and Mr. Wells bade us come with him. Mr. Wharton helped me down, and we followed Mr. Wells through tree branches and duffs of leaves to a clearing in the middle of a marshy cove.

"Now, watch your step here, Mrs. Wharton," said Mr. Wells. "It's a bit sticky in places."

My face flushed at his mistake, but I assumed he meant to say "Whimble." I would have corrected him, but we were already walking through long, wet seagrass, forcing me to lift my skirts and tread carefully.

"Here we are," he said, spreading out his arms. "About the middle point of Nags Head Woods for the villagers on foot. Deep enough water for boats to come and go. You'd get folks from both the north and south, I expect."

The sound before us reached all the way to Roanoke Island, once a home for Ben and me when I was teaching at the Elijah Africa Freedmen School. I'd sailed a skiff back and forth countless times across that body of brackish water, sometimes alone, but mostly with Ben. He'd proposed to me on his skiff on this same stretch of water. He'd lain his forehead on my knees, then had looked up and asked me to marry him.

"This is it," I said.

Toads hummed here and there, and the water licked the shore grasses as sweetly as a cow's tongue. It thread its fingers through the deadwood of old trunks and fallen branches, where a few turkey vultures rested, watching us warily. Ben's childhood home wasn't far off at all.

"Would you like to see the other location?" Mr. Wells asked Mr. Wharton.

"No. This is just right, Mr. Wells," I insisted. "Perfect, actually."

"She knows what she wants," said Mr. Wharton, his eyes meeting mine.

"Fact is, I showed you the best location first," said Mr. Wells. "The other one lacks the...well, I guess you'd call it the *magic* of this site."

"Magic," I repeated. Ben's blue eyes, small containers of a vast love. "Yes."

Mr. Wells turned to Mr. Wharton for confirmation, and he nodded.

"This bit of land is owned by an elderly couple," he continued. "And from what I've found out, they're happy to donate it for a schoolhouse, though a church might have suited them better. The villagers take turns hosting a preacher from the mainland in their homes on Sundays.

"But I say it's about time somebody built a schoolhouse here. My grandmother grew up in Colington, and she couldn't even spell her name, though it didn't bother her one bit. Matter of fact, I think it was a point of pride."

When Mr. Wells pulled the buggy around to the hotel entrance, we found it thronged with men and women in heavy, dark bathing costumes lining up for the mile-long wagon ride to the ocean side. Bathing in the ocean had become a glamorous activity.

"I confess, I didn't bring appropriate bathing attire. Did you?" asked Mr. Wharton, as we made our way through the chattering bathers.

"No," I said, recalling the heavy wool contraption Asha had sewn for me, all those years ago. It had never even taken on water.

I certainly couldn't tell him that once upon a time I was accustomed to swimming naked in both the sound and the sea, Ben at my side.

At the door of my hotel room, Mr. Wharton fidgeted with the brim of his hat.

"Would you like me to accompany you? I won't go in the house. Or anything like that."

I couldn't hide the surprised distaste on my face. "Oh no, Mr. Wharton. That wouldn't do."

He nodded to his feet. "No. I thought not."

Bowling balls knocked down pins not too far from us, happy men hollering victories.

"Will you be back for supper?" he asked, attempting nonchalance.

"I'm not sure."

"I hope...it goes well, Abigail."

"Do you?"

The words escaped my lips before I'd thought to stop them.

"Of course I do," he answered, backing away from me.

He tipped his hat and hurried to unlock his own door.

In my room, I took a moment to look into the spotted mirror that hung above my washstand.

My skin was no longer brown from the sun, yet a fair number of freckles still dusted my nose and cheeks, all the more apparent next to the bright green and gold dress I wore. My red hair was still dark and thick and hung to my waist, when not pinned into a bun beneath a bonnet. Faint lines reached from my eyes and lined my brows, but my lips curled into a tentative smile.

Would Ben still find me desirable? I was one year shy of thirty years old—a middle-aged woman.

I retied my bonnet into a shapely bow beneath my chin and headed out the door into the warm afternoon.

I well knew it was only a short walk down the hotel boardwalk toward the ocean, then a detour south through a patch of shaggy brush and stunted trees to the house. Yet as I walked, it seemed those landmarks weren't there. There was nothing but flat sand as far as the eye could see.

My legs ached from lifting them up and down in the sand in my long dress and underskirts, and my breath came short and hot.

I stopped trudging and stared around me. *I should have come to the house by now*, I thought. Perhaps I'd gotten confused; a handful of new houses had been built by the sea, possibly upsetting my sense of direction.

I retraced my steps, all the way back to the boardwalk, then back again, calling forth memories deep inside me. I spun in a circle on the spot where I believed the house to be, righting myself.

The ocean rolled nearby, the seabirds called.

But the house was gone.

Where was Ben? Where was my daughter's grave?

Trying to quell the panic, I hurried back to the hotel and found the entrance swarmed with hotel guests. Baggage crowded the small room, and children and even dogs hopped about. I waited by the open door until the crowd dispersed, trying to catch my breath and tell myself I wasn't caught in a nightmare.

At last I could see the clerk, his deeply wrinkled face red and irritated. I stepped up to the desk.

"Hello, sir. I'm looking for Ben Whimble."

He leaned over and squinted at me with rheumy eyes. "Benny Whimble? He's always snatching up the pretty ones, but darned if I can figure out why."

Spots swam in my eyes; sweat trickled down my temples. His words washed over me, unheard.

I stuttered, "It seems the house he built near the ocean a few years ago is gone?"

"Land sakes, little lady. He moved that house to the sound side three, four years back. Big storm almost did it in. It's over yonder on the water, right past the market."

"He moved it? The entire house?"

"Took all the men of Nags Head just about, but it got moved. That's how he built it, you know. Slide rollers under its boards and hoist it up, then roll it across the sand."

"He built it that way," I repeated.

"Got to plan for the Resurrection, you know."

I mumbled a thank-you as he cackled and hurried out the door again.

Past the market was a narrow sand pathway of sorts, through a few low trees and yaupon bushes and not much else. I scanned the shoreline for a house, and soon made out a weather-blackened dwelling on a sandy rise.

I slowed my pace and walked closer. Was it the same house? It looked to be, but it had been enlarged with a ramshackle kitchen house, its chimney puffing out smoke.

A fenced garden thrived beside it, likely full of root vegetables. Fishing nets were strung along the porch, ready for repairs. Chickens pecked in a pen. A few skinny pigs, left free to roam the island, milled about close to the sound shore, nibbling on the marsh grass. And clothing was strung from the line in back. Women's clothing. A dress of homespun, a shirtwaist and a skirt. Stockings.

And also, men's clothing. Trousers, shirts, a pair of overalls.

Curling my hands into fists, I stepped closer now, invisible steps.

But I heard the front door of the house bang, and I crouched quickly behind some bushes. Footsteps went lightly down the steps to the ground, then silence.

Why was I hiding? What if it was Ben?

I peered around the bushes to see a young woman strolling to the laundry line with a basket swinging from her hand, her glorious blond hair blowing free, no pins or knots to hold it secure. A girl still, on the verge of womanhood.

She placed the basket down and began pulling the pins from the line and folding the clothing into the basket with easy movements. At last she turned back to the house, and I saw that even with the strain of the heavy basket, her face was beautifully arranged.

He's always snatching up the pretty ones.

She exuded a sense of belonging there in that resilient, simple house, with the calm sound and sailing boats a constancy.

How naïve I'd been, believing Ben to be waiting for me after all this time. How selfish, to leave my daughter's grave, my home, the people who'd mattered the most to me.

Mr. Wharton had been right; I'd waited too long to return.

When the woman went inside, I turned to go. The pigs followed me, squealing in derision, back to the hotel.

I limped into my room, blisters already bubbling on my toes and ankles. I'd somehow forgotten about proper Nags Head footwear. My suede shoes were completely wrong for sand walking. I reached down to pull them off and saw that they were already scratched and dirty.

I untied my bonnet and lay on the bed, expecting to cry, yet no tears came.

The dingy white walls of the room, the loud voices in the dining room, the stale, humid air and sand-covered window conspired to convince me that I was not at home on the Outer Banks. That I'd never lived here, never been a part of these barrier islands. *I was merely a visitor*, said the room, like many others that had come here.

But a stubborn anger grew.

This was my home, I answered. The life I'd lived here had been sanded into my bones.

I rose up from the bed, shoved my sore feet into my shoes, grabbed my sweaty bonnet, and left the room to its anonymity.

CHAPTER FOUR

Abigail Whimble
Nags Head, North Carolina
June 30, 1881

I could forgive the boy, now, if he'd committed a million sins!
—Aunt Polly, The Adventures of Tom Sawyer

I found myself at Ben's old cabin, surprised that at least something was where it should be. It should have collapsed—in spite of Ben's repairs—long ago.

Yet the windows and door had been boarded up and weeds grew window height all over the yard. The roof was still crooked, with multiple wooden patches all over it, and the doorknob was still a discarded spool.

No one had lived there in a long while, from the looks of it.

Ben had moved on.

Jacob and Ruby's cabin was just across the way, surrounded by flowers and gardens; smoke huffed from the chimney, and a shaggy brown cat welcomed me at the threshold.

I stood warily at the door, realizing that I'd never been invited inside; I'd always figured that Ruby had never quite warmed to me, knowing the history of my family.

As a girl, she'd been a slave for a farming family toward the north end of Nags Head Woods; when the war ended, she and her mother had chosen to leave the family but stay in the woods, at a location a few miles south. She and Jacob had married a few years later and built the house where they now lived, right next door to Jacob's best friend, Ben.

"I'm Abigail," I told the cat. "You must know my...well, he grew up in these woods."

The cat peered at me with suspicion, then got up and scampered through the tangled brush. As it went, I spotted on the step a small pile of tailbones, likely those of rats and squirrels the cat had caught.

My feet throbbed in my shoes as I stood there, staring at the bones. Sweat gathered in my armpits, and I felt foolishly as if I was going to cry. At last, I took a deep breath and knocked on the rough-hewn door.

A little girl in braids soon pulled the door open, a tiny Ruby. Her lips were smeared purple with the probable juice of blackberries. In spite of my trembling lips, I grinned at her, full of happiness for Ruby and Jacob.

"Good afternoon. Are your mother and father at home?"

She didn't say a word, but her eyes grew large as she took in my dress and bonnet. "Mama, there's a fancy lady here!" she called. "She's from off, for sure."

"Fancy lady," scoffed Ruby from inside the house. I heard her bare feet stride across the floorboards to the door.

"Miz Whimble?" said Ruby, hands to her chest. She too seemed occupied with my clothing and wouldn't look straight at me. "Is that you?"

"Have I changed that much?"

She looked exactly the same as I remembered her: vivid and strong. Despite her homespun shirtwaist and skirt, covered with a stained and tattered apron, and her bare feet, Ruby exuded regality, with her lustrous, placid face, her soft hair pulled loosely into a knot. The memory of all those hard days caring for Oscar lit up like a lantern in the dark; Ruby had done her best to help me, to help my family.

I reached to grab her hands.

"I've come home," I declared. Ruby was the first person on the island I'd seen whom I knew; slowly the sense of unreality began to lift.

"You're back for good?" she asked softly, pulling her hands away and gazing at me with eyes gone suddenly serious.

"Yes, I am," I said with too much defensiveness.

She nodded thoughtfully. "Well, then. This is a happy day for me. A very happy day. We've all missed you terrible."

"You've been blessed with a child, I see," I said, looking down at the girl. "You must have birthed her soon after I left."

Ruby wiped the girl's lips with her apron. "How old are you, Frances?"

Frances didn't respond.

Ruby said, "She's four years old."

"And a half," said Frances.

Ruby glanced at her daughter, then back to me, so many unasked questions in the air.

"Frances, this here is Miz Abigail Whimble. She's married to Mr. Ben. Ain't that something?"

"No, ma'am," said the girl, shaking her head. "She ain't."

"Now, listen, Frances. She been off teaching teachers in Tennessee, haven't you, Miz Whimble? An important job, ain't that right? Teachers help little girls like you learn to read and such. Well, she teaching the teachers how to teach, you see? She can't come home regular."

"You never said," whined the girl. "I *know* Mr. Ben ain't got a *wife*!"

She stuck out her tongue and ran back into the house.

"Frances Craft! You get back here right now and say you're sorry to Miz Whimble. She's come a long way."

"No, ma'am!" hollered Frances.

"It's all right, Ruby. Let her be."

She sighed, and wouldn't look at me. "I reckon we should've told her about you. We just..." She threw her arms into the air. "We didn't see sense in asking Ben about you, and he never said a word."

She searched my eyes. "Why *are* you back?"

"To build a schoolhouse. Right there, as a matter of fact."

I pointed behind us, out toward the sound.

Her forehead curled in confusion. "Build a *schoolhouse*?"

"I've got an investor. A good friend, from the Normal College. He's here with me now, at the hotel."

She shook her head in exasperation. "We need to talk, I reckon. Come on in."

I followed her inside the one-room house, my eyes taking time to adjust to the flickering dimness.

"Jacob's out," said Ruby. "He's fishin' and proggin' every day, on account it's off-season at the Pea Island Lifesaving Station. He's a surfman now, did you know?"

"No, I didn't. That's wonderful!"

I stumbled after her, making out her tidy house, with blankets folded on the bed tick and shelves stacked with bowls and plates and cooking supplies. The warm room smelled of crab soup, seasoned with dill. Ruby stirred the pot, hung over the fire, and Frances sat upright on a tick on the other side of the room, watching me with sharp eyes. I stood awkwardly, the ceiling so low that I felt I was crouching.

"An Outer Banks surfman is a hard job to get," I said. "But Jacob's just the man for it. I've seen him in action, you know."

"The Pea Island station is all Negro men. Only one in the country," said Ruby, pride in her voice. "But folks didn't take it all that good. The keeper is a Roanoke Island man, Mr. Richard Etheridge. Had to hire an all-black crew, on account no white man would work under him. Then, right after its first season last year, the station burned to the ground, and they just now built it back up."

"Was it arson?"

She rolled her eyes. "What do *you* reckon?"

My face flushed. "It's a lonely job. And hard on the families. I do know that. It was, for me at least."

"We'll get by," she said, turning to me. "You can sit down, you know."

I sat in one of three chairs set up around the hearth and removed my bonnet. Ruby sat in the chair next to me, looking at me hard.

"Talk about lonely, now. Does Ben know your plans?"

"I don't know," I said with a heavy sigh. "I did send him a letter before I left Nashville. But I confess, we didn't keep in touch while I was gone. Just a few short letters."

"Mmm-hmm." Ruby screwed her lips tight.

"I tried to see him at the seaside house, but it wasn't there! The clerk at the hotel told me Ben had moved it to the sound side, so I went there to find him. But there was a young woman there, taking down laundry from the line. And I wasn't sure...well, I didn't stay."

"Oh, I see," she said, a little smile on her mouth. "You saw Miss Jennie, then. She lives there."

I shook my head, unable to speak as tears sprung to my eyes.

She eyed me. "Miss Jennie Blount. From up yonder in Whales Head?"

At my blank look, she added, "From up near the Jones Hill Life-saving Station?"

I suddenly recalled the letter Ben wrote about her, about how she'd knit him an indigo scarf. He'd told me that she'd reminded him of me.

"I remember her. Ben was fond of her. He felt badly about her family home getting swallowed by the sand."

"That's right. Well, that family been living there for a long while now."

"The whole *family* is living with Ben?"

"A whole mess of Blounts. Though their daddy Jimmy works at a fishery most of the year. Used to have a bad back, but seemed once that family got outta that sad house, he healed faster than you could spit. Ben *himself* lives in Mr. Oscar's house."

I shook my head, despite the wave of relief I felt. "But...it's all boarded up."

"He ain't here. Hasn't been for months!"

My thoughts moved as if mired in mud.

"Where is he?"

She shrugged as if she didn't know, but then said, "Jennie gets his letters, and Abner Miller reads 'em to her. Something about Beaufort, working some kind of job. He wasn't right, you know, after the sickness. Left without a word, even to Jacob."

I put my hands to the sides of my head. "He was sick?"

"Powerful sick, for weeks and weeks. I helped nurse him, but he never did seem to get back to himself. No strength for nothing. Hardly hold a fishing pole."

"I didn't know," I said, my chest squeezing. "I would have come back."

She raised doubtful eyebrows at me. "You see, Miz Whimble, after you left, we saw how he didn't care much for himself. Dirty clothes, and not eating, you know. He was in a right state, went on for years. And if it weren't for Jennie..."

"Go on."

"She kept him from going down too dark a path, I reckon. He had someone to care for. Her and her family."

I wrapped my hands into the bonnet on my lap.

"Does he love her?" I blurted out.

"Like a daughter. Sure he does."

She nodded her head hard. But then she added, "But folks do talk, you know. Reckon there might be more to it."

People had said the same of Mr. Wharton and me.

Another question burned its way to my mouth, and I spit it out. "Where is my daughter's grave? Surely he didn't move that too."

Ruby's voice softened. "Stone's marked with a wooden cross, same spot she's always been, just a little deeper after that big storm, you know. You got to look hard, though. Gets buried in the sand, time to time."

I closed my eyes and tried to breathe. I felt Ruby's hands on my shoulders, small and strong.

"I know you came here to build up a schoolhouse, and that's real good of you. I can't hardly believe it myself! But you must be thinking of being with Ben again?"

Would I break down sobbing, here by this hearth, little Frances a witness to my obliteration?

"If he'll have me."

"You're still husband-wife, ain't you?"

It was a fact. "Yes."

"If I know Ben, I 'spect that still counts for something. He'll be back, Miz Whimble. I ain't sure when, but he'll come on back. He won't leave that family for that long, mark my words."

She stood and stirred the soup once more.

"You hungry?"

"No."

"Well, you know I'm gonna make you eat anyway."

I laughed, and swiped the tears away, recalling the way she'd hold Oscar's chin just so as she slipped the spoon of broth into his mouth.

All wasn't lost, I saw. Two small hands appeared at my side, one holding a handkerchief and the other holding a bowl of blackberries.

When I left Ruby's house, the sun was beginning to creep its way west, covering the Whimble cabin in both light and shadow. A giant spiderweb glinted in the darkness of the surrounding trees, and as I approached the house, a raccoon scurried off the stoop and into the woods.

With the boards nailed over the windows, I couldn't see inside to glean clues to his life in the past five years. But it didn't matter; Ben was still here.

I slumped onto the warped boards of the stoop and breathed him in the musky air of the woods. So clearly, I saw him coming around the corner of the dappled, sandy road, his easy stride, his sun-streaked hair askew, a bag of fish slung over his shoulder. He grinned, and cried out when he saw me, and ran to me. Folded his arms around me and squeezed me hard the way he used to in the beginning.

He was so real, my muscles melted in his tight arms, my blood bubbled, joy jumped in my chest. I'd come home at last, and he was happy. But in a few moments, the hope subsided. I was alone here.

"Where are you, Ben?" I said to the woods.

I heard nothing but the cicadas, their steady whine echoing the keening of my heart. When would he return to Nags Head? Would he *ever* return? Maybe it was Ben's turn to stretch his wings, to see what the world outside the Banks could offer.

The shadowed woods offered no answers.

On the beach, it was the hour of the gods, the time of day when the air is full of golden dust, and time slows. There, at the spot where I'd known the house to be, was the wooden cross, poking from the sand. Two sanded pieces of driftwood, tied with twine where they met in the middle.

I don't know how I'd missed it earlier.

I sat down beside it and brushed sand from the humble rock it marked. Remembered exactly what it was like, having her grow inside me. The simple joy I'd felt at the pokes and turns. I put my hand on it, cool and vaguely damp.

"I'm sorry I stayed away so long," I told her.

And I heard her ask why, a soft questioning somewhere in the light that glowed around me.

"After you passed, I was so very sad. Everything here, even on this beautiful island, made me sad. I had to leave. I had to grow stronger. Strong enough to come back and live here again."

I raised my head from the stone to take in the beauty I'd missed.

A sky thick with leaping salmon. A sea full of waving rosebushes, buds of every color.

Her lips had been two tiny, pink petals. They'd never opened to make a sound, to nurse, to smile.

"But maybe I'm not as strong as I believed I was."

The hotel, lit from within with numerous lanterns, was easy to find in the growing darkness. The band played in the dining room, and the sound of singing and dancing could be heard through the open windows.

But in the darkness on the other side of the hotel, I spied Mr. Wharton, perched unmoving on the edge of a rocking chair outside our rooms. Waiting for me.

When he saw me, he jumped to his feet, hat in hand. He appeared disheveled, with his tie cockeyed and his hair mussed.

"Abigail! There you are! You've been gone a while."

"Have I?"

"Are you all right?"

"Not really," I answered. "I'd like to rest for the evening."

"Would you not like to eat supper?"

"I ate some soup at Ruby's house."

"Oh! You saw the Crafts?"

"Just Ruby. And Frances. They have a daughter."

He turned his hat around and around in his hands. "And...Ben?"

"Mr. Wharton. Please, I need to rest."

I was reminded of how much he didn't know about me. The other side of me that he tried to ignore.

"I see. Of course, you must be exhausted."

I hobbled toward my room, not caring that I smelled, that my back was bowed into an arc of disappointment. In my room, not even a shred of moonlight made its way through the sand-covered window.

I sat on the bed, forgetting that I'd laid the copies of the architectural drawings that Mr. Wells had given to Mr. Wharton right there by the pillow, just this morning. I'd insisted on taking them myself.

I ran my hands over the paper, several large sheets. Even in the darkness, I knew what had been drawn on them.

Taken together, the marks sketched out a symbol of hope. Moving beyond what had been. Growing something from both the sand and the water that would nourish, just as much as the fish and the wild-fowl pulled from their expanses.

I would not give up on it.

CHAPTER FIVE

Benjamin Whimble
Beaufort, North Carolina
August 15, 1881

It seemed glorious sport to be feasting in that wild free way in the virgin forest of an unexplored and uninhabited island, far from the haunts of men, and they said they never would return to civilization.
                              —The Adventures of Tom Sawyer

I'd spent the last week cleanin' the boats and packin' nets and bottles away for the next season of learnin', and all around me, the men were leavin' for their colleges, lookin' forward to still more learnin'. I watched 'em go with sadness, all of 'em with browner skin and a looseness to their shoulders that told of a couple months spent in learnin' and leisure.

Dr. Brooks too had a healthy redness to his round cheeks, as well as sparks in his eyes, which I knew had to do with the fact that he had at last got all his *Lucifer ancestra* stages sketched in no less than ninety-nine pictures. It had been my own victory too, and we'd celebrated in town with a bottle of port and a couple of beefsteak suppers.

Dr. Brooks didn't mind muckin' about in the mud one bit—fact, I think he liked it, brought out the boy in him. But I'd never seen a man more delighted than when I brought him nets full of prawns from my collectin'.

He liked that *Lucifer* the best, though. He said the creature was a mystery to most, and he aimed to find out every little thing there was to know about it and publish it all in a special book for scientists.

The critter was a new one to me as well, it being so rare and shy, so my learnin' went hand in hand with his.

Lookin' high and low, I'd at last found where they collected and bred, so many an evening we'd both set out on the skiff to a particular salt marsh during the first hour when the tide ebbed, when the prawns left the marsh to breed in the ocean. As he'd hoped to learn specially about their eggs and young'uns, we were keen to find and capture the females. So catch the females we did.

The way he watched those fine ladies in the tanks put me in mind of how I used to watch for those lost ships on the horizon of the sea, eyes frozen from the wind and spray. Lookin' away could cost lives. And lookin' away from the eggs and young'uns could cost Dr. Brooks his entire scientific article, all his summer's work.

The students worked hard to keep their specimens alive, seemed like they were as important as their own young'uns for all the work they put into it. They used a bellows pump to bring fresh air into the tank waters, and chopped up crab meat to feed 'em. But some creatures died quick in the tanks, and I can't say as I blame 'em.

Jellyfish in particular. Some didn't last a day. And the jellyfish was what they all wanted to learn about, it being the kind of creature that connected many different creatures together into one big circle of animal life.

They didn't look like much, but deep down beneath the blobby flesh of a jellyfish, the innards were little miracles, and could even be compared to those of real people. I got them eggs, young'uns and grown jellyfish all the time, and the race was on to draw them and scratch down their notes.

Now it was all over, and I found myself missing it more than I ever thought I would.

I watched Dr. Brooks talk with the buggy driver, telling him to watch out with all his boxes and crates on their way to the railroad station.

He found me, lingering in the shade of the house porch.

He clapped me on the shoulder. "What will you do now, Ben?"

I hated to leave my shoals, but I knew it was time.

"I reckon I'll head back to Nags Head, see to my people back home. Jennie and her family."

"Jennie the art prodigy."

Many a time Dr. Brooks had called out in vain for an artist, wantin' a quick sketch of a critter before things went south. Many a night, I'd seen him hunched over a table, drawin' those ninety-nine pictures himself.

So I'd told him about Jennie and how she could draw anything, living or dead. How many a time I'd sat on the porch, or the beach, or the soundside, and watched her pencil fly over the paper wherever her bright eyes willed it. And how before I knew it, she'd declare her drawing finished, and hold it up for me to see—a perfect crab, or jellyfish, or sand dollar, lookin' like I could scoop the creature from the paper and hold it whole in my hands.

Her only problem was findin' enough paper and ink. I'd given her some of the paper I'd bought when I figured I'd be writin' to Abby, after she'd left. But after a while, when no words had come, I gave the lot of it to Jennie. She'd used it all up years ago.

Matter of fact, some of the money I'd made from my labors this summer went straight to paper and pencils, which I boxed up and mailed every other week.

"Send some of her samples to me in Baltimore, if you would, for consideration for next summer's season. I'll pay her room and board and a salary for the summer."

I stared at his sunburned face. "You'd give her the job?"

"As long as she's fast, she's hired."

"She's quick, all right. And you'll see—it's not just her art. She sees the *hearts* of the critters, if you catch my meaning."

Dockin' *Tessa* in Nags Head two weeks later, I heard the poundin' of hammers on wood, and I figured a new summer home was going up in the woods on the soundside, which surprised me, since most folks were puttin' up new houses on the ocean side, the same way Abby's pap had done all those years ago and everyone had called him crazy. Which he no doubt *had* been, but still, the man had been on to somethin'.

My belongings I left in the skiff, but I lugged the crate of the best specimens I'd collected for Dr. Brooks and the students up to the Blounts'. Specimens they didn't need any longer, for they'd already wrung out the knowledge to be gained from them.

I walked around to the porch, and there sat Granny Blount in a chair, snuff paddle in her mouth. When she saw me, she let out a cackle and stood up slow as I set down the crate and bounded up the steps to catch her afore she fell off the porch. It had happened a time or two before.

I gave her a big hug, felt her whole skeleton at once.

"You've come back at last!" she cried, snuff paddle still held between her gums.

"Hello, Granny," I said. "You're looking bright and bushy-tailed."

She snorted. "I've the look of a dead fish the dog dragged up from the shore. But go on."

She checked me out with her milky eyes. "You're still skinny as a rooster's neck, I see."

"Where is everybody?"

"Oh, they're around. Here and there. Della's mending. Been out all day."

She sat back down with a heavy sigh. "Jennie's in the kitchen house. She's been cursin' your name for weeks. But she'll be chirked to see you, just the same."

Jennie was sittin' on a stool in the open door with her head down, peelin' carrots and beets. Even in the kitchen house, she'd tacked up some of her drawings on the unfinished walls. They fluttered about wild in the breeze from the open door.

I set down the crate in the sand and said, "Hey there, Jennie."

Jennie jerked up her head, then dropped the bowl and rushed at me, huggin' me so tight I feared she'd crack a rib. She smelled queerly of both soap and manure, but her skin shone fresh as a washed peach.

"Well, well. The voyager returns at last," she scolded. She wouldn't look right at me, the tell-tale sign she was harborin' a grist of anger. "I thought Granny was hollerin' at folks sailin' by on the sound. She's always doin' that these days."

"Tryin' to make friends, I reckon."

"Not hardly. Her words have a mean streak to 'em."

I laughed, but Jennie narrowed her eyes at me.

"I thought you'd forsaken us."

"I wrote you! Had to be a dozen letters! Didn't Abner read them to you?"

"He did." She nodded, already bent over and lookin' through the crate. "Read to me about that smart man you were helpin' to learn about piddly old shellfish, of all things. How you were helpin' all the students navigate the waters and showin' them how to catch fish and such things so they could learn about them in the...what was it called?"

"The laboratory," I said, seeing in my mind that good room full of glass tanks, its tables and jars, its many books.

"I'd started collectin' for *you*, you know. You wouldn't believe your eyes, all the flora and fauna I came across down there."

"Listen to you. Flora and fauna."

She pulled out a type of mollusk the men had taken a particular shine to and held it to the light from the window.

"This crate is a mess, Ben."

"I know it, Jennie."

Jennie's big blue artist eyes at last took me in top to toe. "Doesn't look to me like they fed you very well."

"Oh, Jennie, I ate."

"Those new clothes?"

"Not so new, anymore."

I found myself close to laughin' out loud with joy. "It was the best time...well, one of the best times of my life, Jennie, learnin' from those smart men."

Even now, their voices ran quick through my mind, spoutin' off their knowledge like porpoises do air, in great bursts of joy. My hands always busy with nets and sails, I'd tried to keep all those words and facts moored inside my head without writin' them down in my little notebook.

But the notions from Dr. Brooks's class I did write down in my slow print, and nights, back on Carrot Island, I'd tried to make those sloppy words clear up by lamplight. *Metamorphosis, segmentation, adaptation.*

A whole other language for a world I already knew. A whole other way to think. Critters I'd known all my life now seemed naked, like I'd taken off their clothes and was now privy to their insides. In the name of learnin', their small lives got lifted up, out of their sands and waters, for all to see.

And in my view, all the science learnin' was much better than talkin' about books of fiction. There was a feelin' that the problems of science had solutions, you just had to work to find them. They were always there waitin'.

But books were heavy with feelings—all that sadness, and revenge, and loneliness that mired a reader down. Feelings never had answers.

"There's a wide world out there, Jennie," I said. "*Mayhaps* you'd like to see it for yourself."

"Why would *I* want to see it?"

I could hardly wait to tell her. "Dr. Brooks needs an artist down there. Somebody who can draw the creatures and plants we pull from the sands and waters. I told him about you and how good you are at drawing, and he said to send some of your best to him in Baltimore, for a job next summer."

"A job? Where I'd get paid money to draw? You're pullin' my leg."

"I'm tellin' you, there is a world out there we've never seen, Jennie," I said. "And I'll be there too, working as a collector again."

She narrowed her eyes at me. "You'll be there too? You're going *back*?"

"Sure am. And you should too. It's the start of somethin' for you, I can feel it."

Jennie's gaze shifted to the windows, where the sound crept up the strands with high tide.

After a while she shook her head. "I don't think I'd be good enough for that job. You said yourself, they're some real smart men. I can't even read or write."

"He just wants you to draw."

"Livin' and workin' with a grist of men? Mama would never let me go."

"You can live with me. He'll pay for rooms in town, where all the students bed down for the summer."

"A *room* in *town*?"

She started to laugh then, a warm, wonderful sound to my ears that'd grown used to the grunts and textbook words of men of science.

"You seem a changed man, Ben Whimble. I haven't seen you so full of spirit ever in my life."

I thumped my chest with a fist, felt its newfound strength. "I am happier. It feels good, Jennie."

She whirled around to take in the papers flutterin' on the walls. "Which ones should I send him, then?"

I took note of all the new drawings—she'd given Digby and Bert darned good likenesses, and there was Della and her pap and Granny too. Could have been photographs, but they were even better than that. She must have been using the paper I'd sent for a new brand of art.

She could send any of them, and Dr. Brooks would hire her.

Just then, Della walked in the door, saggin' from a day of mendin' nets with a crew of local women. Della tied knots so fast, you couldn't hardly see her hands moving; she took after Granny, who couldn't do much these days with her gnarled fingers and milky eyes.

She let out a cry and gave me a fierce hug, and while she and Jennie commenced chopping the vegetables for a soup, we caught up on the goings-ons in Nags Head, which didn't amount to much. 'Twas like I'd never been gone a-tall.

"So that's it, huh? You skipped over the new abode on the sound-side. Heard the hammers from the docks."

"Dear me, it slipped my mind. Word is, it's not just a house, but a *school*house. They broke ground in July."

My heart and belly locked fists in a duel. "How could you forget such a thing as a schoolhouse? We've never had one afore. I've got to say, I don't rightly believe you."

"Believe what you will. A local crew, so that's a blessing."

My legs slowly stood me up from the chair. "Who's behind it?"

Della shrugged. "I ain't one notion. Some addled Yank and his schoolmarm wife."

Jennie said, "Who's going to go there for learnin' I couldn't say."

I was halfway out the door now. "What do you mean? Everybody can go to a schoolhouse. You. Bert. Digby. Della. Even Granny!"

Della rolled her eyes. "A bigger boat and more nets are all the boys talk about these days. Don't need schoolin' for fishin'."

"A school," I said, my feet headin' down the steps. "Here in Nags Head. It's a wonderful thing."

"Ben!" hollered Jennie. "Where are you off to?"

But I was too far gone to answer.

Folks bade me to stop when I neared the hotel, backslappin' me left and right at my unforeseen arrival in town. I would have stopped for longer, for I'd missed them all more than I'd thought. But I kept on toward where they pointed me to—the site of the new schoolhouse on the sound. I still couldn't fathom it, and I felt to be movin' as if in a dream, with the hammers marchin' me home.

And sure enough, there grew a brand-new frame of freshly cut pine, right near the water on the edge of the sound, places for four windows on either side and a door in front. Not too big, but not small either. A just-right size for a schoolhouse.

Men hammered on top of it, shapin' up the roof, and some carried planks here and there. I knew the lot of them, Nags Headers mostly.

"Ben!" called Jonah Garfield from the ladder, wedged into the sand beneath the water. "You come to help?"

I walked over to the edge of the water and peered up at him.

"I sure did," I said. "A true schoolhouse, right here in Nags Head. I couldn't say no. How did all this come about, anyhow? I just got back to town."

"Did you now?" His hammer hung limp and his mouth gaped. "Well, just you hold on. I'll tell you the tale."

Jonah climbed down the ladder and waded through the shallows to stand himself before me.

"Lemme just start by sayin' there's a slicked-up Yankee and a *schoolmarm* who's puttin' up this here school. They ride over on Andy Proctor's wagon sometimes, and there she sits, big bonnet and fine dress and little umbrelly. Uppity, you know. All trimmed up and tight. Aims to teach here, if you can believe that! All the luck to her, for she'll need it."

"A schoolmarm, huh?" I swallowed hard, sweat rollin' down the sides of my face. "What's her name?"

He shrugged. "How should I know?"

"What did she look like, pray tell?"

"Hard to tell, with all the garb. But I've heard tell she's a fine one."

"And the color of her hair, Jonah. Did any of you simpletons catch sight of her hair?"

He guffawed at me. "Look at you, wonderin' on the color of her hair. You gonna court her? Naw, you ain't, on account she's with the Yank. I heard tell they're married."

"So...no one could make comment on the color of her hair, is what you're tellin' me?"

"Ben Whimble. You been gone too long, I reckon. You need to fix yourself up with a woman right quick, if you ask me. You can have mine—she's a handful."

I opened my mouth to ask again, but he said, "No, I ain't heard tell of her hair. It was put up in the bonnet, you recall?"

I left him then, and went round asking the rest of the men about the schoolmarm, but they couldn't tell me any more than Jonah did. And what's more, they agreed the woman was married to the Yank anyhow.

So I gave up and started pickin' up planks and carryin' them into the water and handin' them to the men sittin' on the sides of the frame. Then it was hammerin' and holdin' ladders and climbin' boards and dippin' ourselves in the waters below to cool down.

But all the while my body worked, I thought on my lost wife. How foolish I'd been to think she would ever come back here to build a schoolhouse. How easy my mind was tricked.

She was gone.

Gone so long, the folks here thought me a bachelor again.

Even her face was a thing of watery mystery to me now, the way it shifted and warped when I tried to bring it to clarity. And I'd never thought that could happen to me.

Her back—now, that I recalled with great detail. A back was a right terrible body part to conjure of the woman you once loved— the source of a body's work and, as such, the unlucky receptacle of near constant pain. A woman didn't want to be remembered for her back.

Her eyes, yes, her lips and skin and white teeth and tiny waist. Even her hands, if they've never seen much work and appear to a lesser man's eyes to be so fine as to be wearin' soft white gloves.

But Abby's back was what I recalled the most. So straight and proud, even when she was walkin' away from me through piles of sand.

CHAPTER SIX

Abigail Whimble
September 8, 1881
Nags Head, North Carolina

She ran to the door; he was not in sight; she flew around to the play yard; he was not there. Then she called: "Tom! Come back, Tom!"

She listened intently, but there was no answer. She had no companions but silence and loneliness.
—The Adventures of Tom Sawyer

I awoke to a turning of the weather.

The air of my room had an unfamiliar chill to it, and sand pattered over the windowpanes in periodic gusts of wind. I stretched, relishing the feel of the chilly linens on my bare calves. I arose, still wrapped in the linens, and peeked around the sand piles, catching snatches of blue sky and white clouds, racing quickly along.

I washed and dressed quickly, before Mr. Wharton could join me, and set out for the construction site. I hadn't been there in weeks.

As soon as the crew had broken ground in July, it became apparent that Mr. Wells preferred to speak to Mr. Wharton about the construction. I'd found myself stranded in the hot sand, gripping my parasol with damp gloves and watching the boats sail by on the sound.

I'd kept myself busy elsewhere. Long walks on the beach, looking for shells, watching the fishing boats. Hours in the hotel room, ordering readers and books and even a stove. Cramping my hands with letters to Asha and Martha, whose three children filled her house and heart with love and laughter.

But today, I would not be deterred.

I stepped from my room and was greeted with a stiff breeze that smacked my cheeks and pushed me about. And all along the Nags Head Woods road, the canopy of loblolly pine, oak and hickory trees swayed and creaked in the wind.

Here and there, I glimpsed fresh ponds that pooled in the crevices of land, some of them very deep, their surfaces bunching in the breeze and catching green leaves in their folds.

The road dipped lower, where the sweet gum and black gum, red bay and black willows blew. Down, down through tall marsh grasses I stepped, to the packed sand of the sound, where I could see the schoolhouse, its former skeleton now fleshed with bone and muscle.

Fresh pine planks glowed like gold in the morning sun, and the sound edged it in skirts of white-capped green. I knew that the main section of the schoolhouse was already complete, and construction had moved to the apartment in the back, where I planned to have a narrow bed, a table, a chair and household items for the busy days I knew from experience were undoubtedly coming.

I held tight to my bonnet as I walked carefully up the long beams and stepped onto the unfinished floorboards of the classroom. The wind blew straight through the empty window frames, stirring up sawdust in wild gusts.

I spun about in the middle of the twinkling motes, full of gratitude, but jerked to a stop by the sound of faint grunting coming from the back room. I was soon faced with a man, who rounded the corner carrying a plank on his shoulder.

The light from the sun shone across his bearded face; when he strode toward me, I found that, beneath the unruly facial hair and whittled frame, I recognized him.

It was Ben.

We stood as if ghosts, accidentally haunting the same special space. I watched his blue eyes as they made their way from my bonnet to my face to my dress, a slow process of recognition. A mix of shock, confusion, and dread filled his eyes, but nothing close to happiness.

"Abby," he rasped, staggering back a step, the plank thundering to the floor. Both of his hands reached for his heart, grasping his shirt, as if he was in pain.

"Ben!" I cried. "Are you all right?"

He stepped back even farther, so that he stood against a wall.

"What are you doing here?" he whispered.

I attempted a smile, though my mouth was trembling. "I've come back."

He shook his head, still rubbing his chest. His eyes were round with horror.

I spread out my arms out in a numb arc. "This is my schoolhouse."

"You *are* the schoolmarm," he breathed.

"That's right."

He barked out a laugh, soaked in a bitterness I'd never heard from him. Silence fell between us, our hard breaths bouncing about the unfinished wood. He looked me up and down in confusion.

"*This is...you are...*" he spat. "Dear God."

He bent over double and started to moan.

I took a step toward him; every muscle in my body yearned to bring him to me.

But he moved even farther away from me.

"Ben," I said thickly, tears falling down the back of my throat. "I'm so glad to see you. I've been waiting for you. You see, you were gone when we arrived. Back in late June. I wrote to you..."

He squinted at me. "We?"

"Mr. Wharton and me."

Ben was slowly making his way around the edge of the classroom now, keeping as much distance between us as possible.

"You and him."

I hurried to explain. "He's helping to fund the school. We're staying at the hotel."

He was almost to the door now. He stopped and looked about the schoolhouse as the sun disappeared behind the clouds. He shook his head, a grim smile on his face.

"Seems like I'm still building things for you. After all this time. Why is that, Abby?"

His voice was foreign to my ears, hard and unmerciful. I found that I was holding out my arms, reaching for him.

"Ben, please. Don't leave. I want to talk to you."

I searched for the right words to keep him here.

"Stay away from me," he said.

And he was out the door and striding upward through the sand toward the woods.

I sprawled flat on my back inside my unfinished quarters, listening to the heavy splashing of the water on the pilings, driven into the sand. The hide-and-seek sunlight reflecting off the water created a cosmos of light on the pine walls around me.

Such natural grace—it was everywhere here. The kind of grace I'd dreamed of back in bustling Nashville. The nearness of it almost seemed impossible.

Like the sudden nearness of Ben.

My husband, who had somehow returned.

My husband, who I realized didn't care for me the same way I still cared for him.

The folly of my presence here was clear to me. I'd believed there had been time for us, but really, there had been no time. Not even a minute. Not even a second. The wind blew harder now, with strong hints of coming rain.

The sound of men's voices outside reined in my darkening thoughts. I stood shakily and picked up my bonnet, then walked to the door to see Mr. Wells, three men, and an ox-driven cart.

I made my careful way down the planks, feeling my hair tumbling here and there from its pins and blowing in the wind. The men watched me, surprise in their eyes.

"Good morning, Mrs. Wharton," said Mr. Wells, tipping his hat. "You're here quite early. Is your husband around? I'd like to speak to him about a few final adjustments."

Outraged laughter burst scalding from my throat.

"My name isn't Mrs. Wharton, and Mr. Wharton and I are not married," I said with force. "My name is Mrs. Whimble. Abigail Whimble. And no, my husband *was* here. But now he's not. He's left me here."

Mr. Wells stared at me in utter surprise, and the men watched, eyebrows to their hairlines and mouths agape.

"I assumed you and Mr. Wharton were married," stuttered Mr. Wells. "As a matter of fact, he never, in his letters...and you and he are...well, never mind that. I do apologize."

Despite the browned skin he'd developed this summer, his face was almost white beneath the brim of his hat.

"Are you...*Ben's* wife? Ben Whimble?"

"I am."

He rubbed his face hard, as if to revive himself. "He's been working here. He was here just yesterday. He seemed to know a great deal about construction."

"He built a fine house for us, five years ago. You're fortunate to have him on your crew."

I centered my bonnet atop my head and wrenched the ribbons into a bow at my chin.

"There's a bad storm coming, I'm afraid," he said, watching me warily. "We've come to batten down the site."

"Yes," I said slowly. "A storm. I knew it."

The ox stamped his feet, and I turned to go.

"Good day, *Mrs. Whimble*," he said. "Again, I do apologize."

As I walked away, the sand blew in swirls all about my feet. *Mrs. Whimble, Mrs. Whimble*, echoed in my head with each sinking step. And in my wretched state, I almost ran directly into sixteen-year-old Andy Proctor's mule, pulling the wagon that carried the top-hatted Mr. Wharton. Andy grinned briefly at me and ducked his head.

"Abigail!" cried Mr. Wharton happily. "I wasn't planning on seeing you here, and so early in the morning. Perhaps the weather stirred you."

My glaring face was covered with strands of blowing hair, and I swiped at my face to clear them.

"You!" I cried.

Andy jerked up his head, and Mr. Wharton stared as I approached the wagon, finger pointing.

"What's happened?" he asked.

"Mr. Wells believed that you and I were married," I blurted out. "I disavowed him of the notion, but now I wonder if the entire island is under the same impression. Was that *your* doing?"

Andy slumped on the wagon seat, pulling his cap over his face.

"Of course not," said Mr. Wharton. "Why would I let him believe such a thing?"

"And yet he does! You obviously haven't been clear enough about our relations."

Mr. Wharton shrugged. "Perhaps he thought it only natural that I would be investing in such a structure because my wife was the one teaching in it. I really couldn't say."

"It won't do!" I exclaimed. "What must Ben think?"

"Ben?"

"He's back," I rasped, my voice full of grief.

Andy straightened up. "Ben *Whimble*? You know him?"

"I'm married to him."

He stared at me for a while, then laughed loudly. "You're pullin' my leg."

I shook my head, but I'd run out of words. My breathing grew labored, and Mr. Wharton gazed down at me in alarm.

"Come now," he said, climbing from the wagon. "Andy can take us back to the hotel. Let's get some food in your stomach, shall we? Some coffee, perhaps. Though the staff are all a-flutter, talking of a coming storm. Possibly a hurricane, they say. There wasn't much to eat."

The trees creaked around us. "I'm not hungry."

"A rest, then. You look as if you might faint."

I scoffed. "Rest!"

I'd never be able to rest again.

It was, thankfully, a short ride back to the hotel, due in part to the mule's excitability in the stiff wind. Andy whistled; the clouds steadily darkened as we pulled up to the hotel, yet still the young man was outfitting the mule and cloth-covered tram for an excursion to the seaside.

"Thank you for the ride, Andy," I said.

I stepped off the wagon and clambered inside the tram. Mr. Wharton hesitated for a moment before stepping up and seating himself next to me.

Andy looked doubtfully at us.

"I'm surprised the hotel is still running the tram with a storm coming," Mr. Wharton said to the young man.

"Oh, landlubbers love a good storm," he said, shaking his head at the stupidity of people just like us.

Mr. Wharton paid the man his dimes, and the mule started to pull us bumpily along the rails of the boardwalk. I closed my eyes and heard the waves crashing hard, the wind beating the canvas of the tram above our heads. I measured my breaths, heavy with salt, until the mule came to a stop.

The boardwalk ended at the bathhouse, built a few hundred yards from the ocean. The sea itself was marked with snowy peaks, whipped into the air by the wind, and the sun flickered in and out of ragged, purple clouds.

The very first time I'd laid eyes on the Atlantic, when I was just a sixteen-year-old girl, the sea had looked the same.

So powerful, it wiped away all thought.

A few boys and girls in dark bathing costumes darted in and out of the frothing shallows, their mothers and nannies sitting on the sand, watching closely. They were the families who lived in the handful of summer cottages that had been built on the ocean side, families like mine once had been.

"I'd leave off with that hat," warned the young man. "Looks like it may take flight and never come back."

"Yes," said Mr. Wharton, somewhat reluctantly handing him his top hat. His thinning auburn hair blew wild in the wind.

Raising my skirts, I began to walk south down the empty beach as Mr. Wharton trudged along silently beside me. Debris had already been tossed upon the beach—clumps of seaweed, shreds of drift-wood, shards of shells.

We passed four of the hunkering new houses, windows already boarded, before coming to the bit of land I still knew well. Nothing but sand and sea oats marked the location.

"This was where my family's summer house stood twelve years ago. It burned soon after the only season we spent here."

"It was where you tutored Ben, wasn't it? On the porch."

I'd told Mr. Wharton the barest of details of our unusual court-ship one evening after dining with him at his home a few days after his wife passed. He'd been so distraught that I didn't even think he'd been listening, and afterward, I'd regretted sharing such intimacies with him. The memories I'd kept for my own had felt sullied and cheap, then.

"He was there, this morning," I said, my words coming slow and hard. "At the schoolhouse. He's part of the construction crew."

Silent, he patted his blowing hair while watching the agitated sea. The wind battered my skirts and flipped the fabric of Mr. Wharton's pleated pants.

"It seems he doesn't even want to be in the same room as I. He couldn't wait to be rid of me."

I clenched my teeth at the memory of his hands tearing at his shirtwaist, right over his heart. He was so thin now, and with his long beard, I'd hardly recognized him.

"I was afraid this might happen," he said. "How did you think he was going to take your abrupt arrival?"

I turned from him, hating myself once again for confiding in him. "I wrote to him, two months before we departed from Nashville. He likely never received the letter."

It seemed the wind had eaten my words, for he didn't respond, and was quiet for a long while.

"You'll continue on with your plans here?"

I scoffed. "Did you think I would just pack my things and leave after one obstacle?"

"No, I did not. But this particular obstacle...oh, Abigail. I can always sell the schoolhouse. It's not the end of the world."

The clouds had snatched the sun, turning day into night and erasing my sense of time. Raindrops teased my nose, my lips. I stepped into the middle of the blowing sand, right where the summer house had stood.

The way he used to smile at me. The way he touched my leg under the table. The way he ran his dirty finger under the words, sounding them out in a steady cadence, how he'd showed me a different way of looking at the world.

My experiences that summer—with Elijah Africa, with Ben, with Asha—had molded me. Now, I had returned to build on them. To give back what was given to me.

"Ben knows me." My words emerged more as a question instead of a declaration. I tried again. "He knows me. And I him."

Mr. Wharton sighed. In the gray sky, the deep lines beside his eyes appeared to be carved with a dull pencil. He was getting older, his own time for happiness compressing with each day.

"Does he *still* know you?"

He'll come to me, I insisted to myself, and turned into the wind to head back to the tram.

CHAPTER SEVEN

Benjamin Whimble
September 8, 1881
Nags Head, North Carolina

Tom decided that he could be independent of Becky Thatcher now. Glory was sufficient. He would live for glory. Now that he was distinguished, maybe she would be wanting to "make up." Well, let her—she should see that he could be as indifferent as some other people. Presently she arrived. Tom pretended not to see her. He moved away and joined a group of boys and girls and began to talk.

—The Adventures of Tom Sawyer

One minute, I was battenin' down hatches in a brand-new school-house. The next minute, I was livin' in a fever dream. I couldn't feel the sand under my boots, I couldn't feel my arms a-swingin' at my sides.

Thoughts swirled about my head like flotsam in a tide pool, words and feelings washin' in and out with regular motion. More of a racket in my own head than in the wind rattlin' the branches around me.

She was back. She put up a schoolhouse. She aimed to stay.

Over and over, I thought those same thoughts.

But the one question snagged like a fishhook in the meat of it all: Did *I* account for anything in these plans?

Not a word to anybody, not even me. This livin' in a hotel with the man who'd lured her away from the place to begin with. This choosin' to be a schoolmarm at her very own school in Nags Head. Of all the places in the country.

'Twas like she'd taken out my heart, and put it back inside me, but upside down.

Hadn't I at last let her go?

God, how the sight of her almost struck me dead! And there I thought I'd forgotten her face. 'Twas like not a day had passed us by. Decked out like the fine, upstandin' lady she always was. She'd raised herself up, the way I'd wanted her to.

She was still the Abby I knew, but she was also a new and different Abby, a woman I didn't know a-tall. Abigail, she was.

I got to the Blount's abode without even knowin' how I got there. Granny was sittin' in her rocker on the porch—at least that hadn't changed.

"Storm's a-comin'," she hollered. "Hurra-cane, I'll wager."

"Not to worry, Granny. I'll get you shored up."

I went past her inside, and found Jennie in the kitchen house, scrubbin' the pots with cookfire ashes.

"Hey," she said, not lookin' up from her cleanin'.

My breath was comin' hard, so she spared me an upward glance. Then she dropped the pot.

"What's ailin' you? You look like you seen a ghost!"

"I have."

She wiped her blackened hands on her apron. "Tell me. Is it the storm a-comin'? A hurricane, I knew it."

I shook my head. "She's back, Jennie. She's to be the school-marm. At the new school."

She stared at me, all her rosy color fadin'.

"Mercy!" she cried. "You *have* seen a ghost."

I started pacin' about the kitchen. "I saw her. At the schoolhouse."

More pacin', back and forth. I couldn't form words to speak.

"Where you were helpin' out. Go on then!"

"I was comin' round the corner, pickin' up loose boards, and there she stood. I didn't know her at first—she was all trussed up. I says to myself, *That must be her, the fine-lookin' schoolmarm every-body's talking of. Married to the Yank, you know.*"

I stopped and looked at Jennie, but I didn't see her a-tall. I could only see Abby. Abigail. My long-lost wife.

Jennie broke the spell. "And then what?"

"And then...I saw her face."

"Lord-a-mercy, Ben. You're gonna put me in the grave. What did she *say*?"

"She said...I don't even recall!"

She shook her head in disgust as I tried to reach back to those few minutes to snatch up the words we spoke.

"She said she'd been waitin' on me to come back." I laughed. "*She'd* been waitin' on *me*! Don't that cap the climax?"

Della came into the kitchen then with a basket full of vegetables she'd picked afore the storm took 'em. Jennie told her the news.

"Folks said she and the Yank were married! That just goes to show

how talk gets tangled," said Della, shakin' her head. "She's been here for a right long while, you know. Livin' at the hotel. She likely didn't know where you'd gone off to. I'll wager it was right hard on her."

"Serves her right, don't you think? And who's side are you on anyway?"

"I'm not sure yet. Who the devil is that Yankee anyhow?" asked Della.

"It's the same man who took her away from here, to teach at the Normal College. Mr. Warthog or some such."

"He didn't rightly *take* her," said Della, who'd never said a word against Abby since I'd known her. It was the wife in her, I reckoned. "From what I recall, you sent her away and wished her luck."

"For her to come back!"

"Well, Ben, she's back. And with a Yankee to boot. What's to do about it?"

I slid down the wall to the floor groanin', while Della and Jennie looked on with wide eyes.

Abby. 'Twas hard to even think her name.

I saw her with my own eyes. I know I did. But I just couldn't grab ahold of the notion that she'd come back to stay. My mind kept at it, the way it went round and round, guessin' where the prawns were matin' not four months back. They'd hid away like no creature I'd ever known, their secrets born deep inside them. Living in this world required solvin' mysteries, day after day.

"So are you gonna go speak with her?" Della asked.

"I'm not." I swallowed hard. "I...I told her to stay away from me, I think."

Della barked a laugh. "You're still married, Ben. It's a pickle, I'll wager, but you ain't a young'un by a long stretch. Quit your bawlin' and speak with her. She came back here on account of *you*."

"You don't know that. She's puttin' up a school, number one."

"He doesn't have to do go runnin' to kiss her feet on account she finally saw fit to come back here," said Jennie. "He can take his time if he wants."

I crossed my arms about my chest. "Thank you, Jennie."

"Suit yourself, takin' advice from a girl who ain't never been hitched," huffed Della. "You think you can help me fix some wood over these windows? Or might you take some time to think it over?"

I rode out the storm with the Blounts.

All of us sat on the floor beside the fire, forkin' mouthfuls of Della's fried fish and tellin' yarns and passin' a bottle round. Granny got out the squeeze-box and played her old, thorny tunes, fillin' the house with a racket louder than the wind and rain. Then we played "guess what" with the hodgepodge of treasures Jennie kept in Livy Spruel's crate, passin' round with closed eyes all manner of flotsam rescued from the belchin' sea.

After a while, Jennie decided she was gonna sketch my face. She told me to sit quiet and not move a muscle, so I soon started thinkin' on Abby. How overly pleased she'd been to see me, when there I was, a stammerin' simpleton with no notions about anything a-tall. It was downright queer, was what it was.

Jennie told me to quit hunchin' my brow and put on a smile.

When she'd finished, everybody thought the picture looked just like me. But she'd done me a few favors, I saw. Less lines about the eyes and a trimmed beard. Must have been the lackin' of daylight. Or the sips of corn liquor she'd taken.

Jennie declared it to be one of the chosen ones to be sent to Dr. Brooks, along with her sketches of a sea anemone, a sea pansy, and a mollusk. She held them in her hands like they were sacred scrolls, given to her by Jesus himself.

At last we slept some, and when the morning arrived, I stepped outside to see what the storm had wrought. But I soon saw that its bark had been worse than its bite, rainin' more than blowin'. It must've slunk off in the night, embarrassed for itself, for blue sky was peekin' from the tail of gray clouds and the breeze was almost ticklish.

I took up Jennie's drawings and headed along the sound shore to post them at the hotel. *I'll be quick*, I told myself. No time to dillydally, in case Abby showed up out of the blue like yesterday. One more fright like that would kill me dead for certain.

"Ben Whimble!" somebody hollered. I looked to see Ned Saddles at the back of the market, pryin' a plank off a window with a hammer. He dropped the plank into the sand and started over to me, his face a wicked grin.

I started to run.

"Ben! Hold up, now!"

He was runnin' too, hollerin' for me to stop. We must've looked like young'uns at a footrace, so I just stopped, grippin' Jennie's pictures just so, so I wouldn't mess 'em up.

Ned's face was red, but still he grinned. "What in tarnation's the matter with you?"

"Got to get these in the post, that's all."

He didn't even look down. "Have you heard the talk?"

"Talk?"

"Your wife's back! Is it true?"

"Sure is, Ned."

He wrinkled up his brow. "But now she's married to the Yankee, I reckon."

I shook my head. At times, the basic notions of marriage were tenets of mystery to my fellow Nags Headers.

"I don't reckon so, Ned."

"How's that, then?"

"You can't be married to more'n one person at a time."

"That so?" he queried. "But everybody's been talkin', you know."

"I can just picture it."

I hurried inside the hotel and posted the drawings, and when I came out, Ned was gone, but the area was swarmed with people. Each and every Nags Header was out and about, making repairs or wreckin' along the seaside or headin' off fishin' in the swollen sound.

I tried to skirt by everybody I saw, for each person, horse and pig in Nags Head had now cottoned to the notion that my long-lost wife was back. They fed me little bits here and there.

Seemed like her and Mr. Warthog were right close, stayin' side by side in the hotel, taking their meals in the dinin' room and ridin' in the cart down to the sea. So close that folks had believed them husband and wife, no question a-tall. Nobody had thought for a second that she was the same Abby Whimble who'd been married to Ben. And it hurt a little, I'll allow, to see how small a mark she'd made on the people living here.

"Least they're not sharin' a room," cackled Loretta Weeks. "If'n I'd seen her, I would've known her. Can't never forget that face o' hers. Purty, purty."

They said the two went hither and yon in a wagon driven by Andy Proctor. Seemed Andy couldn't wait to go to school there, but his uncle Whalen didn't think it had a thing to do with learnin'.

"Course he'd want to be sittin' in the first row, makin' eyes at such a pretty teacher!" said Whalen. "No disrespect, o' course, but I'll wager all the young lads about the Banks will be swingin' fists to get the chair with the best view."

But the more folks I talked to, the more that schoolhouse seemed nothin' but a joke. Nobody wanted to go inside the place, seemin' as good as Lucifer's playhouse, a redheaded Jezebel for a teacher.

I lasted about a week afore I just had to see the finished schoolhouse for myself.

At sunset, I sailed over, and the sight of it, all whitewashed and glowin' in the water, gave me such a feelin' of hope, as important as a lifesaving station, or a lighthouse. A true ode to learnin'.

The marsh frogs played a tune as I came up the steps to the door and opened it. In the light of the moon comin' through the new glass windows, I counted thirty desks and thirty chairs facin' straight to the front, where a chalkboard was now hung.

An iron woodstove sat proud in the middle of the room with a pipe straight into the roof, and Abby's big desk sat in the corner. Shelves of books and supplies went round the sides of the room. Stacks of brand-new slates and slate pencils. Notebooks of clean, white paper.

A round, spinnin' map of the whole word sat there on a shelf. I spun it real slow to read all the different countries and oceans, all stitched together like pieces of a quilt. The American flag hung on a pole stuck in the wall, crisp with color, and a round black-and-white clock hung on the wall behind her desk, its tickin' unheard over the wash of water beneath.

My boots rang out clear on the smooth floors as I walked to a set of shelves on the wall. I picked out a brand-new book—a collection of poetry!—and cracked it open, sniffed its new-paper smell. There below sat a box that held a grist of books, all the same. A book called *The Adventures of Tom Sawyer* by Mark Twain. I knew she planned to read this book to the students, them followin' along as she went, and I saw she hadn't changed in that regard.

I stepped to her brand-new desk and sat myself in her brand-new chair. I looked out at the rows of desks, and my heart bulged like a too-full belly with all my buried love.

I could feel her here, in this striving place. Her high spirit, her keen mind, the way she cared for others, cared for me even. It swept me over like the sea, rememberin' her again.

I would have done anything to've come to a grand place like this to learn. Mayhaps I would have turned out different, book learnin' of the kind that Dr. Brooks taught in the university too tough for my simple brain to chew.

I ran my hands over the desk, recallin' the days when Abby taught at the Freedmen's School. How I'd watched her doing what came natural to her, doing what she loved. Echoes of her voice, readin' *Uncle Tom's Cabin* to the students, came back to me, as easy as if I'd heard 'em just yesterday.

Knowin' I shouldn't, I stepped through the door in the back corner into Abby's room in back and saw she'd already put an iron-post bed in there, as well as a table and chair, a washstand with a painted, porcelain bowl, a flannel and a bunch of lady's whatnots.

I picked up a bar of soap and sniffed—'twas a fine, rosy smell that didn't remind me of her a-tall. Same with a tin of dustin' powders. There was a horse-hair toothbrush and jar of dentifrice.

She planned to sleep here some nights, I guessed. She'd wanted to do the same, teachin' at the Freedmen's School. So bone-tired, she could hardly move her feet. Would suffer the dirty floor and a blanket if it meant she could just close her eyes for a spell.

I sometimes carried her all the way home in my arms, her sleepin' head heavy on my shoulder.

And now, in the brand-new mirror hung over the washstand, I saw myself, long brown beard and bleached hair, the mismatched colors giving me a befuddled look. My eyes bore branches of lines at their sides, and Wilson's nice clothes had grown stained and ragged. In this fresh-pine room, I took note of my sour stink, a thing I'd not taken heed of in a long while.

I was not brand-new, and that was a fact.

Not ready to part from the little room, I lay down on the soft clean bed covers and shut my eyes. Soon the room took on the feel of a boat, with water slappin' the pilings under me and the breeze strokin' the marsh grass. The frogs still sang, but slowly now.

Here Abby would lay, on the water I'd known my whole life. The school she'd made, a place of change, with feet in both sand and water.

It nearly made the wildest notion seem possible.

CHAPTER EIGHT

Abigail Whimble
September 17, 1881
Nags Head, North Carolina

Then her conscience reproached her, and she yearned to say something kind and loving; but she judged that this would be construed into a confession that she had been in the wrong, and discipline forbade that. So she kept silence, and went about her affairs with a troubled heart.
—The Adventures of Tom Sawyer

Andy Proctor was more than happy to sail me over to Roanoke Island.

"Squirin' the schoolmarm!" he shouted to every Nags Header he saw in the vicinity of the wharf. People jumped in alarm in the peace of the morning and glared at us without answering.

We took the voyage in his very own skiff. Out here on the barrier islands, even women and children could sail, and did so often. I'd once possessed a modicum of skill, but I didn't trust myself to take it on now.

I tried to seat myself out of the way, but the skiff was so small that Andy kept tripping over my feet and bumping my bonnet, all the while keeping up a steady stream of conversation. He waxed on with stories of mishaps on the water, quite numerous given his mere sixteen years, and I tried to follow along.

But I was thinking of my own past, not young Andy's.

Thirteen years ago, I'd made this very trip on Ben's skiff in the dark of night, when I'd taught at the Freedmen's School into the early hours of the morning. I heard the echoes of his calming voice, his eyes shining by the light of the boat's lantern, the sail belling out in the wind. It had been him who'd urged me to teach the freed people in the first place, and it had changed the trajectory of my life.

Their faces, their stories, still occupied my thoughts. I wasn't sure who I would find in the colony now. There had only been three hundred people living there when I'd taught at the school. Now, I feared they'd all gone, every single one, the colony's promise a dream gone very bad.

"And afore I knew it, I was marooned in ice! Can you fathom it?" Andy asked, pulling me from my thoughts.

"Ice on the Albemarle Sound?"

"Were you even listenin' to me?" he asked with suspicion. "You're fixed on Mr. Ben, I'll wager."

"Of course not," I lied. "You're a fine storyteller. When you come to school, you can learn how to write some of your stories down on paper."

He chuckled. "I don't need to write 'em down. They're all up here."

He tapped his head with a finger, then busied himself with directing the skiff in and out of the many small vessels that were sailing through Shallowbag Bay. The waterfront had been taken up with the docks of packing and shipping factories, and he struggled to find a place to tie up the skiff.

The port town itself had also grown since I'd been gone. It had sprouted a downtown of sorts, with a courthouse, a post office, and a bustling marketplace.

As I stood with my parasol overhead, Andy hailed one of the mule-driven wagons that rumbled here and there, their beds full of wares. The driver, a Negro man with a long white beard and a large straw hat, pulled the mule to a stop, looking down at me with curiosity.

"Good morning, sir. We're looking to visit the former Freedmen's Colony," I said. "I was hoping to buy a ride from someone who's heading in that direction."

He squinted at me beneath the brim of his hat. "You mean that lost colony, I reckon. Raleigh and them."

"No, not that one. I'm looking for the settlement of freedmen who came here during the war, when the Union occupied the island. The houses and buildings that were built to accommodate them. On the northwest side of the island."

He stared at me. "Why you wanting to go yonder to that sad stretch?"

"She's a schoolmarm!" Andy blurted out. "Lookin' for folks to teach in her Nags Head School."

He tipped his hat back to get a better look at me.

"The schoolhouse across the water?" he said, jerking a thumb in the direction of Nags Head. "I can hear the racket from here. You one of those *Yankee* schoolmarms?"

"I'm from Edenton originally."

He raised his brows in surprise. "You sure about that?"

I smiled. "I was hoping to find some of my former students from the Elijah Africa Freedmen's School. I taught there, years ago, and I wanted to let them know about the new school."

He quickly removed his hat and bowed his head. "My, my. Would you listen to this, now. You taught at a freedmen's school, and here you are back in these parts again, building a *new* school. I'm proud to know you. Name's George Chapel, ma'am."

"Abigail Whimble. I'm happy to meet you as well."

"Elijah Africa. I sure have heard a lot about him. I came over from Plymouth, not too long after he got killed. Those folks in the colony talked of him like he was Jesus himself."

"Yes," I said, my throat aching with abrupt sadness. "He was the leader that people needed back then."

He nodded his head slowly and stroked his long beard. "Well, I do hate to tell you, Miz Whimble. There ain't nothing of that colony there no more."

"Nothing? I knew the schoolhouse was taken down... but the houses too?"

"Ain't nothing there but dirt. I am sorry."

I took a steadying breath. "I'd still like to see...what's left of it."

The man just chuckled. "Who am I to turn down a schoolmarm, Yankee or no? Least you'll get a good ride. Old Hester here is steady as she goes."

Mr. Chapel rivaled Andy for the ability to hold up his end of a conversation, telling us all about his craft of boatbuilding and how he helped the occupying Union Army fix their bullet-ridden boats.

He owned a few acres of farmland not far from the former colony that he'd turned into a boatbuilding factory, and Andy just about jumped up on his seat with excitement and said he'd like to see it.

The well-traveled roads near the town eventually gave way to patchy rural pathways the farther north we rode. Farms, some with several outbuildings, appeared here and there.

"Those white folks took the oath when the Union was here, but they didn't care which way or the other whose side they was on. They all just wanted to be left alone. Still do, matter of fact."

As we neared the site of the former colony on the northwest side of the island, the roads dwindled to nothing more than wild thatches of weeds and grasses. I had to blink hard, then, to convince myself that what I was seeing was true: The village that had been carved with nothing but hand tools from dense woods on abandoned or unoccupied land had disappeared.

Twenty-six cross streets and three avenues—Roanoke, Lincoln and Burnside. Assigned plots of one-acre each, for one-room, pitch-pine log houses and small gardens. Blueprints for self-sufficiency for about three hundred families fortunate enough to have a home in the village.

Now, all I could see was the Croatan Sound, glittering in the sunlight.

The former Rebel Army barracks, where many of the freedmen had lived in such desperate conditions, had been taken down too. Even the house that had been built for the missionary teachers that frequented the colony during the war—the house where Ben and I had lived as man and wife—was gone.

Nothing but an act of war or a force of nature could have obliterated the area so thoroughly.

Asha had been proud of her drafty house and her garden full of vegetables, her fat hens. Her yard had been crisscrossed with clotheslines, heavy with others' laundry. With no school to support her as a teacher and a dwindling supply of soiled linens, even Asha had been forced to leave the island. I doubted she knew that her house—that all of the houses—had been demolished.

"Where did it all go?" I whispered.

"One good storm could've taken out those shanties, flimsy as they were. I reckon the wood's likely somebody's chicken coop or barn door now. Wood's scarce in these parts, on account the armies cut down all the trees to build their forts and such. You should hear folks up here belly-ache about all their missing trees. Back during the war, all manner of folks would just up and cut down a man's trees, just like they were public property."

I remembered well the long days of teaching in a cold schoolhouse and returning in the late afternoon to an even colder house.

At the site of the schoolhouse where I'd taught, there was nothing but dirt and weeds.

Andy helped me from the wagon, and I walked the barely discernable perimeter of the former building, calling to mind the faces of my students, people of all ages who'd become as good as family to me. There had once been many buildings in the colony that had served as schools for the eager students, but now, almost twenty years later, there were none.

"This was the site of the Elijah Africa Freedmen School," I told them. "It was a simple log cabin, but it had six large windows that let in the light and many shelves full of curiosities the students found on our nature walks. Plenty of books, and a woodstove too."

The nearby tree where the people had buried Elijah Africa had been cut down, and the cross that had marked his resting place was gone too. I hoped that at least his bones were still buried there, but I no longer felt certain of anything.

"Miz Whimble?" ventured Andy. "You all right? You look right pale."

I closed my eyes as dark memories of my daddy, and hooded men, and burning books, and murder revisited me. Flashes of hope and hard work and happiness came too, and a strong wave of sorrow.

"Ma'am?" ventured Mr. Chapel.

Every morning upon rising from the bed, my only thoughts had been of Ben, and how maybe today was the day he'd appear before me, cap in hand and old love in his eyes. But not now. All had faded next to such an obliteration.

It had only occupied a small edge of the island, but the colony had once held the hopes of thousands of former slaves. Even after the war, when the government had wanted them to leave for better employment opportunities on the mainland, many of the families— some having lived here their entire lives—had stayed, believing it to be their only safe home. They'd been led to believe they owned their bit of land, their house, their garden. But in the end, the freedmen hadn't owned anything at all.

I had felt deeply their reluctance to leave the island for better prospects, prospects that held little promise of equitable treatment or support of any kind. I yearned for Asha; I missed her so very much. I missed them all, more than I knew.

I spoke to the empty land. "I can't believe everyone's just...gone."

Mr. Chapel cocked his head. "They didn't *all* leave, now. A few stayed on."

I jerked my head up to face him. "They did? Where are they?"

"Here and there. Most live in a place they call California."

"California? Like the state?"

Mr. Chapel shrugged. "Reckon it sounded like freedom to 'em."

"I'd like to see this California," I said, my heartbeat quickening.

He grinned. "I'll take you to see Miz Mercy. Mercy Williams. You know her?"

I shook my head.

"Well, Miz Mercy and I have known each other for years now. She was a slave on a farm here, before the war. She is the right person to talk to, for sure."

We rode along the sound shore then, as the tide had gone out. Then we detoured inland, and soon we'd arrived at a settlement of a few houses and outbuildings, with a windmill and a church, whose cross I could see on the roof of a small building. A riot of sunflowers surrounded the rough-hewn logs all the way up to the ample windows.

We kept trundling, soon stopping before a small house with an orchard of apple trees surrounding it. Mr. Chapel helped me from the wagon, and we walked to the door. He gave it a good bang, and in no time the door swung open, revealing a barefoot Negro woman in a faded blue homespun dress and a matching head scarf. I couldn't be sure, but I thought I detected a rounding of her belly beneath the course fabric.

Her amber eyes flicked to me briefly before showering George with smiles. "George Chapel, where you been hiding at?"

"Hey now, Mercy. I've brung over this here schoolmarm to see you. She says she taught in the freedmen's school here a few years back, and she come looking for her students. I told her they all but left, 'cept for a scarce few here in California."

She turned her eyes to me then, and inspected my face. "It can't be. What's your name?"

"Abigail Whimble."

She let out a cry, whether happy or angry I couldn't tell. "My name is Mercy Williams. I married Leopold Williams four years back. Remember him?"

I clapped my hands to my mouth. "Leo, of course! He was a good friend to me."

Leo had been a longtime student of mine. He'd come over from the mainland to live in the colony during the war and had known nothing but farming. So Ben had instructed him in boat piloting, and Leo had quickly become one of the best boat pilots around. He sailed me to Whales Head so I could surprise Ben for Christmas, and was kind enough to sail me right back, in respectful silence, to Roanoke Island when the visit went sour.

"Leo's told me all about you," she said. "How good a teacher you were."

"Is he at home today? I'd very much like to see him."

"No, no, he's out most of the time these days. He's a pilot, you know, and now he has to farm too. Now and then he teaches *me* a little, on account I never went to school."

"Is there no school in your community here?"

With a smirk, she said, "Well, there is a school over yonder near town, but the white children go there. Not enough room in the school for us Negroes, says the schoolmaster."

She sighed. "We do what we can. A few lessons here and there from folks who got learned a bit. Letters scratched into the dirt with a stick. Least we could sign our names on the deed. We ain't a bunch of *X*s anymore," she declared.

"Here in California, it's mostly folks that grew up here, working as slaves, same as me. Eleven families bought this land together. Five hundred dollars for two hundred acres. And we moved this here church from the colony. The schoolhouse...well, I don't recall what happened to it. I wish we'd moved it with us too."

I told her about returning to Nags Head from Nashville to build the schoolhouse, and how I'd been looking for former residents of the colony to try to convince them to come to the school when they could.

"Would the residents here want to come to the school?" I asked. "I could perhaps arrange transportation from here to Nags Head and back again."

She shook her head sadly. "You could ask, but we have got all we can handle with this here land. You know that's why the folks in the colony couldn't stay on—on account the government took back the land they'd given 'em. No land, no work, no food. 'Course they all left. It was a shame, because the way we all saw it, it was a grand thing they tried to do. Too good to be true, I reckon."

She looked over to Mr. Chapel, who'd stepped back a few paces while Mercy and I talked.

"George here was born free, but we weren't all so lucky."

He grumbled, "Lucky! Just 'cuz I was free don't mean I was gettin' handouts or nothing. I bought my land too, fair and square."

Mercy's eyes looked past me, to the fields and orchards beyond. "You know how we came about the name of this place? The word 'California' was written of in an old, Spanish story book. A mythical island paradise, ruled by strong, beautiful Negro women. A rocky and wild land of gold and pearls, where a woman could be anything a man could be. Fact, any man that stumbled on their shores was fed to their beasts."

She laughed. "We ain't quite so bloodthirsty as that, but the name stuck with us. If I had more learning, I'd want to find that story and read it myself."

She regarded me with seriousness then. "If we aim to prosper, and live proud like those women in the story did, we do need proper learning."

She put a hand to her belly and rested it there. "'Specially our young'uns. You should have built up your schoolhouse here on the island."

Perhaps I should have, I thought. Perhaps my preoccupation with Nags Head had been misguided; Ben certainly seemed to think so.

Mercy must have sensed my turmoil, for she placed a gentle hand on my forearm.

"Now, listen. You're doing the right thing, Miz Whimble. You already done had a schoolhouse here, and look what happened. Most everybody left. And I should say, those folks in Nags Head could *use* a bit of learning."

"More'n a bit!" laughed Mr. Chapel.

Andy hollered, "Hey now, we ain't all simpletons in Nags Head!"

I saw the Nags Head School in all its costly glory. And yet I'd taught in a schoolhouse that had had almost nothing, and it had been a beacon for so many in a time of desperation.

"The church could be used as a school," I ventured. "You'll need desks, chairs, books. A teacher too. It can be done."

Mercy stepped away from the threshold and surveyed the church, a few hundred yards down the road.

"I'll do everything I can to help you," I said.

She turned to face me, a big smile on her face. "Leo told me you could do anything you put your mind to. Come hell or high water, you always found a way."

I shook my head. Leo had been wrong.

I'd left this island, left my husband, left my only friends. I'd found a way to leave, and that was all. Now, as I stared at Mercy's hopeful face, I wondered if I could truly find my way back.

CHAPTER NINE

Abigail Whimble
September 20, 1881
Nags Head, North Carolina

They said they would rather be outlaws for a year in Sher-
wood Forest than President of the United States forever.
—The Adventures of Tom Sawyer

Ruby had already filled a basket with biscuits and was now removing fresh ones from the spider with tongs, rather quickly, I thought, for it being so early in the morning.

But I wanted to get started as soon as I could. Today I was spreading the word in Nags Head Woods about Enrollment Day, the day when potential students could visit the schoolhouse and, hopefully, enroll in school.

With Ruby's help, I'd drawn a map of the nineteen homesites in Nags Head Woods, complete with the owners' names and how many children lived at the home. By my tally, there were thirty-two children living in Nags Head Woods alone.

Andy had even brought over his mother's Banker horse, a sweet-tempered girl named Pudding, though I'd gathered that his family wasn't keen on losing his fishing skills to school.

"Let me help, Ruby," I protested, but she just shooed me away.

She had suggested that I bring freshly made biscuits to the families of the woods, but I'd had no way to cook on my own, so she'd offered to help. I was grateful, for I feared I would be more of a hindrance than a help in my state. I'd slept poorly the night before, with recurrent dreams of Ben's dark, angry eyes startling me awake.

Frances, biscuit in hand, pulled at the fabric of my dress. "You gonna get dirty."

Ruby snickered. "She got more dresses, I'll wager."

Frances looked down at the ragged cloth doll in her other hand; her handstitched dress was torn and dirty. She glared at me. "Mama says I'm going to your school."

"Four years old is a perfect time to start learning letters and sounds."

"See Frances? Miz Whimble says you can start."

"Little Bud told me she ain't going, so I'm not going neither."

"Don't matter what Little Bud's doing," said Ruby. "You're going to school. Your daddy already told you so."

"I don't want to go," pouted Frances. She ran to the door and headed outside.

"I promise you'll like it," I called, but Frances was already gone.

"Who is this Little Bud?" I asked Ruby.

"Oh, a girl from the family. She's a little older than Frances, and oh my, does she boss her about. I have to bite my tongue to keep from saying nasty things."

I knew Ruby was referring to the Ruffin family, where she and her mother had worked as some of the only slaves in Nags Head. Ruby had been a girl of fifteen then, but her mother had worked her entire life there, laboring on the farm and in the house. She'd been buried in the Ruffin family cemetery, I'd once heard, but well outside the main plots; her marker was a slab of carved wood on the outskirts of a familial group of engraved stone.

"They live four miles up the road, and let me tell you, if Little Bud lived any closer, I'd have to pick up and move. They got about a dozen children, give or take. You may have to give them some extra biscuits."

Ruby finished up the last of the biscuits and wrapped them in cloth in another basket.

I made to thank her, but she said, "It's not just for you, you know. This is for *everybody's* good."

Before I could leave, I had to ask. "Have you...seen Ben about?"

Ruby sighed. "He stops in every once in a while. Brings us clams by the bucketful."

"And...does he mention me?"

She eyed me carefully. "Not to me. But to Jacob, well...you don't need to know what he's saying. Just pass those biscuits round. Gonna take you all day, you know, even on horseback."

I swallowed my misery, mounted Pudding on the sidesaddle, and began to make my way north up the Nags Head Woods road. But as the first two-storied frame house emerged on a rise of land, cleared of trees and fenced with wire, my heart scrambled up into my throat, cowering.

The property seemed to sprawl all the way to the sound. I spotted a barn and some large gardens as I pushed open the gate, fastened to the fence with homemade hinges. I led Pudding to a tree, where she munched on the patchy grass underneath, and walked up the steps of the unpainted house. As rough as it was, the front porch was spacious and well-placed, and a good breeze from the sound cooled the perspiration on my forehead.

After a few deep breaths, I knocked on the door. A boy opened it, but a woman followed right behind him, wiping her hands on her apron.

And I saw with relief that it was Alice Weeks. Her mother was Loretta Weeks, the local midwife, and along with Alice's sister, Ida, we'd all helped care for Ben's daddy in the house by the sea. They were a dependable, hard-working family; I still recalled when Alice herself had outright wished for a school in Nags Head.

"Abigail Whimble. Standing on my doorstep." She didn't look pleased.

"Hello, Alice. It's good to see you again. I hope you and your family are well. How is your mother?"

She looked from my hat to my shoes with no apology, and I felt foolishly dressed, my breath already shallow from the corset.

"Mama's old as Methuselah. Living with Ida on account of her bad knees. Now shoo," she said, swatting the boy on the head. "Run along and fetch me some eggs from the coop."

But the boy stared at me. "You're the schoolmarm, ain't you?"

"I am. I'm Mrs. Whimble. And what's your name?"

"I said scat!" said Alice.

The boy dragged his bare feet past me, out the door and off into the yard.

"Well?" said Alice, crossing her arms and eyeing my baskets, growing heavier by the second.

"I've come to tell you about Enrollment Day this Saturday. An opportunity to go inside the schoolhouse and talk to me about my teaching methods and what everyone will be learning. Food and drinks will be served."

"You brung some biscuits," she said, her lips curling into something like a smile. "Someone must've told you what our currency is out here."

"Ruby Craft made them."

"Ruby did?" She held out her apron. "I'll take six."

I unwrapped the cloth and counted out six warm biscuits into her apron. Then she retreated.

"Alice," I called. "Will you consider coming this Saturday?"

But she'd already disappeared. I stood there staring into the house, where I saw no furniture, pictures or carpets. I sighed; the day was going to be much more difficult than I'd feared.

I turned and made my way back to Pudding, but in a bit I heard Alice calling my name.

"Where are you off to?" she shouted.

I walked back to the house and saw six children of all ages, the boy included, crowded near the door, each of them eating a biscuit.

"Now you can tell us about the school," said Alice. "And your special day."

I launched into a hurried monologue about teaching them to read and write and do mathematics sums. When I finished, I wasn't sure I'd made any of it sound very interesting.

"Do you think you'd like to come to school?" I asked.

They all shrugged their shoulders.

"'*Course* they want to learn their letters," Alice declared. "Do them some good. Put something in those heads other than fish heads and coon tails. Now go, you all got chores to do."

The children scattered indoors and out, toward the gardens and barn.

"Can't give you money, but mayhaps something in trade would suit you?"

"Of course. Just a small, monthly contribution from each of the families. And a regular donation of kindling."

But it seemed she wasn't listening.

"Why are you carrying on with that man, with Ben back?"

My cheeks flared. "Mr. Wharton?"

"How would I know his name?"

"He's an investor in the school. A mentor of mine."

She glared at me. "Don't like the sound of *that*."

"He's like a father to me and that's all. He cares deeply about education."

She narrowed her eyes. "Fatherly or not. Side by side at the hotel for the summer. Riding about, all slicked up. It don't look right, is what we're saying."

We.

Ruby had told me that the women in the woods were as tight-knit as family. That the children called the adults "aunt" and "uncle" no matter the connection, though there were several generations of families living in the woods. Despite the fact that Frances was the only Negro child living in Nags Head Woods, she frequently found herself welcomed into the homes of the white residents, sampling their jams or helping to stir a pot. In the wider state of North Carolina, such an occurrence was unthinkable.

"He won't be here much longer," I said firmly, though I realized, in all of the activity around the construction and planning, we'd never discussed the timing of his departure.

"It's none of *my* concern," she said with a shrug, and closed the door.

The day only went downhill from there.

The men were out fishing or hunting, and the women had their hands full with all manner of household chores and spoke to me while working. Bent double in their gardens, shoveling manure over their soil. Perched on a stool, milking the cows in the barn. Hunched at the butcher block, mixing cornmeal and milk or kneading dough, or standing by the hearth frying slices of fish or tomatoes. Their backs were strong and straight, and they were simply adorned in homespun and old leather boots.

Most were so busy, they forgot about the biscuits I'd handed to them at their doors. They seemed somewhat interested in the school, but when I asked if they'd come to Enrollment Day, they busied themselves with their tasks at hand without answering. Even Alice's sister, Ida Moore, had a hard time looking me in the eye.

And as I rode from house to house, I felt as if I were being watched from the windows, from the trees, from the patches of sound water.

What I figured was the sprawling Ruffin farm emerged around a bend in the pathway, which ended in the sand dunes and buried trees of Run Hill. The property stretched as far as I could see, by far the largest farm in the village. The cemetery, surrounded by a picket fence, was just visible under a canopy of live oaks.

On my way to the front door, I spotted a rope swing, hanging from a low oak branch, and on it were Frances and a girl with two long blond braids. I called hello and waved, but they both just watched me with narrowed eyes.

I knocked on the door, and a dark-haired young woman pulled it open, a baby on her hip. I saw an upright piano in the parlor behind her, the first I'd seen in a home on the island.

I launched into my practiced speech. "Hello, I'm Mrs. Abigail Whimble. I'm the teacher at the new school on the sound. I wanted to let you know about Enrollment..."

"Mama and Daddy are busy," she said, and made to close the door, but I reached out a hand to stop it.

"Walter!" she hollered.

I heard thundering boot steps from the back of the house, and was soon face-to-face with a young man with a neatly combed thatch of black hair and a round, babyish face that contrasted with his muscled arms. He sneered at me, and I took a step backward.

"The schoolmarm we heard about," said the woman. "This is her."

Walter crossed his thick arms across his chest. "We heard you was coming, spreading your devilishness. You tell her we ain't coming to her place of Satanic worship?"

"I did." She sighed.

"It's just a school," I stammered. "And I certainly don't worship Satan there."

Walter took a menacing step toward me, and I held out the basket with the remaining biscuits. "I brought you all some biscuits."

Walter looked at the basket as if it held days'-old fish. "We'd never take food from you."

"Ruby Craft made them."

The young woman's face showed interest. "Her mama's recipe? With the bacon fat?"

She took the basket from my hand, and the baby reached a hand to it, eyes wide. But her brother hollered, "Louise Ruffin, give her back that basket!"

Louise handed me the basket with an apologetic tilt of her head. "We don't need charity, is what we mean to say."

"It's not charity."

"And we don't need no learning from the likes of you neither," growled Walter.

He slammed the door, just as Frances and her friend came running up the steps. Their faces were screwed into angry prunes, their hands fastened to their hips.

"Frances ain't going to school," said the little girl. "And that's that."

"It's up to her mama and daddy. And I believe they'd like for her to learn at school."

Her face untightened in surprise, but then quickly squished into a prune again.

"And what is your name?" I asked.

"I ain't got a name."

Frances piped up, "This is Little Bud!"

"I suppose you don't want to go to school either, Little Bud."

"Nobody cares beans about learnin'."

She stamped her bare foot and stuck out her tongue at me, but I was too tired to tell her how I thought she'd enjoy school, once she gave it a chance.

Pudding and I began to make our way back down the sandy road, four meandering miles on sidesaddle in a bustled dress. I spotted some of the residents working in their fields, and I waved at them. But they didn't wave back.

I reined in Pudding a hundred yards off from Ben's cabin and tied her to a branch, then strode straight through the live oaks and cedars that blocked the Crafts' cabin from Ben's. Light was visible through the window.

I crept as close as I dared through the underbrush and saw Ben sitting at the rickety old table, reading a book by lantern light. I took in his thin back and lanky arms, his unkempt hair, reaching just past his shoulders. He'd changed, and yet he was still reading.

I watched him for a long while, his forefinger running beneath the line of words he was reading, the way that he used to; it was only when my checks began to hurt that I realized I was smiling.

At times, lying in my bed in Nashville and waiting for sleep, I wondered if I'd ever see him again. Just to rest my eyes on him now was a blessing I didn't deserve. Did I once believe I would find someone better than him? There was no one for me but Ben.

I was eager to know what the book was, but I couldn't see the cover. I wished I could ask him. Just knock on the door and ask him.

But he didn't want to talk to me. I made myself leave him.

I handed Ruby the empty baskets at the door and made to leave, but she took me by my arm and steered me into the house. I was surprised to see Frances, sitting on her tick with a plate of food on her lap.

She laughed. "Your horse sure is slow."

"Well, her name is Pudding, and you don't give fast horses names like Pudding. How did you get here so quickly?"

She took a bite of sweet potato and didn't answer me.

"Frances Craft. You answer Miz Whimble right now!"

Frances took her time chewing, then swallowed with elaboration. "Orson," she mumbled.

"That ain't a proper answer," said Ruby.

"Orson Ruffin's boat!" she shouted. "Don't you know boats are quicker than horses?"

Ruby marched over to Frances and took the plate and fork from her grasp. "That's enough," she scolded. "It's time for bed."

Frances glared at me and yanked a blanket over herself.

Ruby turned to me. "Frances said she saw you at the Ruffins'."

I took a gulp of the water she'd handed me. "That's right."

My thoughts turned jumbled and I had a hard time looking her in the eye, though she stared at me, waiting for me to go on.

"I was met at the door by Louise, and her brother—Walter was his name—soon joined us. He was rather intimidating. Little Bud wasn't far behind."

She cackled. "You met Walter?"

"Has he always been so angry?"

"He came out a-squallin' from his mama and never stopped. I helped raise him, you know."

"I suppose I shouldn't blame you for how he's turned out."

"Oh, he's all right, when you get to know him. Ruffins came to our wedding," she said with a rueful grin. "Gave us a cow and some goats and chickens, to get us started. It was a generous gift."

I nodded. I wanted to say, *But they owed it to you*. I glanced at Frances, who was listening carefully to us.

Ruby said, "Frances knows everything there is to know about Ruffins and me. And listen, I ain't complaining about nothing. I heard about how things are on the mainland for us Negroes, and that's a hard way to live. Jacob's got a good government job now, making regular money. And now look—we got us a brand-new schoolhouse and the best teacher in the whole state of North Carolina. No, ma'am, I ain't complaining one bit."

Just then, Jacob swung the door open, a bag of provisions on his elbow.

"Your ears must've been burning." Ruby laughed.

"Daddy!" cried Frances, throwing the blanket off herself and running over to hug him around his legs.

But he only had eyes for me; I hadn't seen him since I'd been back in Nags Head, but we hadn't exactly been seeking each other out. He'd always questioned Ben's judgment in marrying me, in spite of everything I'd done that might've changed his mind.

"Hello, Jacob," I said. "It's good to see you again."

"Evening, Abigail," he said, offering me a rare smile. "It's been a long time, hasn't it?"

"It has. You look well, though. The life of a surfman must agree with you."

"I wouldn't say that!" He chuckled. "How did your day of visiting go?"

"Not very well, I must admit. Interest in the schoolhouse was low."

He snorted. "I could've told you that and saved you the trouble."

He lifted Frances into the air and held her in the crook of his arm.

"Well, I know you'll have one student, at least. Frances Craft will be there soon as that door opens."

Frances groaned and kicked her way back down again.

Ruby handed plates of fried fish, sweet potatoes and cornbread to us, so we sat at the table by the hearth and ate. The food tasted so good that nobody spoke until the plates were clean. In that short amount of time, Frances had fallen asleep on her tick, her doll in her arms. Jacob leaned back in his chair.

"That schoolhouse of yours," he said, shaking his head. "Never seen anything like it. And neither have the folks here. You're used to highfalutin city things and big thinkers, but out here we're happy just to have roofs over our heads. It's gonna take a grist of time for them to come round. And I mean that for *every*body."

I nodded. I knew he was referring to Ben.

"But I want to thank you, Abigail," he said.

"You do?"

"I see what you're trying to do for us. Now, I'm leaving for Pea Island in a couple of weeks, and it sure takes a weight off my back knowin' my daughter is getting her learning and not running wild around the woods. Ruby and me, we want Frances to rise up. Get off this island one day. These woods ain't no place for a growing Negro girl."

Ruby sighed heavily. "Jacob's been talking about us moving closer to the lifesaving station. Get a place on the mainland. For Frances, we'd do it."

"Asha moved to Bertie County to teach in a school there, near a fishery that employs hundreds of Negroes," I said. "She's grown to like it—the strong community and the steady wages. She says everyone works together, regardless of skin color."

"You hear that, Ruby?" asked Jacob. To me, he said, "I've been telling her I've seen many a place along the waterways where folks just get along. Brother to brother and sister to sister. Something about living and working near the water that calms folks down, I reckon."

"You've told me, all right. But this is my home," said Ruby. "Out here, life's hard no matter *who* you are."

She glanced at Frances, fast asleep. "But I know it's different for Frances. She needs to be able to strive for more, with her own kind."

CHAPTER TEN

Benjamin Whimble
September 24, 1881
Nags Head, North Carolina

"Any other boy!" Tom thought, grating his teeth. "Any boy in the whole town but that Saint Louis smarty that thinks he dresses so fine and is aristocracy! Oh, all right, I licked you the first day you ever saw this town mister, and I'll lick you again! You just wait till I catch you out!"
—The Adventures of Tom Sawyer

I'd seen a paper nailed up on the door of the market, and the date of the school shindig had been branded onto my brain. I'd recognized her pretty penmanship right away, though it had been years since I'd seen it.

Enrollment Day!
*Come see the new **Nags Head School** and meet the teacher!*
Barbecue pork sandwiches, iced tea and sugar cookies will be served.
Saturday, September 24, Noon to 6:00 p.m.
Located a quarter of a mile from the hotel,
just off Nags Head Woods Road on the Roanoke Sound

Most of the locals here wouldn't be able to read that paper, and even if they did, Abby's highfalutin notions would raise their hackles. But I figured word would get around about the pig, barbecued by Hal, the hotel cook, and folks would head over to eat. I wouldn't be one of 'em.

I finished up my morning of proggin' and walked over to the Blounts' abode to hand off some of my clams. Granny was dozin' in her chair, and Bert and Digby were just comin' in from the ocean, catchin' spot and mullet. They were still young, but they'd grown into strong fishermen since I'd known them; they now owned two boats and untold numbers of nets, a rarity even here.

"You headin' over to the school this afternoon?"

"For what?" Confusion came over their sunburned faces.

"The shindig Abby's having at the schoolhouse. Pig barbecue and whatnot."

"'Course not," scoffed Digby. "We're fishermen, not good-for-nothin' scribblers."

"Yeah. We're workin' men now," said Bert, pushing out his chest.

I scowled at them. "That's blasphemy, is what it is. Not even wantin' to learn your letters so you can write your own names. Shame on you."

Bert guffawed. "Are *you* going, Uncle Ben? She's *your* wife."

"No," I mumbled. "I'm not ready yet."

"I knew you could be stubborn, Uncle Ben, but this cold-shoulder business is cappin' the climax. I seen her walking into the hotel one day, you know. She's pretty as a picture. If I were you, I'd be runnin' over there and huggin' on her all the time."

Bert and Digby fell over themselves laughin' while they threw their arms around their own backs, makin' kissin' sounds.

Jennie'd been quiet, darnin' some socks. And she wasn't laughin' one bit.

"You should go too, Jennie."

"No thank you," she said, too polite.

"Not you too!" I cried.

She wouldn't look at me. "I don't want to be taught by the likes of her."

Somethin' like a twig in my chest snapped right in two, and I reached for it, rubbin'. Bert and Digby turned away snickerin'.

"On what account?"

"On account she's not a good person. She's selfish and untrue."

I'd thought the same thoughts, on my darker days. "Don't say that, Jennie."

"It's a fact," she said, anger in her eyes. "She's been gone all these years, and now she wants us all to get learned? Like we're a bunch of gum-smackin' simpletons needing her to save us from our ignorance? Don't we have our *pride*?"

My mouth started workin' on its own. "What if we went together?"

She stared, the anger in her eyes dyin'. "You'd do that? Just to get me to go to the shindig?"

I crossed my arms. "You'd have to enroll in school."

She clacked her tongue. "Not a chance. I'm just going to see it is all. And try the food."

Bert said, "I *could* use a good pig sandwich myself. Too much fish makes a man snappish."

"So it's settled," I said, headin' to the door.

"You're goin' like that, Uncle Ben?" asked Bert. He was yankin' off his stained shirt to change into a laundered one.

I shrugged, lookin' down at Wilson's ragged clothes, topped by a moth-eaten sweater.

"You really don't care for her anymore, do you?" laughed Digby, who was also changin' his shirt. "I reckon I'll look better'n you by a long shot. Look at that beard!"

I could see it just by lookin' down at my chest, a nest of thick brown hair.

Lucky for me, Bert and Digby poked fun at me the whole skiff ride to the school, so I didn't have to think on what I was gettin' myself into.

There was a pig on a spit all right, but hardly anybody was there to partake of it. A few folks I knew to be from Kill Devil Hills shoved sandwiches in their mouths while their young'uns splashed about in the water. And Andy Proctor was marchin' up the steps into the schoolhouse. But that was about it.

"Andy's already beat us here," said Bert. "He always fancies himself better'n us."

"Andy's sweet," scolded Jennie. "You could try to be more like him."

"Why don't you marry him then?" sneered Bert. "Where is everybody?"

Just then, Abby appeared in the doorway, lookin' down at us from on high.

"There she is!" rasped Bert. "Just look at her dry goods! Must've cost a pretty penny."

She did look special, with a different dress on than when I first saw her and a hat to match. She gave a little wave, and I raised my arm to her. She started walkin' down the steps; at the same time I started inchin' backward.

"Go say how-do," I said to the boys.

But they were just as skittish as me.

"You go first," whispered Bert, pushin' Digby forward.

"No, you go," whispered Digby, wrigglin' away.

And in no time, Abby was standin' before us, her skin fresh as a peeled sweet potato. I looked away from all that softness.

"We came over to see...see the school, and all," I stuttered. "This here is Bert and Digby Blount. They're thirteen and fourteen years old, not a lick of learnin' between them."

They dropped their eyes down and mumbled hello.

"And this is Jennie Blount, their sister. Age eighteen."

Jennie just looked out at the water.

Abby held out her hand to Bert, who didn't notice on account he was still lookin' at his own bare feet.

Digby dug his elbow into Bert's ribs and said, "Bert!"

Bert jumped and saw Abby's hand in front of him, so he reached out and shook it like he was jiggin' a fishin' line. Then she shook Digby's hand.

"I'm Mrs. Whimble." The spoken name hung charred as the pig in the smoky air. "Welcome to the Nags Head School."

"Nice to meet you, ma'am," said the boys, grinnin' ear to ear and givin' me looks.

Then she reached out a hand to Jennie, who looked at it like it was a dead fish.

"Please, help yourselves to the food," Abby said, droppin' her hand. "I fear that pig will go to waste today."

Jennie put on her sweetest face and said, "The pig won't be the only thing goin' to waste here."

And with that, she walked toward the food table. Bert and Digby went after her, but I stayed behind. In the quiet, I could hear the ocean, all the way over on the other side of the island.

"Ben," she said.

"Abby." I tried hard to look her in the eye, but my sight flickered in and out.

"I hoped you'd come today," she said. "Thank you for bringing the Blounts."

I licked my lips, all of a sudden dry. "'Twas good thinkin', those pork sandwiches."

"Andy Proctor said I should've served beer, but I didn't think that would have been appropriate for a teacher trying to convince people to send their children to school."

"Mayhaps not." I tried to laugh, but it came out soundin' like I needed to hawk somethin' from my throat.

"I'm surprised Jennie came along. Something tells me she doesn't like me very much."

Jennie, I saw from the corner of my eye, was starin' over at us beneath her floppy bonnet, pig sandwich sittin' uneaten on her plate.

"She's just lookin' out for me, I reckon."

Abby's eyes sparked. "Am I that dangerous?"

I was ponderin' a good answer to that when a man appeared at Abby's side. 'Twas none other than Mr. Warthog, I reckoned, and like Abby, he was slicked up in fine clothes and shiny shoes. What a picture they made.

And yet I saw Abby ball her hands into fists.

"Mr. Wharton, this is Ben."

We shook hands, his clean and tidy one mixed with my hard, gray one.

"At last we meet," he said, eyeing me all over.

"Yeah," I said. "At long last."

We all stared back and forth. Once upon a time I would've been shy of him, with his white shirt collar and fancy learnin'. But not any longer. I'd been with men twice as smart as him, and they treated me as an equal. I met his eyes and didn't blink.

"So, *Mr. Wharton*," I said. "I've been wantin' to know somethin'. Is this here your schoolhouse or Abby's? Or is it both of yours? You catch my meanin'."

Abby answered for him, too quick in my view. "Mr. Wharton is an investor."

"He paid for it, is what you're sayin'."

"That's right," she said. "But I bought the books."

I nodded. "A pet project for the two of you. I see now."

"No, Ben," said the Yankee, shakin' his head like I was an ignorant coot. "Abby wanted this. She fought for it."

"And you gave it to her."

"I did," he said, lookin' to Abby. "She was very convincing."

I saw the love he had for her—might as well have been written in ink all over his trim-bearded face.

"You plannin' on livin' here in Nags Head?" My lips twisted into a nasty grin. "Sleepin' in her room in back? Because you paid for it and all."

"Ben," said Abby, scoldin' me.

"I don't need shamin' by you, Abby. Fact, should be the other way around."

I hurried over to the Blounts, who were now partakin' of the cookies and talkin' with Andy Proctor. The lonely schoolhouse stood there behind them, half in the water and half out.

"Something amiss, Uncle Ben?" Bert said, his mouth full of food.

"Let's go," I said. "I can't abide the two of them."

"We haven't been inside the schoolhouse yet!" said Digby. His mouth was stained blackish red from the meat.

"Oh, now you want to go in? I see you've changed your tune."

"Andy says it's the grandest place he's ever..." babbled Bert.

"*I'm* ready to go," said Jennie. "The pig was too dry anyhow. Goodbye, Andy."

"You comin' when school starts?" Andy asked her.

"*No*," said Jennie.

With Bert and Digby laggin' along, Jennie and me hopped right into the skiff, and I made to pole out from the cove. I could feel Abby watchin' me, and this time it was *my* back she'd remember.

With the spirit of youth to burn, Bert and Digby changed back into their fishin' clothes and left for their boat. Jennie and me sat in the rockers on the porch, where down at the water the gulls cried and cried.

"I reckon that was a mistake," said Jennie at last.

"I don't want to talk about it."

I rocked some more. And still the gulls cried, always hungry.

"Do you think they've been...together?" I blurted out. "He's old enough to be her pap."

"I thought you didn't want to talk about it."

I grunted and rocked hard. "He cares a great amount for her. Buildin' her a schoolhouse!"

Jennie sighed. "I don't know, Ben. They're both foreigners to me. But the word is, they're not together. Andy told me she was hollerin' at him for lettin' folks think they were hitched."

I smacked my hand to my forehead. "And you're just gettin' around to tellin' me?"

She glared at me. "I'm not sure what to tell you and what not to. You're all in a tither."

"And do you blame me?"

"Not a bit," she said. "The way that man was hoverin' all over your wife. I'd have knocked him into a cocked hat if I was you."

I grunted. "I just might, at that."

At last the gulls had settled, their squabbles over for now. I could just see 'em, lookin' out to the water, wings rufflin' in the breeze. Watchin' for the next morsels that might come their way.

"Fancy a walk?" I asked.

Jennie got up, wrapped a shawl around her shoulders and grabbed her bucket. We walked across the island to the seashore and checked on the headstone first, as usual, for the marker got buried time to time, 'specially after a storm.

But lo and behold, the cross was clean of sand and reaching for the sky. And the stone had been piled on with bits of seashell.

"This your doing?" I asked.

She shook her head and bent to pick one up. "They're all broke up."

But I couldn't look, for all I saw before me was Abby, walkin' the shore alone. Leavin' washed-up and broken bits from the sea for our lost baby girl.

Me and Jennie kept on, pokin' our way along the shoreline. The ocean was as flat as a lake and shiny as a gemstone. The waves curled in girlish ringlets, leavin' spots of foam and seaweed in little piles.

Every once in a while we'd bend over and pick up a shell or some other piece of flotsam and drop it in the bucket for Jennie to draw later. But in my mind, it was Abby beside me, walkin' down this same shore, her with child and holdin' tight to my hand. Pickin' up shells, not for that gravestone of the future, but for the shelves that lined the walls of the house. She used to look for the perfect ones, but they were right hard to come by.

Jennie's collections now filled every inch of those same shelves. It was Jennie that lived in the house, the house I'd moved all the way to the safety of the sound, away from our daughter's gravestone. And I had such a queer feelin' of wrongness that I stopped my walkin' and stared at her.

This young girl who I'd watch grow, as fond of her as a pap would be. With Jimmy gone at the fishery most of the year, I'd tried to help raise her right, best I could. And she was turnin' out just fine. The boys too.

"May God help me, Jennie, but my wife has come back to Nags Head," I blurted out. "It appears she's come to stay."

She bent to pick up a shell. "You just now catchin' on?"

My heart was as good as a broken rudder. "What am I to do?"

Jennie just rolled her eyes and kept steppin' slow down the beach, and I gnashed my teeth at her, for she hadn't yet loved a man the way I loved Abby. A big part of me hoped she never would.

Never afore had I done so little work.

I did a little fishin' in the fresh ponds of the woods now and then. Caught silver perch, mullet, a little chub. Enough for me to fry over my fire with a bit of spoonbread mixed up. I did a little huntin' there too. Got a sack full in just five, six shots, yellow shanks and brown backs and willets.

But mostly I looked about for specimens for Jennie to draw. So far I'd found all manner of things, even a whole sandbar shark, washed up on the shore. When Jennie was through with her sketches, I wrote where exactly I'd found them, then measured 'em and dissected 'em at a rough-hewn table where I usually cleaned fish. I wrote about what they looked like on their insides, all for Dr. Brooks to read about next summer.

And I have to say, I did feel a little like my good friend Bishop. A real man of science.

But today I had to eat, so I stood barefoot in the sand of the sound at low tide, with one eye on the schoolhouse as I dug my shovel around and plopped the clams into my bucket.

I was close enough to see the clean glass of the windows beneath the propped storm shutters. I spent more time looking in the windows than I did in diggin'. Lookin' for the glow of red hair atop pale skin, but all was shadow.

Just like the days she'd spent away from me, where I couldn't even picture the buildin' where she taught, or the abode where she lived, or who she talked to of a day. 'Twas like she'd been swallowed by a whale, and now here I was, trying to pull her out of its mouth.

Bucket only halfway full but my back achin', I walked home, hopin' and fearin' to lay eyes on Abby. But all was quiet on the sun-shady path.

Settled in my abode, I sat at the table to read some more of the book that Bishop had lent me, back in Beaufort. The laboratory's own copy, matter of fact. *On the Origin of Species by Means of Natural Selection* by Charles Darwin.

I opened up the worn, green book up to the page I'd last stopped at, still in chapter one. The book had been chock full of science words and Darwin's deep thinkin', and I'd had a devil of a time even makin' my way through a sentence, much less a paragraph.

Cover to cover, the pages held all the notions I didn't yet know about things I thought I knew right well. I started in where I'd left off, on page six.

CHAPTER ELEVEN

Benjamin Whimble
October 1, 1881
Nags Head, North Carolina

Now he found out a new thing—namely, that to promise not to do a thing is the surest way in the world to make a body want to go and do that very thing.
—The Adventures of Tom Sawyer

Calvin was there at the hotel desk, asleep and snorin' on a mess of letters.

I rapped on the desk with my knuckles, and he jumped like a spooked snake. He peered at me with sun-bleached eyes.

"Land sakes, Benny, don't *do* that! I already got a foot in the grave as it is."

"Any post for me, Calvin?"

He squinted at me like he'd already forgotten my name. But the fact was that Calvin had been a good friend to Pap, back in the day. The sea had washed him up too, of course, for now he was like a gray hull of a ship, wrecked on the sand.

"Matter o' fact...lemme see here...Ben, Ben, Ben."

He took his time sortin' through a few envelopes and holdin' them up to the light. The rumor was Calvin couldn't read all that well, but I reckoned nobody else in Nags Head could read better to get the job.

"Don't worry, now, take your time, Calvin," I said, rappin' my knuckles on the desk again.

At long last, he pulled two envelopes from the stack and handed them to me. I let out a whoop, seein' as how the first was a letter from Dr. Brooks. Hadn't taken near as long as I thought it would. The second letter brought me back down. The post stamp on the top was marked April 22, 1881. And the script was none other than Abby's.

"Where has this been?"

I shoved it under Calvin's hairy chin, and he peered at it with strainin' eyes.

"I can't keep track of every little piece of mail that comes through those doors," he cried. "You ever see the post that comes for the summer folks? Enough to bury me six feet under."

I took a deep breath. "It's got an April post stamp. That's almost seven months ago."

He shrugged. "You were gone for a spell, as I recall. I reckon I put it away, to keep it safe."

I smacked a palm to my forehead. "This here letter...well, it's important, that's all."

He chuckled. "Sure it is, Benny. You're as important as the president of the United States, whatever his name is."

I shoved Abby's letter into the pocket of my britches and walked outside without answerin', my heart beatin' hard. She'd written to me, just as she said she had.

Not wantin' to read what she'd written just yet, I opened instead the letter from Dr. Brooks. But his letter wasn't one to boost the spirits. He thought highly of Jennie's ability, and I'd been right—he'd said each critter (and man!) had had a livin' soul inside of it.

But he'd matched the handwritin' in the letter to the written names of the creatures beneath the sketches. 'Twas *my* mess of sticks and loops, doing the work of writin' for her.

He wrote, "If she's not literate, I'm afraid I won't be able to take her on. She must be able to take down notes when needed, label parts, etcetera. Decipher information."

Why I didn't think of that sooner, I couldn't say.

I found Jennie around back of the house, pumpin' water into a laundry basin. The Nags Head surfmen's clothes were in canvas bags nearby, ready for soakin'—a bit of extra money for the family. She started throwin' the salt-stiff britches and dirty shirts into the basin and pushin' them around with a paddle.

"I got a letter from Dr. Brooks," I said to her.

She took a look at my face and stopped her stirrin'.

"He didn't like them?"

"No, he liked them right much," I said. "But he wants you to be able to read and write. Said you'll have to scribble notes and write out names of the critters and such."

She tossed the paddle to the ground and buried her face in her hands.

"I knew it. That job was too good for me."

"It's not too late to learn, Jennie."

She scoffed. "It is."

We stood there, the chickens struttin' about in the seagrass.

After a while, I said, "Abby could teach you quick, if you let her."

"What's this now?" she cried. "You know darned good how I feel about her and her school."

"You gonna mend nets like your mama this winter?"

She sucked her teeth. "I was plannin' on it. We need the money."

I looked her square in the face. "You have a gift, Jennie. You know you do."

Her eyes filled with tears. "I wanted that job. You talked me right into it, and now look."

"You can get it. Just gonna take a little learnin' is all."

"Well, then, can't *you* teach me?"

"Not when there's the best teacher around, livin' right here in Nags Head."

She grabbed the paddle once more and started to push the clothes about.

"Mama's not gonna like it."

"She wants what's best for you. You tell her how bad you want the job and she'll come around."

"She wants me at home with her."

"I reckon she does. It's hard to...watch folks leave. But it's not for too long. Just a summer. And then, well you never know where it might lead you to."

Her eyeballs rolled around in their sockets. "What are you sayin'?"

"Dr. Brooks might need you someplace else, come the future. You're so good, you could go, see the world! Draw things you never thought to draw! There was a time when you dreamed of the world outside the Banks. You and Livy Spruell. Where all of the treasures of the world came from. Across the sea and beyond."

She stared at me for a long while, then started stirrin' even harder.

"I'll never leave here. Who would I know anyplace else? My home is here. My family's here."

"You meet new people. Live a new kind of life. And you can come back. It'll always be your home here."

She glared at me. "Your own *wife* can't even come back. You've heard the talk, I'm sure. Nobody wants to be taught by her. Folks think she's touched in the head, comin' back here like she has."

She grunted with her efforts now. 'Twas hard work, stirrin' clothes, and even harder work scrubbin' 'em. I took the paddle from her hands and started in myself.

"You even *going* back to Beaufort, with your wife here now?" she asked.

Too quick, I said, "'Course I am."

"I wasn't born yesterday," she scoffed. "I know how this is gonna go."

"Now stop pitchin' a fit," I said, my arms already achin'. "This isn't about Abby. This is about a schoolmarm, right here, ready to teach you. I'm goin' to write Dr. Brooks, tell him you can read and write."

"You're fixin' to lie to him now?"

"It won't be a lie if you learn what you need to know. I don't want you to scrub and mend and cater to surfmen and summer folks your whole life. Not if you don't have to."

She didn't talk to me for a long while, churnin' the soap around the clothes in the basin, makin' the water foam. She was so much stronger than she knew.

At last she turned to me, her face colored red with work. "You know, I grew up watchin' that big sand hill come closer and closer to our home. Year after year, living in dread our house would crack open, drownin' us with sand. And even though we moved, I still sometimes feel like I'm a sittin' duck, just waitin' for something bad to swallow me up. Livin' fearful."

I nodded. "I've lived that way too."

"Mayhaps it's time for the *both* of us to climb atop those sand hills that we picture. Ride the wave, instead of scurryin' around beneath it. Mayhaps what we're afeared of ain't all that bad for us."

She was a lot wiser than me, I saw. "So that's a yes, then."

She sighed, all her strength to fight me gone. "I reckon we'll soon see how good a teacher she really is."

Tonight, with the full moon fillin' the tide, there was to be a twilight haul on the beach. Most of the fishin' men in Nags Head would be there, pullin' a seine net of fish from the sea. And their families would stand by, ready to pick out the harvest, and take a share back home.

Time I got there, a couple of bonfires were blazin' on the beach, and the young'uns too small to help with the net were ridin' ponies along the shore. That October chill was in the air at last, and the women were sittin' by the fires, blankets wrapped around them. Soon the weather would turn cold and oftentimes nasty with wind and rain, but tonight, Mother Nature was sweet as sugar.

There was a time not too far back when Pap and me would help set the net for just such a haul. Eliza and Iola would be the ones sittin' by the fire and helpin' pick the fish from the net. Those two had moved north, but there sat the newcomers, mixed in with the old. Everybody loved Jennie and Della, and Bert and Digby gave young muscle to the group. There they were out in their own dory, pullin' the end of the net slowly in to the beach.

Ruby and Frances mingled with the lot of them but looked a bit lonesome without Jacob, who'd gone back to the lifesaving station for drills and a season of rough seas and patrollin' the beach.

My people, I thought. The sight of them all here, on this fire-licked night, brought a tear to my eye.

Once upon a time Abby had come down to the beach to find me. That July Fourth evening, after her pap had bought the wild red pony for her. Seeing her there in the bonfire-dark, lookin' for me, had given me so much joy back then. She let that horse go not too long after that, watched her walk away free. And now I saw what I couldn't see back then—freedom was a notion she held in high regard.

I looked about for her in the crowd of women in spite of myself. And there came Della, marchin' over to me with an angry look I'd never afore seen. Jennie was watchin' close from her spot near the bonfire.

"Jennie tells me she's goin' to school," she barked. "She said you're *makin'* her go. You want her to spy on your wife, is that the way of it?"

"'Course not! And I'm not makin' her do a thing, Della."

"Well, why on earth would she want to go, then? It don't make sense. The things she's said about that school and your wife would burn your ears to hear."

"She didn't tell you why?"

"Tell me what?"

I shook my head. "I'm not buttin' my nose into the middle of this."

She laughed out loud and reached for my nose to tweak. "It's already there, Ben Whimble!"

"Look here. She's got a good reason for wantin' to learn how to read and write. But you'll have to ask her."

"Good reason? Hogwash."

Della turned in the sand and marched back to the bonfire, crashin' down next to Jennie and startin' in with her. Jennie shot harpoons at me with her eyes.

But the net was bein' pulled our way, and all of the men headed into the wash and grabbed ahold. We hauled with all our strength; the net was heavy, fit to bustin'. And I welcomed the way my arms and back cried out, settin' free the old, tired thoughts that stuck wrigglin' in the net of my head.

Once up on the shore, we saw that it was chock-full of spot, wedged thick into the mesh. With the gulls divin' and cryin' above, the women and young'uns started to pickin' them from the net and puttin' them in buckets. The men spread the net on some stakes to dry it, and then out came the bottles, passed around from man to man.

The stars swam like tiny sea critters at the bottom of a dark sea. The ocean sat happy beside us, our friend for now, a giver of fish. I walked to the edge of the water and splashed some corn liquor into the wash.

Thank you, I said in my head.

"Thank you kindly!" I hollered.

I turned and saw all my people laughin', pointin' at me.

"He's run aground!" they called.

I raised the bottle to them and drank deep of the liquor.

Abby should be here, I thought. Someone should have told her to come.

The liquor hit my skin 'n bones hard, and the moon was full and bright in the starry sky. I got up and said my goodbyes and headed for home. But instead of skirtin' over to the woods, I found my legs walkin' in the direction of the hotel again

Calvin grinned when he saw me, bored to tears.

"Comin' from the twilight haul?" he growled. "How'd you fare?"

"We'll be eatin' spot for weeks."

He licked his blue lips. "Don't mind spot a-tall."

He sniffed the air around me and scowled.

"You up for a hand of gin rummy?" he asked. "Or you too liquored up?"

"I reckon I can play a hand, Calvin."

He pulled out a deck out from inside his desk.

The cards blurred and danced in my hand, and I could hardly remember which cards I'd gotten rid of. Half-blind Calvin won in a few minutes' time.

"Say, Calvin. You think you could tell me which room my wife is in?"

He grinned, more gum than teeth. "I was wonderin' when you were gonna ask me that."

He told me she was on the first floor of the hotel, around the corner on the sound side. Then he cocked his bald head.

"She's been here since June. Next door to that man she come with."

"I know."

He squinted his bushy white brows and shook a crooked finger at me. "Don't know why your pretty schoolmarm wife is sleeping in a *hotel*. You fixin' to take her home?"

No, not home. There wasn't a home for us anymore.

"I'm working it out, Calvin."

He shook his head and sighed deep. I stood there swayin' like a pine tree in the wind.

"She's a rare woman, that wife o' yourn. Ain't never had a school here."

I nodded and nodded at him. My head was spinnin' like a deathly current.

"Well, go on, then, whatcha waitin' for?"

"I'm not sure. It's late, Calvin. She's likely asleep."

"Land sakes, Benny, go to your wife!"

I turned and stumbled outside, then veered around the back of the hotel. Lookin' for room number twenty-eight, the painted numbers on the doors hard to read in the dark. I soon found it, right on the end. Mr. Warthog next door to her, the no-account.

I stood out front of the room for a long time, tryin' to tell myself that it wasn't my wife in there. It almost worked, but then it was like I could *feel* her in there. Just like a flame, lickin' at the bottom of a pile of sticks.

Heart thuddin' in my throat, I walked through the piles of creamy sand to get to the window in back, but when I got there, I saw that the sand had piled itself right up to the whole back of the building. It blocked the window so that I couldn't even see a thing through it.

I knew it must have bothered Abby, not bein' able to see the water or the sky. Smothered by sand.

I stumbled back around to the parlor of the hotel.

"Now what?" cried Calvin.

"You got a shovel somewhere?"

"In the shed over yonder. What you fixin' to do? Pull your wife through the window? She's got a door, you know."

I found the shed, itself almost buried by the sand dune, and went back around to Abby's window. Started to shovelin' the sand away from her window, in the direction of Mr. Warthog's.

I worked at it 'til my back started to ache, though the liquor in my blood numbed my hands. And when I could see her bottom windowsill, I stopped. I peered inside her dirty window, saw nothing but darkness.

But after a while, I made out her bedstead, and there on the pillow was her head. Red hair all over like a rare breed of seaweed, spillin' over her face, smooth as a shiny white nautilus. She was all wrapped up in the bed coverings, hidin' from the chill.

The night ebbed, and I took my fill of her, 'til I wanted to lay down and rest in the cool, fresh sand. Right near her, 'til the sun rose in the east. The way I used to, afore all those hard times.

Could I love her again, the way I used to? Could we trust each other again? Could we hold our hearts in each other's hands and not squeeze the lives from them? I wasn't sure of a thing.

I made myself turn around and leave, though the moonlight had at last found the glass. 'Twas shinin' on her face, as if I needed a thing else beggin' me to stay.

Back at my cabin, I stretched out on my tick with my head still heavy. I opened up Abby's letter, expecting' to see all kinds of slippery words. But to my surprise, there were hardly any words on the paper a-tall.

We'd moved past all those tired, inky words, we both agreed.

Instead, she'd drawn a picture of a schoolhouse, nothin' like Jennie's art but good enough, and beneath it, she'd written *Nags Head School*.

Then she'd written, in small script at the very bottom of the page, *I'd like to come home now.*

I folded it up neat and held it gentle with blistered fingers, my eyes blinkin' hard to keep out my liquored tears.

CHAPTER TWELVE

Abigail Whimble
October 2, 1881
Nags Head, North Carolina

She listened intently, but there was no answer. She had no companions but silence and loneliness. So she sat down and began to cry again and upbraid herself; and by this time the scholars began to gather again, and she had to hide her griefs and still her broken heart and take up the cross of a long, dreary, aching afternoon, with none among the strangers to exchange sorrows with.

—The Adventures of Tom Sawyer

I awoke to the moonlight on my face, as a bear would emerge blinking from his den into the bright new day. Though the window was coated with sandy grime, the light was so bright the window appeared almost clean.

I got out of bed and looked out; sometime after I'd fallen asleep, someone had shoveled the great piles of sand away from my window. Though all was dark, I could now see the waters of the Roanoke Sound, winking with the light of moon and stars.

With all my strength, I shoved the window up and swung myself over the ledge, down into the sand. Barefoot and clad only in my nightgown, I surveyed the scene, concluding that someone had stood here and shoveled the sand for a good amount of time. I also noted that this same someone had made sure to pile the sand even higher at the window of Mr. Wharton.

My heart began to leap about in time with my thoughts. *Was he here? Was he waiting?*

I walked through the cold sand around the hotel and looked about, but all was still. No boats in the sound and nobody in sight. Yet the fat slice of moon reached her arms of light toward me, as benevolent as an old friend.

I shook the sand from my feet and crawled back into the room. Burrowing back under the thick layer of coverings, I couldn't close my staring eyes to beckon sleep.

In his own way, Ben had come to me. He'd sent me a message, a message without letters or speech. A message from the heart.

I pulled the pillow over my face to catch the bubbling laughter. There was no sleep to be had. Memories of our past rolled in—happy days, and hard days too. They piled up around me, as heavy as the sand, and I decided to shovel it all away and arise.

Pulling from the wardrobe my new dress, indigo homespun stitched by Ruby, I readied myself for the first day of school.

Even in the gray dawn, every small thing seemed animated: the water waved hands of greeting; the branches waltzed with me; their coloring leaves sang a chorus. Birds and chipmunks and squirrels emerged from the woods to usher me along the path.

The day opened for me, full of hope.

And there was Ben, sitting on the steps of the schoolhouse. I forced my shaking legs to continue to walk forward, a grin already on my face.

Ben took off his cap to loosen locks of shaggy hair that spilled over his thin face. He pushed it all away with a swipe.

"Morning, Abby."

"Good morning, Ben."

"How...?" he started, then paused, looking down at his boots. "How's your view these days?"

I took a deep breath of the marshy air. "Clear enough to give the window curtains a purpose again."

A little smile was visible beneath his beard. "Today's the first day of school," he said. "Wouldn't do to start the day with a view full of sand."

"Thank you, Ben. Though I daresay I won't be enjoying the view for much longer. I'm moving into the schoolhouse today."

"That so?"

I stepped closer to him. "Staying there...wasn't meant to be for long."

My words hung in the air, full of weight, and we both fell silent.

"I know it's early," he blurted out, "but I wasn't sure...well, what time school would start, and we didn't want to miss anything, you know."

He turned his head and pointed to the water's edge, where Jennie Blount stood watching us. Her unpinned blond hair puffed about her head like dandelion fuzz.

"I won't be staying, myself. But Jennie here, she wants to get started on her learning."

He beckoned her closer, and she crept over to us, as if each step brought significant pain.

"Welcome, Jennie," I said.

I tried to sound cheerful, instead of disappointed that Ben's purpose here was to help Jennie, seemingly the most important woman in his life.

"Morning," she muttered.

"I'm teaching two sessions—four hours in the morning and four hours in the afternoon. There will be an hour break for a meal at noon for those students who choose to stay on for the afternoon session."

"She'll stay for both sessions," declared Ben. Jennie huffed and crossed her arms about her chest.

I filled the bucket at the pump, and Ben hurried over to take it from me. I opened the schoolhouse door and breathed deep of the pine-scented, chilly room. Ben walked straight to the woodstove and shoved some of the wood from the pile beneath into its belly.

"Choose a seat anywhere you like," I told Jennie. "I'd recommend the seats nearest the stove."

Instead, she sat down hard in a chair with a desk near the door, nowhere near the stove.

Ben's eyes traveled around the classroom, lingering for a while on the shelves of books.

"Jennie, I hope you know what a good thing this schoolhouse is," he lectured, his chest pushed out. "It's a rare treasure, and you're lucky as heck to be able to learn here."

Jennie sighed.

"You do whatever she says, now. And you'll be reading and writing by the new year."

Jennie looked away from us. "What should I call her?"

He put his hands on his hips. "What do you mean?"

"If I have to speak to her. Abby? Abigail? Or should I call her *Mrs. Whimble*? That doesn't sound right to me."

My face flushed with embarrassment.

"'Course you should call her Mrs. Whimble," he spluttered. "That's her name."

Ben's eyes met mine, and he shook his head in apology. Jennie shrugged.

As I gathered up a new slate, a slate pencil and a brand new primer, I heard the door open.

"Thank you, Abby," called Ben, and he was out the door before I could respond.

Jennie looked to me, a sly smile on her lips. Rather reluctantly, I sat down in the desk next to her and opened the primer.

"Have you had any instruction in letters and their sounds?"

"Sure haven't," she said, crossing her arms about her chest. "Guess that makes me right ignorant in your view."

I got up and walked to the bookshelf, pulling down the dictionary. I set it down before her and recited through the alphabet, flipping the pages until I arrived at words that began with the letter "I."

"The definition of '*ignorant*' is: 'lacking knowledge or awareness in general.'" I looked to her. "Would you say you lack knowledge or awareness?"

"No," she admitted. "I know a lot. Just not about..." She pointed at the dictionary. "Those things. Letters. Words."

"So there you have it. I don't think you're ignorant." I angled the reader toward her again. "We'll start here, with the first letter of the alphabet. 'A.'"

We worked for a while in the primer, going through the letters and their accompanying sounds. At a point somewhere around the letter 'J,' her eyes grew livelier, and she began to take more of an interest in the exercise, repeating after me more quickly and flipping the pages on her own. Just as we were sounding out the letter 'Z,' Ruby opened the door, pushing a pouting Frances ahead of her. When Frances saw Jennie, she brightened and ran to hover over her desk.

"Why are *you* here, Jennie?"

"I'm here to learn, same as you I reckon."

Frances peeked at the slate on which Jennie and I had been writing the letters of her name.

"What's that say?" Frances asked Jennie.

"That's my name. J-E-N-N-I-E."

Frances looked shyly up at me. "Can we do that with my name too?"

I took up another slate and wrote F-R-A-N-C-E-S, sounding out each letter as I wrote it on the slate.

"See, Frances?" said Ruby. "Miz Whimble can teach you how to write all the letters in the alphabet. And how to put those letters together to make words that folks can read. You *might* even be able to teach Little Bud what you learn. Won't that be something?"

She bit her lower lip, studying the letters of her own name. Ruby kissed her on top of her head in farewell, but Frances hardly noticed. She picked up the slate pencil and started tracing her name.

When Ruby opened the door, Andy Proctor rushed in. He grinned when he saw Jennie and sat down in the desk on the other side of her.

"You said you weren't coming to school," he said.

"I changed my mind," she said. "Well, more like *Ben* did."

"Well, I'm real glad you're here," he said cheerfully.

As Jennie flushed, I opened the schoolhouse door, peering out at the woods that surrounded the schoolhouse. All was still and silent. I walked to a window to see if I could spot any boats coming toward us. But the water in both directions was strangely empty of life.

Just as I was writing my own name on the blackboard, the door opened, and I turned, expecting a flood of students. But it was only Mr. Wharton, dressed in a wool frock coat and silken tie. He carried a pail, which he brought to my desk.

"You missed breakfast," he said. "Lila packed a biscuit and bacon for you."

As the students watched him warily, he removed his gray top hat and seated himself at a desk in the back of the room.

"A small gathering, I see," he declared.

I struggled to summon my composure; we had never discussed his presence in the classroom before. A heavy foreboding settled on my shoulders, so that I felt I may bend over double with its weight.

I cleared my throat. "Students, this is Mr. Wharton. A scholar in the field of education, and a benefactor of the school," I said. "He'll be observing this morning. Please, pay him no mind."

He smiled at me grandly. "I'll be observing *every* morning," he said. "And in a year's time, you all may find your names in a book I'm writing."

I shook my head, very small movements, left and right.

But he merely pulled a notebook, pen and ink from his case and set them before him on the desk.

144

That evening, Mr. Wharton and I seated ourselves for supper in the empty dining room, a lone flickering candle on our table. The hotel visitors had dwindled to a handful; there were hints from the manager that the hotel would close for the season very soon.

As much as I'd wished for the crowds to disperse, I felt the guests' absence around me keenly. I craved their noise, their exuberance. I could not look Mr. Wharton in the face.

"A good first day, was it not?" he asked, breaking the silence.

I narrowed my eyes. "It was. In spite of the uninvited guest?"

He didn't smile. "I'm sure you knew of my intention to observe your teaching. I don't know why my presence came as such a surprise."

"You never told me of your plans to observe. Every morning? The students will never feel comfortable with you hovering in the back of the room, taking notes on their very behaviors. *I* will never feel comfortable."

He laughed. "I must say, I'm surprised at you. After all I've done to make this school a reality, I'm to be barred from its daily operation? That doesn't seem fair."

I felt anger growing, from my belly to my chest to my tongue. "Don't you have important work waiting for you in Nashville?"

He shrugged. "*This* has become my important work, don't you see? This school means as much to me as it does to you."

It was hard to fill my lungs. "How can that be? It was *borne of my own desire*."

Seventeen-year-old Lila Pugh strode over with the water pitcher, but she took one look at Mr. Wharton's pinched brow and inflamed face and turned on her boot to retreat to the kitchen.

I ground me teeth. "How long are you planning on staying in Nags Head?"

"I couldn't say at the moment. But I agree, it's time to discuss where we will live when the hotel closes. I must say, conditions are deteriorating quickly. Have you seen the giant dune of sand that now lies beneath my window?"

"I'll live at the schoolhouse, of course."

His gray brows rose high. "The schoolhouse? I never thought you'd actually *live* there." He laughed. "No, no, that won't do. I've made some inquiries."

"Mr. Wharton," I said, my voice too loud. "You aren't listening to me. I will live at the schoolhouse. *You* may do what you want."

He sat back in his chair, his eyes full of outrage. "You are rather heartless, Abigail," he rasped. "I never wanted to believe it of you, but it's the truth. You are a hard woman."

He'd never spoken to me in such a manner before; the fire in my blood turned quickly to ice.

"I always wondered why you never came back to visit your husband. But I now see that you have quite an unnatural ability to forsake the people who matter the most to you."

Was it true? It seemed that it was, as much as I wanted to disbelieve him. My life had changed quickly, from a surfman's wife on a barrier island to an instructor at the seminal Peabody Normal College. And the change had eroded relationships, most especially with Asha and Ben and even my sister, Martha. I hadn't seen her or her two young children since my first and only visit, five years ago.

And yet, didn't they all know I loved them still? That I carried them as carefully as precious gems in the hold of my heart? I was sure they did. In my heart, they were mine, and I was theirs.

But maybe I'd been wrong; maybe I'd been selfish. I had used Mr. Wharton's money for my own objectives. He'd done everything he could for me, and now that the goal was in sight, I was ready to be done with him.

"I never forsook Ben," I insisted. "And I would never forsake *you*. We...you are...my good friend."

He exhaled loudly, then grabbed my hands from my lap and squeezed them hard.

"I *saw* you, Abigail. *Me*," he said, his white lips trembling. "Your invigoration, when we traveled the East Coast. When you observed different methods, new techniques. Met new people. All of our conversations about education, about the country's promise, about progress itself. You came alive, and it was a magnificent transformation to behold. You are not meant for this forgotten stretch of sand. Even your own husband saw that. *He let you go*. And you let him go as well."

He would not understand. "Everything I did led me back here."

He searched my blurring eyes, then let go of my hands with an abrupt push.

"You will see, in time. From what I've heard and seen, it's going to be quite difficult to convince these Nags Headers to come to the school. They don't mix with outsiders, and it seems to me that they certainly don't trust you. What if our hard work was for naught? What if your marriage cannot be resurrected? Then what will you do?"

"Why do you believe they don't trust me?" I cried. "If you hadn't poisoned their minds from the moment of our arrival, leading them to believe that you and I were a happily married *husband and wife*—when I was in fact still married to a local man—I wouldn't be facing such hostility."

He shook his head sadly. "You are still an outsider, Abigail. You may never earn their trust."

"Who has forsaken whom?" I seethed. "Why would you have ever agreed to build the schoolhouse if you believed such things?"

He softened his gaze. "Because I love you. Not as a father loves a daughter, nor as a good friend. But as a man loves a woman. And I'm not planning on leaving you here like this. I would never put you in such a precarious position. *That* is what love truly is. Certainly not *running away* when love stands before you."

I shook my head back and forth, for words escaped me. I watched helplessly as he shrugged on his overcoat and affixed his top hat firmly to his head.

"Good night, Abigail. I'll see you in the morning."

He marched out the door, passing Lila in the doorway, water pitcher still in her hand. She gave me a sad little wave and retreated back to the kitchen.

I gazed about the empty dining room, with its empty chairs and empty tables. Not much had changed in the room since 1868; the ghosts of my family—Mama, Daddy, Charlie and Martha—were still seated at a round table by the window. As I watched them eat, the picture of a perfect family, their images slowly slipped away, leaving only empty chairs in their places.

The cold room chilled me to my bones.

The following afternoon, with Andy's help, I settled into my little apartment, which I found to be about the same size as my previous bedroom in Nashville.

But that was the end of the similarities.

That night, a storm descended. The blows whistled along the corners of the schoolhouse and rattled the battened glass in the frames. Rain flew against the fresh pine boards, a barrage of tiny bullets, and the sound flooded clear to the woods, marooning the schoolhouse in turbulent water.

Falling asleep, I felt to be in the hold of a ship. But strangely, I wasn't afraid. It was a ship of my own making.

The next days arrived dreary and cold, yet the same three students arrived on time and eager to begin where they'd left off. And in spite of my growling belly and bitter hands, I was filled with the forgotten joy of teaching others how to read and write.

Of course, Mr. Wharton was there too, offering me sad smiles but no conversation. One day, he arrived even earlier in the morning than Jennie.

"How are you finding your new accommodations?" he asked.

I forced myself to meet his eyes. "Quite cozy, thank you."

"Indeed," he said archly. "This schoolhouse is too cold. Your apartment must be frigid."

It was true; I was going through the pine wood left over from the construction faster than I would have liked. I resisted the urge to rub my hands together, a newfound habit. Instead, I picked up a piece of chalk and began to write the date on the blackboard.

"The students don't seem bothered."

I felt his eyes on my back as I wrote.

"I hope you're eating, Abigail."

"Ruby brings me slices of cornbread and handfuls of chinquapins for my breakfast."

The thought of the warm cornbread soon to arrive incited a hard rumble from my stomach. Just yesterday afternoon, on my return from my daughter's grave, I'd detoured through the woods to pick hickory nuts, my only supper.

"That won't do. You must find another solution or you may not make it through the winter."

I turned to face him. "I don't want you to worry about my meals."

"You can't teach on an empty stomach."

"I've done it countless times before."

I consulted my plan for the day's spelling words and began to write them on the blackboard.

"I suppose you should know—I've found lodging with Mrs. Keets, though everyone here calls her 'the widow.' Do you know her?"

"Not very well, though she was kind enough to help me with Ben's daddy when he was sick. She made a good dish she called 'old drum.' Oscar took one sniff of it and grinned. Then he ate a few bites of the fish, and no one had been able to get anything down his throat but broth."

"You're in luck then. She has agreed to provide you with breakfast. She makes too much food as it is."

"Thank you, but I don't want Mrs. Keets's food."

"You've lost weight, and it's only been a few days since you departed the hotel! And your coloring is extraordinarily pale. In fact, I've considered calling a doctor from the mainland to see to you."

"I don't need a doctor," I scoffed.

"You need someone to take care of you."

At his desk, he removed his notebook from his case. "One more thing. Have you considered getting a lock for the door here? I believe it might be for the best."

"Of course not. I trust the people here, Mr. Wharton. And you must have noticed by now, no one uses locks here. It's not that kind of a place."

He nodded. "I worry about you."

In the sagging of his shoulders, I was reminded of the good friend he'd once been to me.

"Don't worry. Please. Everything is fine."

He cocked his head, just as Jennie opened the door. "Well, it's not exactly fine. Three students out of the three *dozen* that could fill this schoolhouse."

A bitter cold arrived with November.

Yet not one of the Nags Head Woods families I'd visited had sent their children here. Not even Alice and Roy Weeks.

Every afternoon, Ben would appear, waiting for Jennie. But he kept his distance, sitting in his skiff, docked beneath the schoolhouse and out of sight. I could only watch him sail away with Jennie, back to the house that used to be ours.

In the evenings, I sat at my desk as the lamp flickered, nursing my bruised heart as I planned the next day's lessons.

Jennie, however, had slowly warmed to me, and I to her. Andy hadn't a hope of keeping up with her, though he tried hard to impress her.

This morning, she was already sitting at her desk when I emerged from the apartment. I slid some of the remaining wood from the pile into the stove, and when the room started to fill with a little warmth, we sat down in the chairs nearby with the next-level reader.

But she soon grew frustrated with the new words and the complexity of the sentences and sat back with a groan.

"You've made some remarkable progress," I said. "I hope you know that."

"I have to," she said with a heavy sigh. "I have a job waitin' on me come summer, and I need to be able to read and write. Ben says, learn Latin."

"*Latin?*"

She pinned me with her big blue eyes.

"Ben worked at a scientist's laboratory this past summer, down in Beaufort. As a guide for the scientists. He helped 'em to find specimens to study. Even took a class for college students."

"Oh, I didn't know," I said, trying not to sound too surprised.

"I've never seen him like that afore, so chirked with himself." She laughed. "It was like he'd found some buried treasure inside himself he never knew he had."

I'd seen him that way before, many years ago, when he'd been offered the surfman's position in Whales Head. How eager he was to take it, to strike out for a new land.

"He passed along my name to the head professor there—Dr. Brooks—on account he'd told of his need for an artist to sketch the critters. All manner of plants and fish."

"And you're an artist?"

"I am. At least, that's what Ben thinks."

My heart squeezed with envy. She was a lucky girl, to have Ben's admiration. "Well then, you must be."

"Ben sent some of my sketches to Dr. Brooks in Baltimore, and he wrote back. Told Ben I needed to be able to read and write. And Ben wrote him back and told him I *could*! So here I am. I just don't think it's goin' to pan out. There ain't enough time."

The job of marine artist was a rare opportunity for a woman, and even more so for a young woman on the Banks. But packing a lifetime of education into less than a year would be almost impossible. Of course Ben surmised it was possible; he'd once believed he could learn to read *Moby-Dick* in one summer.

"You'll have to work hard," I said. "But I'm going to help you. Any time you want assistance outside of school, come to me. You know where I live."

She gave me a little grin. "I do."

"I'll order a Latin grammar book from the bookstore in Elizabeth City. We can learn some words together."

Her eyes popped open wide. "Thank you, Mrs. Whimble."

"That's why I'm here."

She cocked her head. "Is it?"

"It's...one of the reasons."

She nodded, and picked up the slate. With the pencil, she drew a perfect Scotch bonnet in about one minute. Even with a nubby slate pencil, the rendering was expertly done.

"What a coincidence. I recently found a Scotch bonnet on the beach."

I'd found the shell on one of my late-afternoon walks along the seashore and had placed it on my daughter's gravestone. It was whole and barely scratched, yet I placed it among the broken ones.

"I saw it," she admitted. "We visit the grave every now and again, to clean the sand off. So we've seen all your shells."

The image of the two of them visiting the gravestone together, examining all my broken offerings, robbed me of breath.

She went on. "I have a collection myself. Every once in a while I have to dump some, on account they won't all fit in my buckets. They're about the easiest things to draw, so I use 'em for practice."

In the quiet, I heard the crackling of the logs in the woodstove and the swishing of the sound below.

"I used to think they were special when I first came here. Gifts from the sea," I said. "And then, after we lost her, I thought they were nothing more than empty homes. Parts of an animal that had once lived."

"They still make you sad?"

I shrugged. "They'll always be little homes, whether or not anyone lives there. To me, they seem ready to be filled again. Maybe not with a living creature, but with...something. Something might make a home in them."

Jennie stared out the window, across the sound. "What was it like? Being gone from here?"

"It was many things, all at once."

"But you came back here. After seeing all those big cities and slick people and all that. After teaching the teachers. You came back."

"I did."

She turned her eyes back to me. "Ben is like a daddy to me, you know. Or mayhaps an uncle, more like."

"I know," I said, swallowing back the strange mix of relief and grief. "I'm glad to see that he's had the chance to be a daddy. I always knew he'd be a good one."

I wanted to talk more with Jennie, this young woman who knew Ben better than I did now, but Ruby and Frances opened the door, ushering in the cold air.

"I'd like to stay today," Ruby announced, unwinding her scarf from her neck and handing me the warm cornbread, wrapped in a dish towel. "Me and Frances, we gonna learn together."

Frances nodded happily, and directed Ruby by the hand to a desk. Just then, Andy came rushing in, slamming the door behind him as usual.

Mr. Wharton arrived soon enough, placing a pail of the widow's food on my desk. Even though I'd already gobbled up Ruby's cornbread, my mouth watered traitorously at the smell of warm fried chicken and biscuits.

"I had to try not to eat your portion on the way here," he said, patting his belly, which I noted had indeed grown rounder.

That evening, I stayed at the schoolhouse to make some notes in my journal about my progress, but I found that I hadn't much to write. So I sat at my desk, staring at the small fire in the woodstove, at last absorbing the continued rejection of the community I'd wanted to help.

In spite of myself, I began to question the usefulness of a traditional education here. I heard the voice of Mr. Wharton, his judgment and lack of hope, wearing me down.

I wrote in my journal:

The Nags Headers are not interested in learning anything but how to net great hauls of fish or strings of duck. They are concerned only with their survival on this isolated island.

And yet...

There was Jennie.

And there were Ruby and Frances.

And Andy too.

Instead of more scholarly thoughts, I wrote about Jennie. How she was on a path to a more intellectually vibrant life, and she needed education to get there. I wrote about Jennie's love of shells, and how I'd loaned her my book of seashells so she could learn to write their names in both English and Latin.

Then I wrote about Ruby—how she'd been a slave on the island just sixteen years ago, yet still hadn't received access to education. I wrote about Frances, her daughter, who'd convinced her mother to come learn along with her.

I wrote about the young fisherman Andy, who came to school in spite of his family's objections. Who preferred to stand, or roam about the room, when learning. Who always helped me wash the blackboard and wipe the slates before hurrying off to help his uncle.

And then I wrote about Ben. My very first pupil. How he still read books, all these years later.

CHAPTER THIRTEEN

Benjamin Whimble
Christmas Eve, 1881
Nags Head, North Carolina

Then at once they reached and hovered upon the imminent verge of sleep—but an intruder came, now, that would not "down." It was conscience. They began to feel a vague fear that they had been doing wrong to run away...
                    —*The Adventures of Tom Sawyer*

I stood at the bottom of the schoolhouse steps, listenin' to the sound of Abby's teacher voice as she wrapped up the day. Jennie'd told me they got to leave a little early today, as it was Christmas Eve, and that Abby was goin' to give them each a gift.

Soon Ruby, Frances, Andy and Jennie came down the steps, bundled in coats, mittens and wool hats. The wind blew cold today, but the sky was jingle-bell clear.

"What's in the box?" asked Jennie, pointin' to the crate at my feet.

I shrugged. "I brought Abby somethin' for the school, that's all."

"Like a Christmas present?" asked Jennie, her eyes shinin'.

"Mayhaps," I mumbled, my boots shufflin' about. "So tell me. What did your teacher give you for Christmas?"

Frances shoved a book into my face. "We each got a book," she said, a big grin on her tiny face.

"I should've guessed." I laughed.

"She said we wouldn't be able to read 'em all *every word* just yet, but if we kept on learnin', we could read all the books she has on her shelf," said Jennie. "Even that big one, *Moby-Dick*."

My stomach flopped over in my belly. That book would always remind me of cold dark winters and stingin' sand and great loss. In fact, it was Christmas Eve, five years ago, that Abby'd brought me *Moby-Dick* itself, along with a dictionary to help me read it. And I'd given her nothin' but sorrow in return.

Face aglow, Jennie showed me the cover of her book, *Alice's Adventures in Wonderland*. "She said I'd like all the talkin' critters in the story. Said I should try to *illustrate* 'em. That's a fancy word for drawin' pictures."

Andy got *Robinson Crusoe*. My favorite.

I knocked on the schoolhouse door and heard Abby's footsteps drawin' near, my heart beatin' in time to her boots. I hadn't seen her proper since the day I'd brought Jennie to the schoolhouse, two months back.

And now she was openin' the door, and I had to catch myself from throwin' my arms about her. Even in her gray homespun, she lit up the spaces around her.

"Ben!" she said, her green eyes round as china plates, with dark lines beneath them, and red splotches around her nose.

"You feeling all right?"

She shrugged. "It's just the cold weather. It gives me congestion."

The warm woodsmoke was driftin' quick out the open door, so I hurried to tell why I was there.

"I brought you somethin'. For Christmas."

"You did? I don't have anything for you...I haven't seen you in three months."

I waved away my long absence and pointed down at the box at the bottom of the steps. "I'll just...lemme fetch it. It's a touch heavy."

I hurried down the steps and picked up the box, then brought it inside and set it on one of the desks. I lifted the tank from the box and set it down, its glass shinin' clear in the light through the windows.

"It's an aquarium!" she said, her eyes sparkin' up her tired face.

"That she is," I said. "I figured you could use one in your school here. For your science lessons."

She turned to me with such happiness on her face that I wanted to tell her all the things I did last summer, all the things I'd learned. How much that life of learning grew on me, even now. The words piled up inside my mouth like fish in a net.

"The State Normal didn't even have one of these," she said. "I hope it wasn't too dear."

"Naw, but I did have to fetch it in Elizabeth City. I can help you, if you want. I know how to operate these tanks now, on account I worked down in a laboratory in Beaufort this past summer. Good group of scientists down there, come every summer to study the flora and fauna."

"Jennie told me."

"She did?"

"We mostly talked of the artist's job," she said with a little grin. "Not you. Don't worry."

"I took a class taught by the head professor there. I reckon it was kind of like takin' one of your classes at the Normal School. They had so many of these here tanks, I didn't even try countin' 'em. Fresh water and salt water both. All kinds of critters."

I then told her the tale of my bad sickness, Carrot Island, and Bishop and Dr. Brooks, and how I came to be the guide for the scientists. It felt good talkin' to her again, like rememberin' somethin' special I'd forgotten I'd even known.

"I'm to go back next June and work there again. I hope Jennie can come with me. We can rent a place to live in town."

Her eyelids dropped over her eyes. "Oh…that's a good opportunity for you both."

She blew her nose into a handkerchief, then pulled out a desk chair and sat down with a thump.

"It *is* a good chance for her," I said. "So I want to thank you for all you're doing for her. She's got a little bit of you in her, matter o' fact. Big ideas, you know."

She smiled a little. "She's a hard worker, and very bright."

"See? Just like you. You must have been the best teacher at that school."

"I was the most unconventional, that's for sure."

"I'll bet," I said with a chuckle.

Pictures Jennie had drawn were hung on the walls here and there. I spotted the faces of Ruby and Frances, and Andy too.

Feelin' more easy, I pulled out a chair and sat down, not too close, but not too far either. Took my time in askin' the next question on my mind.

"You think you'll go back one day?"

She shook her head. "No, Ben. I want to teach in a schoolhouse, not in a college," she said, so soft I could hardly hear her. "To start back at the beginning."

She closed her eyes and sort of swayed back and forth on her chair. I reached out to put a hand to her forehead, and we both jumped when I touched her skin. I drew back my hand quick.

"You've got a fever," I said, standin' up. "Time for you to rest now."

Abby made her way to her room in back and stretched out on her nice bed. I just stood there, not sure what I should be doing with myself.

"I *am* tired," she said, closin' her eyes.

"I'll be back," I told her, grabbin' her tin cup.

Outside at the pump, I filled her cup with water, then brought it back to her. But she'd already gone to sleep.

I put the cup beside her on the floor and looked at her all curled up, her hand still holdin' her handkerchief and her feet laced into her boots. I untied her boots and slipped them off her stockinged feet. Then I reached my hands under and around her to lift her a bit, so that I could grab the blankets beneath her.

As I lifted, her warm body leaned loose into me, smellin' of chalk dust and fever. Though the urge to hug her tight to me was strong, I lay her gently back down and pulled the blankets up to her chin.

The sun was quick in settin', and the room was getting' dark. There wasn't much more I could do but curse. It was Christmas Eve, and I was leavin' Abby to tend to her own sick self. Headin' to the Blounts' for Christmas supper and a bit of frolic.

It was shameful.

I wasn't myself at the shindig, sittin' dead in a chair by the fire and watchin' the Blounts sing and dance around as Granny played a strange Christmas tune on her squeeze-box. The room was strewn with holly and mistletoe they'd picked in the woods, and the fresh smells mixed in with the scents of roasted duck and fig cake.

"What's the matter with you, Ben?" asked Della, in mid-jig. "It's Christmas Eve, not a funeral."

"Nothin's wrong with me. Fit as a fiddle."

Jennie stopped dancin' with Bert and came over to study my face.

"He's in love," she said softly. "He's in love with his wife again."

I shook my head, but I couldn't help but smile down at my lap.

With his mouth full of pie, Digby said, "Took him long enough."

Old wool socks were hung from nails over the hearth. I could see the apples and oranges already stuffed into their toes. I got up and turned my back on the group, fished in my britches. Slid pieces of candy I'd bought in Elizabeth City into them one by one.

I turned back around, and everyone was looking at me, as if waitin' on me to give a speech.

"Abby's not well," I said. "Got a touch of fever."

"How bad?" asked Della.

"I'm not sure," I said. "Went to sleep right when her head hit the pillow."

"All right then," said Della. "I'll fix her up a poultice."

Jennie hopped up. "I'll make her some ginger root tea."

Della grabbed a cabbage head from the basket of vegetables and peeled off a couple of leaves. Then Granny took up an onion from the basket, gave it to Della to chop up and pile the bits into the cabbage leaves. Sprinkled some herbs in there and wrapped 'em up tight.

When the tea had steeped and been poured into a tin flask, the women handed me a basket full of all their homemade care.

"Be sure to stick it tight in her pits now," said Granny.

"We can help too, Uncle Ben," said Digby. "Rub her feet and sponge her face."

"After all, it's Christmas Eve," said Bert.

"The only thing you two can do is fetch up some more kindlin' for her stove."

They moaned at that but did follow me into the woods with their ax and a lantern to look for scraps of wood.

In her cold little room, Abby still lay in the same ball that she was in when I'd left. I set down my basket and lantern and crouched down to put a hand to her forehead. It was scorchin' hot and slick with sweat.

"Abby," I whispered. "It's me."

Her eyelids creeped open and looked at me. "Ben," she croaked. "I'm so hot."

Her hands looked to be tryin' to pull the blankets off herself, but they just flicked at them.

I pulled them off for her, and a wave of summer heat washed over me. She fumbled with the buttons at her neck, and I saw with a fair amount of dread that she wanted to undress.

She let out a little cry when she couldn't get unbuttoned. So I started to do it for her, startin' with the button high on her neck. Then the next one, and the next one, and so forth, pullin' the dress off her shoulders, then down her legs and off.

"Your...underclothes?" I whispered.

She nodded a bit, her eyes closed now. But I just stood there, sweat comin' even in the coldness. I poked my fingers around her belly and then the back for some kind of ribbons to untie her woolen petticoats, as I tried not to look at her face or breathe the warm air comin' from her lips. At last I found them, and I wriggled the blasted things off.

Then came the woolen stockings, which I pulled gently down her legs, my knuckles touchin' brief on her damp skin. All that was left was her chemise, and I couldn't take that off her, no matter how much she wanted me to.

Even in the dark, her pale legs shone like the moon. My eyes moved further up, to her chest. Her chemise stuck to her belly and breasts. Nipples warm and round beneath the shiny cloth.

Then I looked up to her face, and I saw that her eyes were wide open now. Starin' at me starin' at her.

"Nightdress," she said. She pointed to the trunk against the wall, so I took up the lantern and opened it up, found clean clothes and bedcoverings. Rummaged around and found the nightdress, cold white cotton.

I turned about to see Abby pullin' off her sweat-sticky chemise. I shut my eyes tight, afore I saw a thing.

I stepped to the bed, eyes still closed, and handed her the nightdress. She took it from me and I heard her grunt, tryin' to get it on herself.

"All done?" I whispered.

Whisper words only, like I was afraid to break the spell of magic that had come over me. A wicked spell that cast me back to those early days of love. A powerful spell that pulled deep from my mind each bend of her body beneath my hands, as if I'd made love to her just yesterday.

"Yes," she said.

I opened my eyes and there she lay pantin', fresh as a maid in her white nightdress. Her red hair had come unpinned and now fell all around her. I had to remind myself to breathe.

I took up the tin cup of water I'd filled earlier and held it to her mouth.

"Drink it all down, now," I said, but I didn't have to say that, for she drank it all and wanted more.

Went outside and fetched more water in the pitcher, poured some into the tin cup. She drank all that down too. Then another cupful.

"Della and Granny Blount made a couple poultices for you," I said. "They're to go in the pits of your arms."

A little smile curled onto her lips. "I smell the onions."

"Right." I looked at her lyin' there in her clean, cold nightdress. Didn't seem right to stick cabbage and onions under her arms.

"Why don't you just drink some of the tea Jennie made?"

I poured some tea from the flask into her cup, but it was too hot to drink. So I pulled up the chair and sat beside her. Her eyes closed, and it seemed she slept.

But after a while, I heard her whisper, "When you were ill. I should have been here. To help you."

I was quiet for a long while then, thinkin' of those terrible days when I believed myself too sick to keep livin'. Those terrible days after, when I was too weak to earn my livin'.

"You were there, in a way. You came to me in my fever dreams."

But she didn't answer. Sleep had taken her again.

A loud bangin'—the droppin' of wood—outside the school-house door didn't even wake her. I heard Bert and Digby yammerin' loud enough to wake the whole of Nags Head Woods.

It was time for me to take my leave, but I found my rear side tacked down in the chair. I bade my legs to stand and carry my weight; at the door, I turned to look at her one last time.

"Merry Christmas, Abby," I said, too loud for the sickly circumstances, but I didn't care. I was done whisperin'. From now on, we'd talk to each other.

165

'Course I didn't sleep a wink that night, and got up early to see to Abby. Brought her a bit of cornbread and apple jam, a sprig of holly from the woods.

She was sittin' on her bare mattress, dressed in a mornin' robe from her trunk. Her hair hung in clumps, and her skin looked yellow next to the brown of the cloth. But her eyes jumped from their sockets, full of life.

"You're better," I said, puttin' the holly sprig in her hands and the cornbread on the table.

"I am. The fever broke last night."

I spotted her nightdress and bed linens, balled up in the corner of her room. She'd drunk the cup of tea I left too.

"Well. Ain't that a merry Christmas for you."

She sniffed a laugh and said nothing more. The spell from the night previous had been lifted. We couldn't even meet the other's eyes. I went out to fetch up the newly chopped wood, then threw a couple logs into the classroom stove. Then I stood there starin' at my feet again.

"Thank you for caring for me," she said.

"It's what anyone would do. You're the schoolmarm, after all!"

She looked away from me, at my not mentionin' the fact that she was also my wife.

"You feel like eatin'? Brought you some corn bread."

I handed her the cloth with the corn bread, careful not to touch her fingers. She opened it up and took a little nibble, smilin' at the apple jam inside.

"You know what I think we should do today?" I sounded just like a knee-baby, so I lowered my voice. "Fill up that aquarium. You don't have to do a thing but rest abed. I'll fetch everything and bring it here."

166

She nodded, as she couldn't speak with her mouth full of bread.

I went down to the pump again and filled her pitcher with water. When I came back, she was stretched out in bed again, her eyes closed, the holly sprig in her hand.

Comin' down the steps, I spotted Mr. Warthog picking' his way through the sand, all dressed up and with a box in his arms.

"Good morning, Benjamin, and Merry Christmas to you," he said, his eyes not on me but on the schoolhouse. "This is quite a surprise, I must say. I suppose you've beaten me to it."

"Beat me to what?"

"Wishing Abigail a Merry Christmas, of course."

I cut my eyes at him. "She's been right sickly, you know."

His eyebrows disappeared under his top hat. "No, I didn't know. I saw her just yesterday morning, and she seemed fine. How bad is she?"

"She's better this mornin'. Her fever broke in the night, but she's sleepin' now. I wouldn't go in there disturbin' her."

He looked down at his box. "I won't disturb her. I'll just leave her this gift and be on my way."

If I were a dog, I would have pissed right there on the schoolhouse steps. "I'll bring it up to her."

I made to grab the box from him, but he moved it away from me, pretty quick for an old man.

"That's quite all right," he said. "I'm perfectly capable of doing it. And if she's sleeping, it certainly won't matter who leaves her the gift."

I saw, then, how he thought in his mind that the schoolhouse was his. And if the schoolhouse was his, then Abby was his too.

"I'm her husband. And I say who sees her and who doesn't. And as for your habit of gift-givin' when it comes to my wife, I'd say it's time to break it. She doesn't need anything from you."

He grinned a nasty grin. "Doesn't she? To my mind, she's been lacking in companionship these last few months. Lacking in a great number of things, to be sure."

I ain't sure what came over me then, but it wasn't a-tall nice. I ripped that box from his arms and tore the ribbon from it in one swipe. Out from the box tumbled a creamy white shawl, lookin' soft and fine as snow.

We both reached to fetch it from the ground, bumpin' our heads together and knockin' the top hat from his head. He cried out as I ripped the shawl from the sand and marched to the waters of the sound, where I tossed it hard as I could into the murk. And there it floated, its wool woven so tight it hardly took on water.

Mr. Warthog came rushin' hatless to the edge, but I knew he wouldn't step a shiny-booted foot into the water to fetch it back. We watched it float about like it was nothin' but a pretty goose, head down in the water for a bite of weeds.

He turned to me, his face red and eyes dark. "For heaven's sake, Ben! Why did you do that?"

I only chuckled, arms crossed about my chest.

He pointed a finger at the shawl, where it flapped happily about in the current. "Retrieve it at once."

I wiped his spittle from my cheek with the back of my hand. "No."

We eyed each other like a couple of wild hogs, our breaths foggin' in the cold. I squared my hips and puffed my chest, tried to make my skinny bones fill a bigger space than they did. And it seemed to work, for he turned about to leave, takin' up his hat and the empty box as he clambered away.

I had the urge to laugh at his back, but I knew he'd come around again. After all, he was a man who owned things. And I was, I saw, a man who threw things away.

CHAPTER FOURTEEN

Abigail Whimble
Christmas Day, 1881
Nags Head, North Carolina

He worshipped this new angel with furtive eye, till he saw that she had discovered him; then he pretended he did not know she was present, and began to "show off" in all sorts of absurd boyish ways, in order to win her admiration.
—The Adventures of Tom Sawyer

I spent most of Christmas Day drifting on a skiff, rocking gently over the sound's swells. Christmases past sailed by, hearty meals of roasted ham and potatoes and pie with Mr. Wharton. Church service and carols and wreaths of holly and mistletoe. Sparser dinners of roasted duck and collards with Ben, and elaborate meals with every kind of food as a girl in Edenton.

In my sleep, my belly growled for sustenance, but I couldn't find it in me to wake.

Ben came and went. I at times heard him in the classroom, bumping the glass of the aquarium or grumbling to himself. In the afternoon, he came into my apartment and set a bowl of Ruby's chicken soup and a cup of water on the table.

The previous night lingered in my mind, as fragile as a dream.

I yearned for him to put his rough hand on my forehead again. To help me undress. But just having him near me seemed to pull my body back together again, to knit my fibers into a stronger fabric. I pushed myself into a sitting position.

"What are you putting in the aquarium?" I asked as Ben lit the lantern beside me. I wanted to keep him with me as long as possible.

He shook a finger at me. "Now, that's a surprise. You have to get well enough to get up and look at it yourself."

"Alright then, I will."

"No, no, no," he said, as I made to get the bedcoverings off me.

"I'm feeling better," I assured him, swinging my legs from the bed, realizing too late that I likely smelled of sour sweat and sickness, that my hair must be a mess of knotted tangles. As I stood, my head tilted as if caught in a hard current, and I closed my eyes until the feeling passed.

"Take it easy, now," said Ben, rushing to fetch my morning robe and slippers from the trunk.

He helped me into the robe with a quick slip up the arms and grabbed the lantern, as it was dark in the cold classroom. In the flickering light, I spotted the aquarium, set on a desk near the woodstove.

Ocean water filled it almost to the top, and sand lined the bottom of it, which was strewn with rocks and shells of different sizes. And when I looked closer, I made out a little crab, its clawed legs creeping its gray shelled body along the sand. Another one sat on a rock, and seemed to be staring at us.

"The little buggers are called hermit crabs," said Ben fondly.

"Where did you find them? And so quickly?"

"I'll never tell," he said, his eyes glittering with pride in the light of the lantern. "That's why those scientists pay me, you know."

The crab on the rock slipped tighter inside his shell, but his eyes, perched on the end of little stalks, still watched us.

"One of those scientists studied marine hermit crabs just like 'em last summer, so I learned a lot from him. Such as they're more related to lobsters than crabs. These are *Pagurus longicarpus*, otherwise known as the long-wristed crab. See how their right front claws are bigger than their left ones? You've got to have at the very least two of the critters to keep 'em happy in the tank. They like company, you see. And you've got to keep the water pretty warm. That's why I put the tank so close to the woodstove."

He pointed at the tank. "I put some different sizes of shells in there too, so they can change their homes every now and then. I will say, it sure is a sight to watch 'em creep out of one shell and try on another."

"What do they eat?"

"Plants and animals both. But don't worry, I'll bring some fish and seaweed bits for them to dine on. Gotta feed 'em once a day. They're hungry little crustaceans."

"Crustaceans! What a word."

"Comes from the Latin word 'crust.'"

I laughed, but he said, "It's the truth! I learned it in Dr. Brooks's class."

I couldn't hide the hope in my voice. "You're planning to come here every day to feed them?"

"I was," he said, squinting at them. "You have too much to do as it is, I reckon. I'll have to clean the tank every now and then too."

Somehow, in half a day, Ben had given me a piece of the ocean, and a part of himself as well. Our faces reflected back at us in the glass, as close as they'd been in many years.

"This is the best Christmas gift I've ever received."

I saw, in the glass, a shadow pass over his eyes. "I suppose I should fess up. Mr. Wart...Mr. *Wharton* stopped by earlier, to give you a present. 'Twas a fine white shawl, and I...well, I sort of...I threw it into the water."

"You threw it into the water?"

"I did. And I ain't sorry about it neither. Why's he giving you gifts anyways?"

My face quickly burned hot, but not from a fever. I stepped away from the aquarium so that I could face him directly.

"I've told him that I don't want anything from him."

Ben huffed, his eyes blazing with naked fury. "Just the best schoolhouse that money can buy is all."

I walked away from him, collapsing in a chair at the other side of the room.

But he wasn't finished with me. "You took a lot from him, Abby. Don't you think he's gonna want something back in return?"

I pressed the heels of my hands into my eye sockets. "I'm trying to make it a successful school. If it's successful, he'll leave for Nashville to write about it and take the credit for its existence, I imagine. But the school is still struggling, so he's still here."

He cackled. "He's here because of *you*, not the school. Jennie says he sits there watchin' you all day. A student in the subject of Abigail Whimble. I've seen the way he looks at you. It's sickenin', gawkin' at a married woman like that."

My happiness dissipated as anger rose. "A married woman? Is that what I am?"

I left him there and went back to bed, pulling the coverings over my head. But even through the mound of wool and linen coverings, I heard the sound of Ben marching to the door and slamming it shut behind him.

In spite of the poor night's rest, I felt I was well enough to teach the following day. My arms trembled a bit when I dressed and pinned up my hair. But the sound of the squeaking schoolhouse door hurried me along, and I stepped from the apartment to see Mr. Wharton, already inspecting the aquarium. He straightened when he saw me and doffed his hat.

"Oh, good. I'm glad to see you're feeling better." He stepped closer to me. "Merry Christmas, Abigail."

"Merry Christmas," I mumbled, shoving some wood into the stove and stoking the embers. "Ben told me you visited yesterday."

"I'm surprised. Did he mention how childishly he was acting?"

The image of the waterlogged shawl floated about in my mind, and I grinned in spite of the severity of Mr. Wharton's expression.

"Yes, he has a bit of a temper at times. But his sentiments are warranted, don't you agree? He'd just given me the gift of this aquarium, you see. He found the hermit crabs as well."

He sighed deeply but didn't respond. Instead, he pointed at the tank.

"Are you planning on keeping it here? It certainly takes up a good deal of space."

"I am. It's for science lessons."

"Science lessons!" He laughed. "Is Ben in charge of curriculum now? You don't even *teach* science! I've never heard of such a thing in a classroom before."

Just then, the schoolhouse door swung open and Andy barged into the room, slamming the door behind him.

"Uh-oh," he said, taking in our faces. "Somebody die?"

He made his way to the aquarium and stood mesmerized, his nose pressed right to the glass. "What is this thing anyway?"

"It's called an aquarium. It's a way of displaying aquatic life for the purpose of learning..."

"What are those, some kind of crab? I reckon they're takin' their rest," he exclaimed. "What else is in there?"

"Nothing, as of yet. Ben is in charge of acquisitions."

Andy stood up and grinned at me. "This is the best thing I've seen ever in my life! Mr. Ben is clever as they come, I swear."

Mr. Wharton coughed and headed quietly back to his desk.

Though it lent the room a fishy scent, the aquarium was such a novelty that I had a difficult time redirecting the students' attention. Under Mr. Wharton's watchful eye, I decided to use their distraction to my advantage.

"I'd like you to think of words—descriptive words called adjectives—to describe the creatures you see in the tank. When I spell them on the blackboard, I'd like you to write the words on your slates."

Their eyes jumped to the aquarium, and Frances began hopping up and down in her seat. Andy got up, as usual, and walked to the tank.

Jennie said, "Shy."

I wrote the word "shy" on the blackboard, enunciating the "sh" sound.

"Naw, they're just grum," said Andy, squinting inside. I wrote "grum" under "shy."

Frances said, "Their shells are green and white. Or no, maybe they're gray."

As if on cue, the crabs began to emerge from their shells. "They're comin' out of their shells! Come look!" cried Andy.

Ruby, Frances and Jennie got up and rushed to the tank.

"Their right claws are bigger than their lefts!" said Jennie.

"Their big claws are striped down their middles," said Ruby. "Like tiny little socks."

As their words came faster and faster, I began to wonder if we were all describing the same creatures. Struggling to keep up, I heard the door of the schoolhouse open and turned to see Bert and Digby standing in the doorway.

"Hey, Miz Whimble," said Bert. "We don't want to bust up your teachin' or nothing' but...well, we wanted to see this tank Uncle Ben told us about."

"Of course," I said. "But you'll have to squeeze your way through the crowd, I'm afraid."

After the students made way for them, they spent a good deal of time at the tank looking and whispering.

"We happen to be writing descriptive words about the hermit crabs in the aquarium," I said. "Perhaps you'd like to sit for a while and listen to the lesson."

They snuck looks at each other, then shrugged.

I brought over the beginning readers, slates and chalk. "Why don't you watch Jennie?"

They sat down next to Jennie, one on either side. "You boys stink," she said, wrinkling her nose.

They looked to me in horror. "We can't smell ourselves, ma'am."

"It's all right with me," I said. "It's Jennie you should worry about."

They laughed. "We don't give a care about her. She smells us every day anyhow," said Bert. "She should be used to it."

Bert and Digby stayed until lunch, when Ruby and Frances usually headed home. Because Jennie stayed for both sessions of the school day, she usually opened a tin box packed with a biscuit or corn bread and fruit.

Andy stayed as well, but he never brought a thing to eat. So Jennie would offer him some of her food, which he would refuse, saying he wasn't hungry. And now my own stomach rumbled, despite the plate of eggs and corn bread that Ruby had brought me that morning.

"We should make soup tomorrow," I said. "For our lunch. Each of you could bring an ingredient or two for the pot, and it will cook all morning on the stove."

Andy clapped his hands together. "I'll bring the fish. That's easy."

Jennie said, "I'll bring a cabbage. And some herbs. We got a surplus."

Ruby said she'd bring some chicken broth and a potato, and we all laughed, wondering what strange kind of soup it would be.

"I wouldn't say no to a bowl of that soup," ventured Digby. "What about you, Bert? You think you want to come here tomorrow and try it?"

"I might, at that," said Bert. "Got to see to Stinky and Smelly, you know."

"Sure, Miz Whimble. We'll come back tomorrow."

"We'll be happy to have you. Maybe you can get a little learning in as well while you're here."

They laughed and donned their caps before skirting around Mr. Wharton to the door. He'd been watching and listening to everything, I knew; his hand flew over the pages of his notebook throughout the morning, and when he at last got up to leave, he actually smiled at me.

And I could, for a moment, see what he saw today from his station at the back of the room—a community of excited learners, where different-colored skins stood closely together, marveling at nature and new things to learn. The aquarium had been the key, not books or readers or slates.

I wished Ben could have been there to see it all.

I was sweeping sand out the schoolhouse door that afternoon when I spotted a man walking toward the schoolhouse with what looked to be a bellows in one hand and a glass jar in the other. I watched as he made his way through the sand to the bottom of the steps, and when he looked up to me with shining eyes, I saw that it was Ben.

He'd shaved his beard and cut his hair so that it swept off his forehead in a thick blond wave. His face was pale where the hair had been. But there were his clean strong bones, and his blue eyes like circles of sky.

He laughed. "Figured it was time to shave." He ran a hand over his smooth face.

My tongue lay useless in my mouth; I couldn't speak as he started up the steps toward me.

"Brought some fish food for your friends in the tank," said Ben, holding up the jar filled with tiny bits of fish. "And these here bellows will put oxygen into the water so the critters don't die off on us."

"Oh...that's...yes," I stammered.

He chewed his lip. "I shouldn't have said all those things yesterday, and I apologize," he said. "I won't ask you about him anymore, I promise."

My head bobbed with sudden dizziness.

"You still feeling poorly?" he asked, his brow creasing. He was so close, right on the landing in front of me, inspecting my face. "I told you it was too soon for you to start teachin' again, didn't I?"

"I'm fine," I said, clearing my throat. "Come in."

We walked inside to the aquarium, where he sprinkled some of the fish bits into the tank. They floated to the bottom, where the hermit crabs hurried to the food, as fast as I'd seen them move.

"Stinky and Smelly are hungry," I said.

"Stinky and Smelly?" he asked, an eyebrow raised. "I'm guessin' you weren't the one who named 'em."

"Bert and Digby did."

Ben chuckled. "I knew they'd show up. I told 'em about the tank, and they were right curious about it. How'd they do?"

"They could write their names by the end of the day," I said. "Seems they were curious about learning some letters as well."

"Well, I'm not takin' any glory for *that*. That's all your doin'."

"The aquarium was a rousing success with everyone," I said. "Even Mr. Wharton came around."

"Mayhaps he ain't as dim as he looks."

He took up the bellows and gave it a few short pumps, casting air into the water, visible as tiny bubbles making their way throughout the tank.

"That should do it," he said, turning to me.

His face was so familiar, as comforting as a blanket tucked up to my chin. So warm, my face flushed just standing there.

"You know, Andy could bring the fish food for them, and I can probably master that particular bellows skill, if you'd prefer not to come here every day."

His eyes widened in dismay. "Oh, I don't mind. Stinky and Smelly are like kin to me now, you know."

I laughed, and then he laughed too. And the time that had passed us by fell away, and I raised my hands up toward his face.

But he looked down and saw them coming, trepidation in his eyes. Embarrassed, I stopped them halfway, but then I couldn't help myself. I lifted them all the way to his face and rested them lightly on his cheeks.

His skin was warm and smooth, but hard as well, like a turtle's shell resting in the sun.

He stared at me in surprise for a moment, then put his hands atop mine. We stood like that for a long while, our hands trembling.

"Your hands are right cold, Abby," he said, his voice crackling.

"Yours aren't," I said.

I turned my hands backward and laced my fingers through his. I squeezed them hard, soaking up their rough comfort. Just our hands, but we knew they were everything. I felt the width between each of the fingers, the deep lines of his palm, the patches of rough skin. At last, he squeezed mine in return.

Ben took a deep breath. "Where to now?"

I shook my head, but smiled so big my cheeks strained. "I don't know."

We swayed slightly, as if blown by a wind.

"Hellooooo!" called a voice from the sound. "Abby Whimble! You in there?"

"It's Abner," said Ben, shaking his head in amusement. "Are you in here?"

"Where else would I be?" Slowly, our hands came apart.

I lifted a window open and stuck my head out to see Abner in his U.S. Mail sailboat, grinning up at me beneath his long drooping mustache.

"If it ain't Nags Head's favorite schoolmarm," he said, his breath puffing in the cold air. "Good to see you back, Abby."

Ben stuck his head out, right beside me. "You happy to see me too?"

Abner made a show of squinting at Ben in confusion. "And who, pray tell, are you? A little old for a student, ain't you?"

"Never," said Ben.

Abner hopped from the boat and tied it to a piling. "I'm comin' up."

He soon appeared in the doorway, limping over and swooping me into his long arms. He smelled of a life lived on the water.

"I been watchin' this schoolhouse go up, you know," he said. "Now at last I get to see its insides."

He gazed around, whistling. "Ain't never seen a grander place, schoolhouse or no. Even Eliza says it's a real good thing, what you're doin' here."

"She does?" I didn't believe I was high on the list of Eliza's favorite people.

"Sure she does. You know, I taught her the rudimentaries, but she's gone way beyond all that. Now she's smarter than me, I daresay! She says a schoolhouse is just the thing Nags Head needs, everybody being dumb as donkeys. In *her* words, you know."

Ben snorted. "That's Eliza for you."

Abner shifted his weight from leg to leg, a big grin spreading on his face.

"She married me, if you can believe it! Been hitched about a year now. I finally wore her down in askin'. She's been guiding'for the

Yanks goin' on almost five years now. Livin' in the caretaker's house, high as a hog. And course, mama to our infant young'un. She don't have a second to sleep, but don't let her tell you she minds a-tall. She soaks up every minute."

"Congratulations on the birth," I said. "Boy or girl?"

"A boy."

Ben suddenly shuffled over to the bookshelf.

"Name's Benji Jon Miller. Now, I know how it sounds, his name so close to Ben here. But it was what she wanted, so I went along with it. Since Ben is a good friend to the both of us, and plus it's a real easy name to say. But she calls him B.J. now, you know, so it's not a circumstance to me either way. Ain't that right, Ben?"

Ben grunted, picking up books and putting them back.

"It's a good name," I said.

Abner stepped over to peer into the tank. "Me and Eliza are set to teach B.J. our own selves, on account the teacher who travels our way only comes to the lighthouse and lifesavin' families two times in a year. Eliza says that ain't near enough time for all the learnin' she's plannin' for B.J. This here Nags Head School...well, it's a special thing for the folks out this way."

"Try telling that to the Nags Headers."

He nodded, as if he already knew. "No one comin'?"

"Just a handful of students. And I tried to bribe them with Ruby's biscuits!"

Abner chewed his lip, his green eyes skirting between Ben and me. "Takes folks a while to warm up, out here. You know that, Abby."

"I do," I agreed.

I looked to Ben, his back narrower than I'd remembered. He stood taller, now.

"They'll come around," said Abner. "And if not, I'll just stop readin' their letters and news to 'em. Then they'll be knockin' down your door, I'll wager."

Ben turned and stepped over to me. My skin ached, sensing the warmth so close, yet again out of reach. Abner narrowed his eyes at the two of us, then grinned.

"I know, I know," he said. "Time for me to go."

We both protested, but he just waved a long arm about and hobbled out the door.

Ben and I went to the window and watched him sail north with the setting sun, taking him home, eventually, to Eliza and his son.

To break the newfound silence between us, I asked the first thing that came to mind. "What are you reading now?"

"How did you know I was readin'?"

"I saw you," I admitted, my cheeks flushing. "One evening, on my way back from visiting with the families in the woods. You were reading a book by lantern light."

He glanced over at me, a pleased smile on his face. "You were spying on me."

"I was."

With great aplomb, he announced, "*On the Origin of Species* by Charles Darwin. You read it?"

I'd heard of it, of course. It had been published many years ago, but it had caused such a sensation that I frequently heard discussion of it in both religious and scientific circles at the Normal College.

"I haven't."

"It's tough as new leather, let me tell you. Friend of mine from the laboratory this summer loaned it to me. Said I had to read it, it was such an all-fired good book. And not just for science folks, but for all the people in the world."

His whole face shifted upward with hope. It reminded me of when I taught him how to read, the way he held *Robinson Crusoe* so reverently. I was impressed that he'd taken on such a challenging book as *Origin*—not a work of literature, but of science.

"I'll order a copy and read it too," I said happily.

"Oh," he said, and I heard the disappointment in his voice. "Not...for us to, you know...read together?"

"No, no," I hurried to say, though I realized that that was exactly what I'd wanted. "On my own. We don't have to...even, you know. Talk about it."

He breathed a sigh of relief. "All right then. That's good."

I cringed all over as I hastened to the door. I swung it wide for him, ushering in the cold.

"But listen," he blurted. "Would you fancy a sail on the sound sometime? *Tessa* would sure like to see you again."

"I would, but my only day off is Sunday. And even then, I've been teaching Jennie most of the day."

He grinned. "I'll talk to her. She'll soon see sense."

"I'm not sure of that at all." I laughed.

"She's a sharp one, ain't she?" He gave me a casual salute, though I was hoping for more of a farewell, and made his way down the steps.

"'Night, Abby," he called.

Too soon, he was gone into the gathering darkness.

CHAPTER FIFTEEN

Benjamin Whimble
January 3, 1882
Nags Head, North Carolina

Tom found himself writing "BECKY" in the sand with his big toe; he scratched it out, and was angry with himself for his weakness. But he wrote it again, nevertheless; he could not help it.

—The Adventures of Tom Sawyer

I figured I'd get to school at the crack of dawn so I could have Abby to myself for a bit. But it wasn't meant to be; Jennie had beat me there. 'Twas dark, with a couple of lanterns and the bowels of the stove throwin' off some light, but I saw Abby, up at the chalkboard, loopin' *January 3, 1882,* across the top in her pretty penmanship. She caught sight of me just standin' there in the doorway, cap in hand.

"Hi, Ben," said Abby, her smile lightin' up the dark.

"Hi, Abby," I said. "I brought fish for the crabs and crab for the soup."

I dropped the bits of fish into the pot, then fed Stinky and Smelly and blew the bellows over the water.

After that, I just stood there, lookin' about. Jennie smirked at me.

"Do you need something else?" asked Abby.

"No. Well, truth be told, I'd like to stay and learn my script. I should have learned it long ago."

"Oh! Why script?" asked Abby.

"The scientists wrote in script, so they could get all their big thoughts down in a hurry," I said. "Not that I have any of those, but I've been writin' notes in my zoology notebook on *Origin of the Species*, and my fingers are set to snap."

I sat down at a desk next to Jennie, already turnin' a page in her reader. I peeked over at the page and saw it was a good bit easier to read than old Charles Darwin.

I read aloud: "'Ellen, do look at Fido! He sits up on a chair, with my hat on. He looks like a little boy, but it is only Fido. Now see him shake hands. Give me your paw, Fido. How do you do, sir? Will you take dinner with us? Fido? Speak! Fido says "Bowwow," which means "Thank you, I will." Isn't Fido a good dog, Ellen? He is always so polite. When school is out, I will try to teach him some other tricks.'"

I chuckled at that claptrap she was made to read, thankin' my lucky stars that Abby taught me to read with *Robinson Crusoe*.

Jennie glared at me. "Stop that, Ben. This book is for *me* to read, ain't it. Not you."

"Sorry, Jennie. I'll let you get back to Fido and Ellen. I wonder what-all tricks she's gonna teach him next."

Abby sat down at the desk next to me with a copy of the same reader Jennie had.

"Not to worry, Jennie," she said, her eyes creased in a smile. "We'll soon see what tricks Ben has up *his* sleeve."

She showed me the page with the dreaded script letters in it, and I flexed my fingers, hearin' the knuckles pop. "That's right. Watch careful, Jennie."

Abby picked up the slate pencil and started writin' the alphabet in cursive letters. But try as I might, I couldn't pay much attention to the grand curlicues she was makin', for I was watchin' her strong fingers and her soft hand with its freckles like the smallest of fadin' blooms, and then the bone of her wrist, its sweet little knob. How I'd like to sneak my rough fingers up under that homespun sleeve, feel that warm arm once again.

Her teacher voice made me jump. "Once you learn the forms of the letters, you can learn how to connect them. Like so."

She started with a capital cursive "B," then looped the bottom of it to another letter, then another, until they connected in a line. *Benjamin Whimble.* All the letters linkin' up like a happy family, on the way to somewhere good.

Abby and me almost had that, once upon a time.

I was so far gone in my thoughts, I didn't feel Jennie right next to me, watchin' over my shoulder, her own slate and pencil in hand.

"You try," Abby said to me.

I tried to copy what Abby had written, but my fingers felt like five little twigs about to snap. My name came out a mess of slaughtered letters; that poor family was no more.

Abby took a look at Jennie's slate, where she'd written *Jennie Blount* in perfect cursive. Least it looked that way to me.

"Better than trusty Fido here," said Abby proudly.

"Ho, ho!" laughed Jennie.

"Take a slate home to practice," said Abby to me, winkin'.

"Bowwow," I muttered.

Andy and Ruby and Frances came in after a while, and then Bert and Digby too. Not too long after, in came none other than Mr. Warthog, big coat on and top hat too. He couldn't spare me a nod. The rest of the folks in the room rustled about, same as if a fox had entered the hen house. Their eyes darted from him to me to Abby, whose jovial mood soured up quick.

"Good morning," he said grandly. "I see we have a new addition today. I daresay I didn't recognize him without all the facial hair."

"That's right," said Abby. "He's brushing up on some penmanship."

"Penmanship? Whatever for?"

I turned to glare at him. "I'd watch what you're sayin' in here because it *sounds* like you're sayin' folks here don't need to know how to write script."

He chuckled. "You've misunderstood me, I'm afraid. I'm sure there are plenty of good reasons for a fisherman to possess perfect penmanship. Please, carry on."

Abby glared at him. "Penmanship will be taught in this classroom, no matter the occupation."

Mr. Warthog sat quiet in the back like a cut of rancid chuck.

I tried to ignore him as I worked at my slate. *The pond is still. How it shines in the hot sun! Let us go into the woods where we can sit in the shade.*

Abby and I liked to swim in the fresh ponds in the summers, once upon a time. Naked as the day we were born. I never could take my eyes from her body, my hands neither once we were in the water. When I set pencil to slate to copy the words, the letters curled about like her red hair, dryin' messy in the sun.

The crab soup cooked the whole mornin' through, makin' all our bellies growl. When she heard it was crab in the pot, Ruby had run home to fetch a jar of her tomatoes and a handful of her special spices. Even Bert and Digby had brought along a couple ears of dried corn and two carrots fresh from Della's garden patch, which they peeled and chopped right into the pot with Bert's fishing knife. Andy came empty-handed, but no one seemed to care.

When it was time for lunch, Mr. Warthog gathered up his papers and went out the door, likely back to Nell's kitchen of plenty. Too good for our humble soup, I reckon.

Abby ladled some soup into the fine bowls and handed us some shiny silver spoons. We all sat there slurpin' and lickin' 'til our bowls were clean as new, and the classroom, though still right empty, seemed filled up to burstin'.

Without Mr. Warthog a-scribblin' in the back, the afternoon hours went like smoke up a chimney.

Abby passed out copies of *The Adventures of Tom Sawyer* and started in readin' to us, with us followin' along the way me and her did with *Robinson Crusoe*. And let me tell you, not even a creak could be heard as they all took in the magic of a story, not in the tellin' of yarns by a fire but in the readin' of words. Now and then, Abby got up, even while she was readin', and wrote words on the blackboard to talk about later.

I saw why she picked a book about boys and girls and their treasure-seekin' adventures to read to a class of Nags Headers—it was simple for folks to understand, and lively enough to keep their attention. The shenanigans of Tom put me in mind of myself at that age, truth be told. Too canny for his own good.

But stories like that didn't do much for me these days.

I settled on watchin' my wife move about, full of spirit. It put me in mind of when I first met her. How she'd lived like she'd swallowed a glassful of sunshine every morning. And how every time she spoke, she breathed a little of that light over everybody. Almost dancin' about between the desks, her homespun dress as pretty as the fanciest gown on her. Getting' us to learn somethin' we didn't know before, makin' us grow strong. Makin' it seem, if just for a minute, that all wasn't lost.

Even a blind man could see why she'd come back here; she fit in as easy as the ladle into hot soup. And I thought, *Dr. Brooks and a whole roomful of scientists ain't got a thing on Abby Whimble.*

I wanted that for the whole of Nags Head.

At the end of the day, I helped everyone sweep up the floor and wash the soup pot and bowls and wipe the blackboard and slates.

All of a sudden, Abby hollered, "Smelly is out of his shell!"

Everybody crowded around the tank, and Jennie hurried to get her journal and a pencil, then settled herself right in front of the tank. Her pencil moved quick over the paper, eyes flittin' fast from the tank to the paper, as Smelly pecked his way over to a shell a bit bigger than the one he came out of and took his time in wedgin' his body up inside of it. He took a few jaunts around the sand, then settled down for a bit, likely tuckered out.

When it seemed the fun was over, Jennie had two different sketches that mirrored the happenings in the tank: naked Smelly and newly shelled Smelly.

"What should I write beneath the drawings?" she asked me.

"*Pagurus longicarpus*," I said. "Don't ask me how to spell it."

Abby gave her some hints about proper spellin', lookin' in her Latin book for the meanin' of *longi-* and *-carpus*.

"*Pagurus* means a type of crab fish," I said with pride.

They turned to laugh at me, as if that was the easiest thing in the world to know.

I left the schoolhouse and walked straight to the Weeks's abode, knockin' hard on the door. Alice pulled it open, already fit to bust.

"Ben Whimble. What on earth do you want, and at the supper hour too."

"Hey Alice," I said. I smelled fryin' fish, and my belly growled loud enough for her to hear. That bowl of soup was long gone.

"Come on in," she said, rollin' her eyes. I followed her back to the kitchen where I spotted the fish spittin' in a pan on a grate in the hearth. Her oldest girl was tendin' the food, tongs in hand.

"Haven't seen you about much," said Alice, throwin' sliced pota-toes into the pan. "Where you been?"

"Oh, you know. Proggin' round."

She snorted. "That ain't much."

"Been getting a little learnin', too. Over at the schoolhouse."

Her girl snuck a look over at me, and Alice shook her head, a little grin on her hard face.

"I'll bet you have," said Alice. "I see you're fresh shaved."

"'Twas past time to clean myself up."

"Well, you had a good reason, I reckon."

I couldn't help but smile. "She's a real good teacher, Alice. Even better than she was when she taught at the Freedmen's School."

She blew out a raspberry. "You sure it's the *teachin'* that's dazzled you?"

"Enough of that." I shook my finger at her. "You best get your young'uns over there tomorrow. No more time to waste, now."

She guffawed. "Tomorrow?"

"Why not?"

"I already told all this to Abner Miller, but I see I'll have to tell it all again. *I shouldn't have to spare my children.* There's too much to do on this here homestead for them to go runnin' to that school-house every day. Good teacher or no."

In my mind, I saw my wife, standin' in the schoolhouse, waitin' for the young'uns of Nags Head that wouldn't come. Mr. Warthog's money sittin' like the devil's hoard, holdin' sway over her. I stepped over to Alice and grabbed up her rough hands, and she was surprised enough not to pull 'em away.

"You have to heed me now," I said, my voice loud and strong. "They can do the chores and get their learnin', all in one day. Ask Jennie and the boys. Ask Ruby too. They're just about bangin' down the door to get inside that schoolhouse. They've never seen such a place. A place to learn about things you and Roy can't teach 'em. How to read, and write, and do sums. She's readin' them a real good book called *The Adventures of Tom Sawyer*. Hijinks galore. Everybody follows along in their own books."

Alice yanked her hands from mine, all in a pucker.

"I want to go, Mama," her daughter squeaked from the hearth.

"You see what you've done?" huffed Alice. "You've gone and put highfalutin thoughts into my girl's head. What does she need with readin' and writin', if she's to be married with young'uns?"

"It's called education, Alice."

"Pshaw!" She cut her eyes at me. "Don't you think I know that? I always pined for a school here."

"Well, you sure ain't actin' like it."

She let out a growl. "Keep an eye on the fish, Mabel."

She grabbed me by my elbow and marched me to the door.

"You want to know why no one's comin' to that schoolhouse?" she hissed.

"Folks see it as strange that Abby and me aren't together. That she's plumb crazy, even comin' back here at all. I've heard the talk. Is that what you think too?"

She nodded her head big, hands on her skinny hips. "She don't seem right in the head, Ben."

"She's more right than all of you folks put together, Alice."

"You back together as man and wife then? Is that what you're tellin' me?"

Her eyebrows arched all the way to her thin head of hair. "We all want to know, on account we know she's a-livin' at the schoolhouse, but *you* most surely *ain't*. And that Top Hat she came with still ain't gone, is he? Comin' and goin' at the school more'n you, some say."

"I can't do a thing about him. Believe me, I ain't actin' nice."

"She could do it, if'n she wanted. But she knows who butters her bread, don't she?"

"You can tell 'em..." I wiped my face with my palm, all of a sudden damp. "Tell 'em she's still my wife, and I...*we* still care for each other."

"*Care*? I *care* about my heifers and my fig tree."

Mabel hurried around the corner and handed me some steamin' fish on a tin plate afore Alice swung wide the door and pushed me out.

"Thank you kindly, Mabel," I said, blowin' at the fish. "I'll see you at the schoolhouse."

Mabel grinned, just as Alice slammed shut the door.

The next morning, a deep and cloudy cold had settled, smellin' of winter ice, and I cursed the January weather. Not the best day for a Sunday sail with one's long-lost wife. I packed on all the clothes I could, hauled up all my woolen blankets and brought them out to my skiff, already tied up at the schoolhouse. *Tessa* seemed too cold to move and moaned with the wind.

I made my way up the steps, and with achin' hands, knocked on the door.

She pulled it open, and I hardly knew her, she was so covered up. Not a strand of red hair could be seen beneath the man's wool cap she wore. I pulled up the brim and peeked into her eyes.

"Is that you under there?"

She laughed. "Andy loaned me his hat. And I'm wearing every article of wool I own."

"You sure you still want to go out? Smells of snow, almost."

She shut her door and looked up to the gray sky, hope in the sweepin' of her eyes.

"It might clear up," she said, pulling the schoolhouse door shut.

We walked to the wharf, and I helped her into the skiff. She sat on the bench that faced mine, our knees almost touchin'. She took up a blanket and wrapped it over her legs, and I poled us into open water, passing by cows, huddled in the marsh grass for warmth and watchin' us with doubtful eyes.

We'd barely gotten goin' when we sailed past the hotel, windows boarded up. Then lickety-split, we came upon the house I'd built for us, which in my heart and mind, I now thought of as the Blounts' abode, nothing to do with me and Abby. They'd even brought some of the wood from their old home in Whales Head to build the kitchen house. Smoke now came from its chimney, and the garden twinkled with frost. Abby's head turned, takin' it in.

"It's still in good shape," she said.

"The sound side ain't as hard on houses," I said. "It was a risk, buildin' her closer to the sea. I knew it was. But..."

"You had to try," she said.

And just like that, the house was out of sight.

But the island where we'd lived our lives lay right across the sound from us. Queer, how we were here again, after all this time, and everything backward.

"You been to Roanoke Island since you've been back?"

"I have," she said, soundin' mournful. "There was nothing left of the colony really. Even the schoolhouse had been taken down. But there's a new settlement in the middle of the island called California. Leo Williams and his wife, Mercy, live there now. She's with child, I believe."

"I haven't laid eyes on Leo in a long while, truth be told. But I heard of California from Jacob, who heard it from the keeper of the Pea Island station. He said those folks wouldn't stop 'til they owned their own land."

"Mercy said they work so hard, they don't have time to come to the Nags Head School. They have a church, which could be used as a school too. But the teacher, and the supplies..."

"There's a school on the north end now, I heard," I said. "Could they go there to learn?"

"Mercy said it only has room for the white children," she said, a fair amount of fire in her words. "It's the same everywhere. The white children attend the best schools, and the Negroes are made to scrimp."

"Not at the Nags Head School," I said, hoping to raise her spirits.

The sail swelled with a sudden icy breeze, and we picked up speed.

"I lost touch with Luella and Ruth," she said, duckin' her head down in the wind. "It's too bad, because I have some ideas of how to help Luella learn to read. I promised to help her, you know."

She paused, then added, "And I miss them. I'd give anything to see their faces again."

I chuckled. "They kept us all on our toes."

"Remember those days, livin' in that old schoolmarm house?" I laughed, shakin' my head back and forth. "They were some hard, hard times, but I can hardly recall the sufferin' now. All I can remember is us, just bein' together. It made it all seem easy."

The words took us both by surprise I reckon, and we sailed along in the quiet after that. But after a while, I felt her gloved hand touchin' my thigh.

"I remember."

Her hand singed the skin of my leg, even through the layers of cloth, wool and suede glove. Hot as an iron pressin' down. At last, her hand moved from my leg, and I swear I saw steam comin' from it. And I saw how this love I had for her was a painful kind of love.

I blurted out, "Why *did* you fall out with everybody, do you think?"

She seemed to jump from the bench, so taken aback she was. She looked out at the water, her eyes dim and cloudy.

"I'm not sure how to answer that," she said at last.

The water we crossed broke at the bow, thin as a sheet of ice, and the sky was empty of fowl.

"Do your best," I said.

"I was living a new life," she said, choosin' her words careful, as if lookin' through her big dictionary for just the right ones. "It was...exciting. I traveled with Mr. Wharton to New York City, and Boston, and Philadelphia. Richmond, Baltimore and Atlanta. We visited old schools, new schools. Schools for Negroes, schools for Native Americans. I was learning new things every day, things I would try to bring back to my own classroom at the Normal College."

"So many things, it crowded out all the old things," I said, some bitterness makin' its way into my voice.

She shook her head. "You all were with me, the whole time. Especially you, Ben."

I cocked a brow. "You stayed away for *five years*."

"You sent me away."

"I wasn't a fool. I knew you wanted to leave. And look, I was right. *Five years*, Abby," I said, anger now poundin' in my head like a thunderstorm. "*That* wasn't what I wanted. I could never want that! Even *one* year was too long for me to be away from you!"

"I didn't know..." she said.

"Well, you didn't write much."

She narrowed her eyes. "You didn't either."

"'Course, there was that one letter," I said, my voice full of a rare anger. "The one you wrote after Pap died. A letter sloppy with false sorrow and not much else. After that, I tried to stop thinkin' of you. I tried to let you go."

I'd thrown that letter in a fire one night, then wanted to reach in and snatch it out again. That's how it was with Abby and me.

"I couldn't write," she said, her voice shaky. "I don't know why."

"I can tell you why," I said. The notions driftin' about my mind were as thin and sticky as a spider's web. Sayin' it all out loud mightn't make sense. I took in an icy breath that froze my lungs.

"On account we're two different kinds of people. Like a species and a subspecies that can get along all right but can't make offspring together. Mayhaps we should have just stayed with our own kind. Mayhaps we would have been happier."

Abby's eyes grew dark with a pain that I'd only seen in them once before.

"I'm sorry," I blurted out.

Abby put her face in her gloved hands.

"Dear God, Abby, that's not...Us being different sorts of people had nothin' to do with why we couldn't have young'uns. Not at all."

I rubbed my face with scratchy gloves, wishin' for my beard. "I'm readin' too much of that Darwin, I reckon."

Sleet started to fall on the wood of the boat, tiny pricks of ice that jumped about our feet and danced on the water. It had been wishful thinkin' on our part; it wasn't going to clear up. I turned the boat for Nags Head.

"Darwin says some species change when their homes are isolated, which got me to thinkin' about the wild ponies here."

My words bounced from water to air, trapped by the spittin' clouds above.

"No one knows for sure where they came from. Some say they swam ashore from long-ago sunken ships, Spanish most like. Put 'em next to mainland horses and they're real stocky things, with stubby legs, wild looks. And the skills to live on their own, out in nature. They're still horses, just different."

Abby took her hands from her face, so I kept on.

"It's like us Nags Headers, out fishin' and huntin' to make our livings. In our way, we're a subspecies. Left to ourselves, same as the wild ponies. Different than folks like you."

But Abby, it seemed, had stopped listenin' to me. She stared across the water; her red eyelashes caught bits of ice, and still she didn't blink.

At the schoolhouse, she helped herself out of the skiff and, icy blankets trailin', walked up the steps, me followin' in her footsteps like a scolded dog. At the door, she turned to me, her eyes bloodshot, her face so blue with cold, even her freckles had disappeared.

"You don't see," she said.

Sleet seemed to be in my mouth, my throat. I couldn't speak. "See?"

"See why I came back. After five years away. Why I came back here."

I shook my head; the reason had seemed just out of my mind's reach.

"It was for you," she said. "Only you."

Not the schoolhouse, not the gravestone, not even Nags Head itself. I ground my teeth to keep from bawlin' like a baby. "I c-c-couldn't be sure."

"Some may have seen us as two different species, or as *species* and *subspecies,*" she said. "But I always knew we were exactly the same. Did you not feel that way too?"

My voice shuddered like a sail in the wind when I said, "I still love you, Abby."

She dropped my blankets and turned to open the door. "That wasn't the question."

I lumbered back to my abode in the blowin' sleet and sat in my cold room with my head in my hands for a long while, thinkin' of Abby missin' me, all the way out in Nashville. Missin' me so much that she'd imagined a schoolhouse, a place where she could teach my kinfolk who couldn't read or write.

Two different species! Can't produce offspring! Sometimes words just didn't come out right. Sometimes words meant the opposite of what the person dearly wanted to say. *Doin'* was much better than talkin', in my view.

In those long-ago days, I'd wanted to do it all for her: catch the fish, grow the food, build the fires. Doin' those things showed her my love. But Abby needed the words too. Needed the words more than all the food and fire put together. I fell short in that regard and I knew I always would.

I lit a lantern and picked up *On the Origin of Species,* fanned the pages with a crackled thumb. I'd read the words of the book, as well as I could, but it didn't keep my tongue from manglin' the ideas.

This, this was what the Nags Headers were afeared of. A dark and twisted road of learnin' with an unknown ending. Away from the family, then away from the Outer Banks altogether.

And much as you couldn't hardly break a wild pony to take a saddle and work, the Nags Headers weren't about to be told to take on the yoke of education.

And yet Abby was here to try. Stubborn and strong-willed, she was! There was a time when I thought Abby could change the world. Just her. Her, with me beside her.

CHAPTER SIXTEEN

Abigail Whimble
January 11, 1882
Nags Head, North Carolina

We see these beautiful co-adaptations most plainly in the woodpecker and missletoe; and only a little less plainly in the humblest of parasite which clings to the hairs of a quadruped or feather of a bird;...in short, we see beautiful adaptation everywhere and in every part of the organic world.

—Charles Darwin, *On the Origin of Species*

"You shot a hundred ducks today," I said, writing the number on the blackboard. "The market buyer will pay you five dollars a canvasback. How much money should you be paid in total?"

"That's way too much money for a canvasback," said Bert, shaking his head at my ignorance. "Get around a dollar, maybe two for a pair. And a hundred of 'em? That's a real good day, by anybody's measure."

Everyone chuckled, even Frances.

"Alright then." I erased the five and wrote one, feeling ignorant, once again, of the Nags Headers' daily lives. "Now the challenge will be to calculate how much you'd be paid for a pair, if you still shot a hundred canvasbacks. It was a *very* good day for duck hunting."

As usual, when I connected the mathematical problems to their personal experiences with money—using hunting, cooking and counting stitches—as examples, I heard the excited sound of pencils on slates. Nodding, Mr. Wharton wrote rapidly in his journal.

Next I planned to conduct a lesson on telling time, for the clock behind my desk was still an object of mystery. Most Bankers told time by watching the sun move in the sky. It had taken Ben becoming a surfman for him to learn the concepts himself, but he still didn't own a clock or a pocket watch.

Since our disappointing boat ride three days before, Ben had been absent from the schoolhouse, his penmanship instruction abandoned. He'd enlisted the Blounts to bring bits of fish for the hermit crabs "for a few days," though they claimed he didn't say where he was going.

"That's Uncle Ben," Digby had said, shrugging.

They weren't worried in the least, but I was having a more difficult time of it. Even the smell of today's soup—collards, beans, and some small cuts of pork—wasn't taking my mind off him.

I grew irritated with myself by glancing at the door, waiting for Ben to come through it. And when he finally did appear in the doorway, I had to rub my eyes and look again to convince myself it was really him.

"I brought someone to learn with us today," he announced, and when he stepped away, I saw a thin dark-skinned woman with a head scarf and threadbare coat enter the room behind him. I hardly recognized her, the way life had worn down her youth. But I knew her, without a doubt.

"Luella!"

Her shouted name echoed about the walls of the schoolhouse.

I hurried to her and pulled her into an embrace, but Luella merely patted my hips, her thin body like sticks in my arms.

"Miz Whimble," she said, as if she'd caught me doing something naughty.

"Are you well?" I asked her, pulling away to take in her sunken face. Her eyes were dark and hard as they took in not my face but the schoolhouse around me.

"You ain't got but six measly students in here?"

Ben coughed into his coat collar. Luella had never minced words.

"This big ole schoolhouse, nice as can be, but nobody here. What's the matter with these here folks?"

The students watched me carefully.

"I suppose it's a matter of convincing them of the need for education."

She rolled her eyes. "If you have to do that, then they ain't much worth it. You should have built a schoolhouse for Negroes somewhere. The place would have been packed to the rooftop. Like the Freedmen's School was."

She stepped to the pot of soup on the stove, lifted the lid and sniffed. "They'd bring you some spices for this soup too."

"We all bring spices," noted Ruth.

"How did you get here, Luella?" I asked.

"Mr. Ben came and fetched me in Jarvisburg. I just about dropped dead when I saw him walking up to the house, and there I was at the laundry pot, cursing my very life. Told me you could teach me proper now, and I should get on over to your new schoolhouse so's you could show me your new tricks."

I looked to Ben, who fidgeted with his cap, a smile on his face.

"You knew where Luella and Ruth were?"

"I'd caught wind they'd gone to Jarvisburg, but I didn't know exactly whereabouts. Course, everyone in town knew Luella, so it didn't take me too long to find her."

"The hard bit was convincing Lionel to let me go." Luella chuckled. "Mama can't work in the field like I can. Her heart beats funny, and her feet are all swelled up. But she can cook most days, and minds Bo too, so she stays busy. He's four years old now, and he just about eats all the food we can muster up. He's growing up tall."

She smiled for the first time, speaking of her son. "I told him 'Mama's got to go learn, Bo. However long it takes is how long I'll be gone. And when I come home, I'll teach you too.'"

Joyful laughter boiled in the depths of my throat, and I swallowed hard to keep it all down. Luella was here, standing in my classroom at last, and Ben had brought her here.

"Where will you live?"

"Mr. Ben said I could stay in his shanty."

"Shanty?" Ben protested.

"And what of Ben?" I asked, avoiding his eyes.

"Now, that's a question you should be asking *yourself*, Miz Whimble!" She laughed. "*What of Mr. Ben?*"

Ben hurried away from us, over to the tank, and Luella walked about the classroom and even opened the door to my apartment and looked around. At last she directed her gaze to Mr. Wharton, strangely silent in the back of the room.

"I remember you," she said, wrinkling her nose.

He stood up and bowed to her. "Welcome back, Luella. I'm glad to see you. Perhaps we can converse after school has ended. Get to know each other a little."

Luella snickered. "Ain't nothing to tell that I ain't already just said. And Ben's told me all I need to know about *you*."

With that, she seated herself in a desk at the front of the room, and Mr. Wharton stood unmoving, shocked by Luella's dismissal.

"Let's get to work, now, Miz Whimble. I been waiting long enough."

I walked to the front of the class and said, "This is Luella Washington...Luella, what is your married name?"

She rolled her eyes. "Pitts."

"This is Luella Pitts, a former student of mine at the Freedmen's School on Roanoke Island. I must say, I thought I'd never see her again."

Luella batted a hand at me. "Oh, I knew I'd see you again. We were family, weren't we?"

"We were. Are."

I took a deep breath. "I'll be working with her alone for a bit, so I'd like you to work among yourselves in the readers. Then we'll have our soup."

I rummaged in my desk drawers for the papers I had on Luella's word blindness, and quickly reviewed their findings and suggestions, glancing up now and then to confirm that Luella was actually here.

The day went quickly after that, with Ben reading aloud *The Adventures of Tom Sawyer* and acting out the voices of Tom and Huck and even putting on a high-pitched voice for Aunt Polly.

He would stop every once in a while and ask questions: "Now, why do the boys run away from their homes and set up camp on the island? Well, that's true, Andy, they wanted to escape from the laws of society into the easy comforts of nature, with nobody tellin' 'em what to wear, or do, or say. I reckon that's why folks come to Nags

Head in the summer—to recall themselves to nature. But ain't we the lucky ones, gettin' to live here all the time?"

Everybody agreed. He caught my eye and winked.

It was growing dark by the time Luella and I finished with our work; without my noticing, the students, including Ben, had already cleaned up and left.

We walked wearily to the door and stepped out into the cold afternoon, Luella laden with a thin bag of her belongings. She claimed she wasn't hungry, but I gave her an apple and a biscuit from my bag.

I walked with her up to the road and told her how to find Ben's cabin.

"So how *did* you convince your husband to let you go?"

"Mr. Ben paid him," she said, as if it were obvious. "He won't tell me how much. I asked him the whole way here."

"Oh" was all I could muster, for my throat had closed up tight.

She shook a forefinger at me. "Mr. Ben said that Yankee paid for this schoolhouse. That he comes around every day, watching you with lover's eyes."

"Ben told you that?"

She shrugged. "We had nothing to do but talk on the way over. He told me all manner of things, matter of fact. Seems he's a man of great learning now. I stopped listening to him after a while and took a little nap."

"Mr. Wharton is a…friend. He cares about the schoolhouse as well. He wants to stay on, to see how it does."

She narrowed her eyes. "Oh, I see now. Ain't nothing to do with you."

"He's planning to publish several articles in the education jour-
about the school. Perhaps even write another book. He's an
ic, Luella."

to you. Loyal as a dog. No wonder Mr. Ben's in a dither."

d and walked up the path. Over her shoulder, she called,

ing I'm back, Miz Whimble. Someone needs to set

reckon it's gonna be me."

good to see her again.

d on my
artwork
inner parts
ng.
little specks,
from Latin,
es from Latin,
on, but tinier—
d."

ed up early, smelling of lye soap.
ve up his shanty so easy. I spent all
can't seem to get out the reek.

hering those dark days of
hile to get used to it."

e animal one. You
nt it's got this here
got these little parts
ke sugar from sunlight.
we don't have to make
ed so much last summer."

uella and I shared
pt with Jennie.
r while I was
throat.

ns?" he

just look how neat her writin'
grin. He picked up his bag and

he

s here

Dr. Brooks

8

did and go along from there," he said. "For today, I'd talk about the difference between a plant and an animal."

He must have seen something like confusion on my face, for he said, "Seems like a simple thing to figure, I know, but there are a few things that make them different from one another on their insid I've got little pictures of plant and animal cells that Jennie drew lookin' at my own chicken scratch. You know what a cell is?"

"No," I said, my cheeks flushing. Mama had read books of s but I'd never taken the time. "Not really."

He pulled drawings from the back of the notebook to spre desk. Breathing with life and color, they were as beautiful hanging in a gallery; one circular and one rectangular, their were labeled neatly along the margins in Jennie's handwrit

"Cells are what all livin' things are made up of. Tin can only see 'em under a microscope. The word com o' course: *small room*. Like a cell in a prison, I reck much tinier—than even the fluff of a dandelion see

He moved even closer to me.

"This here is the plant cell, and this here is t can see the plant cell is rectangular, on accou membrane around it to give it shape, and it' called chloroplasts that help the plant cell ma Animal cells don't need those, on account our food. We can just go out and eat it."

I didn't dare look at his face. "You lear

"Dr. Brooks is a good teacher."

"I see that Jennie labeled the parts."

"I helped her with the spellin', but is. And look here," he said, with a sl pulled out a big, black piece of metal. "Dr. Brooks sent me this here microscope, straight from Johns Hopkins University. Now we can look at the cells of all kinds of livin' things, right here in Nags Head."

"First an aquarium, now a microscope!"

"I know I won't be near as good a teacher as you," he said. "But mayhaps we can work together. Like I'll teach 'em some new words, and you can add 'em to their spellin' word lists. Or the students can use the science words for script practice. I don't know, you're the teacher."

"And so are you, it seems," I said. "I'd be honored."

In the warmth of his smile, I saw a hint of the love I used to see. The love I had taken, and then placed into a tiny room—a *cell*—in my mind, until it had outgrown the space and begged for fresh air. Now it flowed through every room of my body.

"What in tarnation are you two doing up there?" asked Luella.

We both laughed, but the students watched us warily.

"Ben is going to teach you science," I announced.

The class blinked at Ben in confusion.

"What's science?" asked Frances.

I racked my brain for a good way to explain the far-reaching subject of science, but Ben stepped forward.

"It's the study of nature," he said. "All the things around us that we can see and feel. Trees, critters, ocean, air."

"Uncle Ben, I'll allow you can do lots of things," said Digby. "But you ain't no schoolmaster. Why can't Miz Whimble learn us some science?"

"I don't know the intricacies of the subject," I interjected. "But Ben does. In fact, he studied it in a class taught by a college professor this summer."

Everyone stared at him, surprise on their faces.

"College? What's that?" asked Andy.

"A place where you can really pack your brain with all manner of information, on any subject you want," said Ben. "But you have to start here, in this schoolhouse, afore you can go to such a place."

Ben took a deep breath. "My own teacher is a real smart man. He made me see that *all* of us here on the Banks are already students of nature. So learnin' science should come right natural."

And with that, Ben launched into a discussion of the microscope and how it allowed observers to see the magnified images of anything slid beneath the lens: a minuscule slice of Stinky and Smelly's crab food, a sliver of leaf, and a bit of a goose feather.

As he worked with the students, I wrote words on the blackboard: *microscope, observe, magnify, lens, vertebrate, cell, specimen.*

But I might as well have been invisible, the students were so engrossed in the workings of the microscope. Being able to see inside the objects they'd handled their entire lives mattered more to them than anything I'd taught them thus far.

I remembered his job in Beaufort, then, and knew I should be happy for him. But the last time I'd lost him to a job, our marriage had been lost as well.

That night, Stinky and Smelly slept deeply in their shells, and the roar of the wind surrounded the schoolhouse, so loud I couldn't dwell on my lesson plans any longer.

Yet I dreaded the dark and empty bedroom, where the classroom's wood smoke had permeated everything in the room, even my bed linens and nightgown.

In the light of the lantern, I washed from my face the daily scum of chalk dust and cold sweat, and gazed at my pink face in the mirror. I removed the pins from my hair and brushed it out, thinking that Ben used to run his hands through this hair, always marveling at how soft it was. "Compared to a horse's mane," he'd said.

I imagined him next to me in the frigid bed and soon fell into a deep sleep, where I dreamed of witches and cauldrons, their whispered spells stealing through the roaring night as they tossed books into the fiery pot. Cackling, as the scent of dead fish emanated from the burning books.

Still exhausted, I awoke in the early morning to the same wretched stench, the wind still howling. Shivering with the cold, I got out of bed and looked out the window to see if perhaps the sound had washed an entire school of fish upon the shore. Yet there was nothing but the water meeting with the sand.

I stepped to the bedroom door and opened it, and as I did, a pile of dead fish tumbled toward my feet. I jumped back with a cry. The door to the schoolhouse was wide open to the dull, morning light, illuminating the room's chaos of small striped fish, poured over every surface.

"Hello?" My voice was foreign in my ears. "Who's there?"

Only the wind responded, a mournful moan.

Fighting fear, I pulled on my coat and boots and took a large step over the mound of fish at my feet to gaze about the ransacked room. All of Jennie's artwork had been pulled down from the nails in the walls and crumpled, their pieces mingling with the wet, rotting fish all over the floor. The desks and chairs, as well as my own, were strewn with fish as well.

But most horrifying of all: All of the books on the shelves had been removed, several fish left in their stead. I had purchased three hundred carefully selected books for this schoolhouse, and someone had made off with every single one of them, all while I slept.

I never thought such a thing would happen in the village of Nags Head.

My body sagged, my breath coming in fits. I had no idea where to start cleaning the mess. I would need barrels, and mops, and plenty of strong soap. I stepped outside to take the air.

When Ben arrived with Jennie and the boys, I readied myself for their shock and disappointment.

"I hope you're hungry," I said. "Someone left us some fish last night."

Ben bounded up the steps toward the open door and stopped at the threshold. Bert, Digby and Jennie followed him up, peering around him to take in the scene. Though Ben was silent, the others gasped and muttered.

Ben turned to me, his eyes clouded with concern. "This happened while you were asleep?"

I nodded. "I didn't hear a thing," I said. "But the smell woke me."

"Who would do this?" cried Jennie. "Our grand schoolhouse! And did you see my sketches? Torn and mussed about the floor. It's the devil's work."

Luella arrived, took in the mess and shook her head. "I knew it. It's black and white learnin' together that makes folks do this kind of hateful stuff. I just knew you were headin' for trouble, Miz Whimble."

"Naw, that ain't it," said Digby. "It ain't like that here."

"It's like that *everywhere*," she declared.

"Well, it was more'n one man, I'll tell you that," said Bert. "'Twas a heavy barrel full to make such a mess. A waste of good perch."

"Somebody who don't come to school," mused Digby.

"That's the whole village," Bert muttered. "Coulda been anybody."

Jennie shook her head. "No, I don't reckon so. I only know of one family who'd have the guts to do this, and that's the Ruffins. That Walter has a black storm cloud over his head."

"We don't know anything yet," I cautioned. "I wouldn't start accusing people. I don't want to put anyone off even more."

"Ruffins," spat Digby. "I'll bet that's who. They never want anybody gettin' the better of 'em."

They left to fetch barrels, mops, buckets and soap, and by the time they'd returned, Ruby and Frances had arrived. Ruby declared that we'd need some sustenance while cleaning and left with some perch to fry over her hearth.

That afternoon, back aching and hands freezing in the cold air from the open windows, I heard a knock on the open door of the schoolhouse. I looked up to see Mr. Wharton, surveying the activity in the room. It didn't take long for him to notice Ben, scrubbing the empty bookshelves with renewed vigor.

"I heard what happened," he announced. "Word travels fast at the market, apparently, and Mrs. Keets informed me immediately. What a catastrophe! Are you all right, Abigail?"

I kept mopping, pushing the soapy water laced with fish scales toward the doorway where his shiny boots stood. "I'm fine. Just angry about the loss of time. And of course the theft of the books."

"But at least *you* are safe. Books can be bought again, but you, my dear, cannot be replaced. Just to think—you were *here!* *Asleep!* While the hooligans proceeded to leave you a day's catch of fish."

"I reckon Miz Whimble can see to herself," said Luella from the front of the classroom. "Just look how she slings that mop."

Bert and Digby scrubbed the desks and chairs with soapy rags, and Jennie was on her hands and knees, scrubbing the floor.

"Glad you're here, Mr. W.," said Digby. "We could use another hand."

He looked aghast. "Oh dear, I'm afraid I'm not dressed for that."

There came a general chuckling from the room, and Mr. Wharton stiffened.

"Mrs. Keets has offered her home to you," he said to me. "We may be somewhat cramped, but I do hope you'll consider taking her up on her invitation."

"That won't be necessary," said Ben, still scrubbing.

"On the contrary," said Mr. Wharton. "I'm sure you share my worry that Abigail is vulnerable out here with no *lock* on her door. Which I will be procuring soon enough, you can be sure. *Someone* should be watching out for her."

Ben turned from the book shelves to face him, his wet cloth dripping onto the floor. "Nothin' to worry over, since I'll be here with her. Door lock or no."

I put some more muscle into my mopping to disguise my surprise, but the rest of the students stopped their cleaning to stare with wonder at Ben.

"It's a gallant gesture, Ben, but I don't think it's appropriate. *Children* come here to learn, after all. You mustn't set a seedy example."

"Seedy? We *are* man and wife, last time I checked."

"Indeed," said Mr. Wharton. "And yet it still wouldn't be appropriate."

"What *you* think, and what the folks livin' out here might think, are two different things entirely."

Both men stared with anger at each other, faces drawn tight and chests heaving.

I stopped mopping. "We've got it all in hand here, Mr. Wharton, but thank you for coming."

"Of course. My schoolhouse is of the very utmost importance."

Ben let out a barking cough, which sounded a great deal like "My!"

Luella muttered, "Mmm, mmm."

As Mr. Wharton walked out the door, I felt the previously stifled laughter fill the newly clean room. And yet I couldn't laugh. My heart was heavy, so heavy that I had to sit down, to rest my newfound weight. I closed my eyes. I feared Mr. Wharton would never leave Nags Head. I feared the schoolhouse would never truly be mine.

When I opened my eyes, Digby was standing before me, a tickler in his hand.

"Thought this might come in handy today," he said. "I mean, you may think it's *seedy*, a schoolmarm sipping on whiskey and all. But it does do the trick."

"Where did you get that, Digby Blount?" demanded Jennie.

"The tickler or the whiskey?"

Jennie just shook her head in disgust, but I took a hearty draft of the liquid before handing it back to Digby.

"Thank you." I coughed. "But don't you dare bring that tickler to school anymore."

"That's the last of my liquor anyhow."

Bert chuckled knowingly, and the students returned to the cleaning.

That evening, the schoolhouse still smelled powerfully of fish, despite the large amount of soap we'd used. But the room was as clean as it had ever been. I ran a cracked hand over the surface of my desk, shining in the lamplight.

To occupy myself while I waited for Ben to gather his things, I took up *On the Origin of Species* and seated myself at the desk, attempting to read. But all I could think of was Ben, reading through these same difficult pages.

As the night wore on, I embarked on chapter four, but my tired eyes burned in the flickering light. I grew chilly as the fire died out, so I pulled a blanket around me. Perhaps he'd changed his mind about staying with me.

Unwilling to go to bed and close the apartment door, I rested my forehead on my arms and closed my eyes. It seemed much later when I heard the door creak open.

I raised my head to see Ben, sitting at the desk near the stove, one leg crossed over the other as he pulled off a boot. He'd brought a tick and had placed it on the floor near the stove, its fire nothing but embers.

"You're here," I croaked, the blanket slipping from my shoulders.

"'Course I am," he said, pulling off his other boot. "Nothin's changed, I see, you readin' afore bed. What is it tonight?"

I held up the book for him with a little grin. "It put me right to sleep."

He rummaged around in his bag and pulled out his own *Origin*. "It's not the easiest book I've ever read, but it does make me think. I dwell on Darwin's ideas all day, just about. You'll see."

I laughed. "Oh, I'm sure you're right."

"How far have you got?"

"Chapter four."

He snickered.

I rolled my eyes. "All right, how far have you gotten, then?"

"Almost through with it, matter of fact. But don't worry, Abby, if you got any questions about anythin', just ask. I'll be right out here."

Ben crawled onto the tick and arranged the blankets over him, so I stood, pulling the blanket across my body. But I couldn't move my sore feet toward the door to my apartment. My heart pounded at the sight of him here. Here with me at last, after all these long months. I wanted him in my bed, not on the floor.

I swallowed hard. "I must say, I think of you when I read."

He propped his head under an elbow so he could see me. "How's that?"

"It's Darwin's curiosity. And his respect for nature. The natural world is everything to him."

"I can see myself settin' sail across the ocean, the way Darwin did. Lookin' for specimens to learn about."

"You can?"

"Well, I did, back when you were...gone," he admitted. "But not anymore. Now I know I can learn more'n I'll ever need to know just by stayin' put. All of this right before our eyes, and we have no notion how special it all is."

He cleared his throat and lay back flat on the tick. The room had grown cold, but I knew Ben wouldn't use any of the precious wood.

"Sweet dreams, Abby."

It was the first time I'd heard those particular words in many years. What would he do if I pulled off the blankets that covered his body and settled in next to him? Would he push me gently away? Or would he wrap his arms about my freezing body, warming me in an instant?

"Good night, Ben."

Gripping *On the Origin of the Species*, I stepped into the apartment and quietly closed the door. I opened the book to where I'd left off and started reading in the moonlight. And as I read, I heard Ben's voice, reciting the words along with me, as if he were lying in bed next to me. Years had peeled away, and we were back where we'd started, living only with each other wrapped up in the words of a book.

I read four chapters before I dozed off, the book still in my hands.

CHAPTER SEVENTEEN

Benjamin Whimble
January 15, 1882
Nags Head, North Carolina

What can be more curious than that the hand of man, formed for grasping, that of a mole for digging, the leg of the horse, the paddle of the porpoise, and the wing of the bat, should all be constructed on the same pattern, and should include the same bones, in the same relative positions?

—Charles Darwin, *On the Origin of Species*

I'd heard the preacher from the mainland was due to visit the Nags Head flock this Sunday at none other than the Ruffin house, the house with hands-down the biggest parlor. So I thought I'd go and see about God again, among other things.

The whole village was there, it seemed like. Alice Weeks rolled her eyes at me, but Mabel smiled and waved. The Blounts were there as well, and surprised to see me.

They used to try to get me to come to church service—they claimed God had saved me from the fate of drownin' the way my fellow surfmen had perished, and that I should come to offer thanks and praise. But the way I saw it was that God had spared the wrong man. And if he'd mistook *that* particular situation, mayhaps he'd been wrong about a lot of other things He'd done as well.

And now the preacher spouted forth, readin' from the Bible just like he was God's own professor. After his blessing, folks turned quick for the door, and I shouted, "Don't leave just yet, my brothers and sisters. I'd like to have a word."

I squeezed my way through the men, women and children to get to the front of the parlor. They watched me with wary eyes.

"Now, I know you all are good, church-goin' folks. I mean, look at you all here, givin' your Sunday mornin' to learn about God and his son Jesus Christ and the gospels."

They smiled shyly and looked about at each other like they all were really somethin' special.

"But all is not as it seems, Preacher. There is evil afoot. *Somebody* in this here village saw fit to dump a day's catch of perch all over the new schoolhouse," I said, pointin' my finger around the room. "And whoever did this then helped themselves to every single book on the schoolhouse shelves, leaving cold, dead fish in their places. All while my poor schoolmarm wife was sleepin' in her room in back."

I looked about at the faces of my fellows and was happy to see outrage and shame on most of them. Except for the Ruffins, who all looked down at their shufflin' feet.

"Now I'm here, as Abby's husband, to see about findin' out who done that terrible thing to the grandest schoolhouse in the state of North Carolina. Took a *book*..." I said, reachin' for the Bible in the preacher's hands and holdin' it high.

"...and left dead fish in its place. A book such as *Moby-Dick*. A book my own wife gave to me, years ago, and still I recall turns of phrase that stick with me, even to this day. A great book, to be sure. Let me tell you, a pile of dead fish ain't near a fair exchange for a grist of quality books."

Bowin' my head, I handed the Bible back to the preacher. "Today I'm here to get 'em all back."

I squinted my eyes at their sorrowful faces. "Now, I know whoever took those books can't even read 'em, on account you don't even go to school to learn your letters. I mean, it would be one thing if whoever took 'em was short of good books and was sufferin' to read somethin' good. But no, whoever took 'em just took 'em to be spiteful. And I can't abide that in this village of good people like yourselves. We've got to root out that evil, don't you agree Preacher McMillan?"

"Oh, yes," he said. "I am sorry to hear of that, I truly am. That is not the Christian way."

He shook his bald head sadly. "I'd hoped that some of you would have attended school by now, in order to better read scripture. That schoolhouse is a gift from God if I've ever seen one."

I grinned. "I couldn't have said that better myself."

Alma Ruffin, holdin' her sleeping baby, spoke from her place at the front of the room. "I do believe you've a future as a preacher, Ben Whimble."

"Naw. I'm more a science man, myself."

Everyone in the room sniffed at that, includin' the preacher. And the Ruffin baby started to cry.

"I'll speak with you outside, Ben," said Alma. She handed the red-faced baby to her eldest daughter and made her way to the door through the starin' crowd. I followed her out, and we walked over to the barn, out of earshot of the folks spillin' out of the house.

"Now, I'm not sayin' my boys were part of the scheme, mind you. But Walter and Jesse were gone fishin' on the sound a couple days ago. Thought you might want to know."

"And what did they catch?"

She screwed her thin lips tight. "Perch. Had it for supper every night they been back. Told 'em to sell it to the market man. But mayhaps they had another ideer."

"Sounds like they did."

"Well, what's to do about it?"

"I reckon you and Erb need to send those boys to the school-house for their learnin'. Not to punish them, as such, but to set a mold for the other young'uns here that schoolin' is important. As important as catchin' fish or huntin' ducks."

"That won't fly, I'll tell you now," she said. "Not with Erb, and not with the boys."

"Well, then, I'll call the law to come over from Roanoke Island. And they'll make a fuss, you know. Those books cost a bundle."

She rolled her eyes. "Wait here."

She marched up to the house and was inside for a few minutes, then came out with her husband and the boys. As the rest of the family stood at the door watchin', they walked real slow over to where I stood. The boys ground their jaws, while Erb smoked his pipe, his arms crossed about his chest.

Alma poked Walter in the back. "Tell him."

Walter eyed me with two hateful eyes. "'Twas me and Jesse done it."

"Shame on you," I said.

"We didn't know she was there!" Walter hollered. "Why's she sleepin' in a schoolhouse anyways?"

I wouldn't answer that. "Why'd you do it?"

Walter glared at me. "Sam and Willis Weeks came here tellin' us how you were goin' around, tellin' everyone to go to school. How their mama was gonna make 'em go, after all this time of not going. It wasn't fair. We never asked for a schoolhouse here. Why'd she even build it? She ain't even from here."

"She's tryin' to help you, you fool," I growled. "Where'd you put her books?"

"Buried 'em on Run Hill. Good luck findin' 'em, too."

Erb unfurled an arm and struck Walter across the back of the head. "You'll show him, boy. And after a good whoopin', you'll go to that schoolhouse too. And you'll get learned just like my grand-daddy was."

"Abby teaches men and women too, you know. Doesn't matter to her a student's age."

Alma spoke up. "We heard she teaches Ruby Craft now."

"She does, right alongside Frances."

She laughed a little. "They'll have more learnin' than me, I declare. Frannie even learned Little Bud how to spell her own name. Should've been me to do that, I reckon."

"You're welcome to come too, Alma. You too, Erb."

They both shook their heads. "Time's past for us," said Erb. "But not for these ones here."

"You said we'd never have to go to that school," huffed Jesse, lookin' to his brother for agreement. "You said learnin' was good-for-nothin' 'cept makin' a man prideful."

"That was afore you did what you did," said Erb. "You wasted and stole, and them's terrible sins. I'd rather you be prideful as Nebuchadnezzar than do what you boys did. Now you've got to make amends."

"Won't she be afeared of us?" asked Walter, a grain of hope in his dark eyes.

"Not hardly." I laughed. "She's stronger than she looks. And too, I'll be there, teachin' lessons."

"You?" hollered Walter.

"I told you I was a man of science."

"Don't you need us for spring fishin'?" Walter begged his pap.

"What do you think I have four other boys for?"

"They should be in school too, Erb," I said. "And the girls."

Erb and Alma looked at one another for a long while, likely summin' up all the extra work they'd have to do themselves while their young'uns were gone.

"We'll work it out," said Alma at last. "They need to learn to read the Bible some. Like the preacher said."

"Fair enough. Now show me where you buried those books," I said to the boys. "And we'll need your horse and cart to bring 'em back to the schoolhouse."

Raisin' his hands, Erb smacked both the boys' heads.

We each carried stacks of books up the steps and into the schoolhouse.

I heard Walter whisper to Jesse, "Still smells of fish."

Just then, Abby came out of her apartment, her face alive with happiness. "You found the books!"

"Buried in the sands of Run Hill. And these boys were involved in their theft and untimely burial," I said. "That's Walter and Jesse Ruffin. And they'll be here tomorrow for school. Along with their brothers and sisters."

Abby stepped closer to us. "I've met Walter. But not Jesse. How do you do?"

"Not so good," said Jesse. "We're sorry about the...the fish and all. We didn't even know you was here a-sleepin'. Well, we did later, when we opened the door to your room and saw you in bed."

Walter snickered and dumped his books onto the top shelf, spillin' a few of them to the floor.

"Set 'em down nice," I barked.

I picked up one of the books to see a river of sand stream from its spine. Abby fetched the broom and dustpan and handed it to Walter.

"I spent my savings on those books. Money I'd saved for five years," she said.

Walter pushed the broom here and there along the sandy boards, not even makin' a pile.

"Ain't you never swept a floor?" I grabbed the broom from him and showed him how to sweep up.

He shrugged. "Sweepin's for girls. It's not man's work."

"Well, sweepin' up sand from this floor is gonna be *your* new job, man's work or no. Now go and fetch some more books, and take care to bang out the sand from each one afore you bring it in here, or else your job's gonna get a lot harder."

The boys moaned and left for the cart.

Abby shook her head. "I must say, I'm not surprised Walter was involved. He almost pushed me off their property when I visited back in September," she said. "How did you figure it out?"

I shrugged. "You can find out a lot at church service. They're of the mind to confess their sins."

Abby laughed, a sound I felt like I'd been waiting a while to hear.

I wanted to take that sound and stick it in a bottle for me to sip on whenever I needed a dose of happy.

"I hope you don't mind them comin' to school tomorrow. They're not gonna make it easy on you, but I think Ruffins being here will be good for the Nags Head School. Believe it or not, the family is held in high regard here."

"I don't mind. And I don't plan on going easy on them either," she said. She gave my hands a squeeze. "Thank you, Ben."

After the boys left, Abby and I counted the books, lined up nice and neat on her shelves once more. We were still missin' a few, but I figured they'd turn up sooner or later. Watchin' those Ruffin boys dig them up from a Run Hill dune put me in a bad temper, recollectin' all of Elijah Africa's books burnin' in a pile on a sad, dark night.

"You don't have to sleep here anymore," said Abby. "The danger is over. At least until the Ruffins start school."

My heart jumped about like a fish landed on a boat. "That's alright, I don't mind," I blurted out. "It's better than sleepin' in the Blounts' house, to be sure. Granny snores like a bear."

She smiled. "Would you like your tick in the same spot?"

She turned and made her way to the apartment, where I stowed the tick durin' school hours.

"No," I said. "I'll keep it in the apartment, if that's all right with you."

She turned about, her face pale. "What?"

"Well, that way, we can talk about *On the Origin of Species*. I have a feelin' you've got some ideers to mull over with me, and I figured we could do it from a spot of comfort."

She stood there starin' at me.

"I'll just be a minute," she said at last, duckin' her chin. "While I change."

When she was done, and I presented myself in the bedroom, I felt to be the dirty young man I'd been when I first saw her on the porch of the summer cottage. Ignorant and bumblin' and unworthy.

Settled on my tick, I watched her take the pins from her hair and use her fingers to smooth the curls. Then she poured water from the pitcher into the wash bowl and splashed her face, cryin' out with the cold of it. And when she grinned at me with her face all pink and wet, I thought, *This was why I could never love another woman. How could I, when I'd had such a fine creature as her?*

She crawled into her bed, and we looked at each other for a long while. I wanted to look at her for hours, but her face was so clear and bright I had to close my eyes. And even then, I could still see her on the backs of my lids, like the sunshine still at work.

Even as we talked a bit about Darwin and his notions, my eyes stayed shut. Seein' her here, so close to me now, was a treasure, don't mistake me. But hearin' her words, and my words twinin' through hers, was like watchin' a couple gulls in the sky, comin' together and then flyin' apart, both of them lookin' for the same fish.

Cryin' out, laughin' loud. Up and down and back and forth. I found I could give her the words she needed. It was easy, now.

I couldn't sleep with Abby so near to me, and her voice still hangin' about the room like the tail end of a lightnin' strike. Not to mention the moon shinin' through the windows, bright as day.

I got up from my tick and stepped quiet over to the window nearest to Abby's bed, but when I got there, all I could do was stare at her sleepin' face. I jumped when I saw her eyes pop open; she wasn't sleepin' neither.

"What are you doing?" she whispered.

I swallowed hard against my beatin' heart. "Lookin' at the moon. She's a fat one tonight."

Abby came out from the mound of coverings and stepped to the window, and there we stood, side by side. The full moon sat right over the sound, leakin' rivers of cream into the water below it. Looked like you could sail right up to it and scoop it into a bucket.

"I've never seen it like this," she whispered, shiverin' against the cold.

"Looks like she's tryin' to be our friend, she's up so close. Mayhaps she wants you to teach her how to read."

I moved behind her and wrapped her in my arms, and together we gazed on what lesser men would charge folks just to look at, like a paintin' or a statue. Holdin' her like this was the finest feelin' in the world.

Her hair smelled of the smoothest soap, her nightdress was of the finest linens. But none of that mattered a lick to me anymore. 'Twas Abby alone that mattered, her flesh and bone. Her big, beatin' heart.

"I should have welcomed you with open arms," I said into her neck. "Not run away."

She didn't say a word, and the quiet between us unfurled wrinkled and bumpy, havin' been wrapped up tight for so long.

I spun her around. "I'm sorry, Abby. Please, say you forgive me."

Her body shook, but from the cold or from my words, I couldn't say. "I do."

I moved my face close to hers, so close that when I next spoke, my lips touched hers. "I'm here now. We won't be parted again."

She pressed her lips hard to mine, and there we stood in the wavy light of the moon. I pushed her gently onto the bed and raised up her moon-creamy nightdress, licked her cold white thighs. Inside her, she was warm as milk, heated slow on a woodstove.

As we moved together, I thought of the moon on one side of the sky, and the sun on the other, winkin' at each other before goin' about their days and nights. Just one good look a day was enough to sustain them.

What a thing it would be, I thought, *for the two of them to at last meet face-to-face.* T'would be the beginnin' and the end of the world, all at once.

CHAPTER EIGHTEEN

Abigail Whimble
January 16, 1882
Nags Head, North Carolina

It may metaphorically be said that natural selection is daily and hourly scrutinizing, throughout the world, the slightest variations; rejecting those that are bad, preserving and adding up all that are good; silently and insensibly working, whenever and wherever opportunity offers, at the improvement of each organic being in relation to its organic and inorganic conditions of life. We see nothing of these slow changes in progress, until the hand of time has marked the lapse of ages...
—Charles Darwin, *On the Origin of Species*

Jennie bent low over the paper on her desk. There was just enough light through the windows to see the color of the palette before her.

Instead of working in the reader as we normally did when she arrived, she'd wanted to paint a gray-green crusty tube of fulgurite that she'd found. She'd been enthralled with the box of oil paints and brushes I'd ordered for the classroom, and she'd made it known, rather aggressively, that they were not to be used frivolously. In short, the paints were hers alone to use.

Ben was excited about the fulgurite. "That's petrified lightning, did you know? Lightning hits the sand and locks all the particles together. Inside, it's hollow, lined with glass."

Jennie was familiar with it, but I had never heard of it.

Ben stood over the puttering woodstove, preparing a pot of coffee and a pan of eggs and cornbread, while I wrote the day's date and some spelling words on the blackboard, words that Ben had suggested from the day's science lesson. He asked me to add "fulgurite" to the list.

As we sat to eat, the door opened, revealing a stream of twelve Ruffins from the smallest—Little Bud—to the tallest—Walter, bringing up the rear with a sallow face. They formed a knot of thin coats and homespun by the door, looking about with wide eyes. I shoved a forkful of eggs into my mouth and stood to greet them.

"Morning, ma'am," said Louise. "Mama said to get here early."

I nodded and tried to swallow quickly.

"It's cold in here," said Walter. "Ain't you got any wood?"

"We're running low," I said. "A donation of kindling would be welcome, if you can manage it. And cuttings for the soup we always eat for our midday meal."

"We ain't stayin' long enough for soup," said Walter.

My gut churned the eggs uneasily as I surveyed the large group. I would now have to divide the class into several different learning areas, according to the various abilities; undoubtedly, most of my time in the next few weeks would be devoted to teaching Luella and the Ruffins.

I spoke to the younger boys and girls I'd never seen before. "Welcome to the Nags Head School. I'm Mrs. Whimble, and of course you know Mr. Whimble over there. He will be instructing you in science later this morning."

Ben gave a salute from the stove as he piled the dirty dishes into the wash bucket.

"Please, be seated. If you would, select desks that are near one another."

They made their way to the right side of the room, filling in an astonishing number of empty chairs, while I distributed the new readers, slates and journals.

Louise sat at the desk next to Jennie, who looked up from her painting to greet her with the kind of look she used to reserve for me.

"What's that thing?" asked one of the younger boys, pointing to the aquarium.

Ben spoke up. "That's the aquarium, home of none other than Stinky and Smelly. Our very own hermit crabs."

The other students arrived one after the other, greeting the Ruffins with a simmering hostility. Luella cast a dark glance to them and walked to the front desk closest to mine where she usually sat, but the desk had been taken by Jesse.

"That's my seat," growled Luella. "Get up."

Jesse glared at her. "It ain't yours. You don't own it."

"It is mine. I always sit there, on account Miz Whimble helps me the most."

He snickered. "I ain't surprised by that one bit."

"Hey now!" shouted Ben.

I held up a hand to him. "Jesse," I said sternly. "There will be no more of that kind of speech in here, or you will be turned out to face your parents. Do you understand?"

He nodded glumly as Ben picked up a desk from the other side of the room and set it down next to mine for Luella.

Ruby and Frances were the last to arrive. Squealing, Little Bud got up and pulled Frances over to her chair, where they both tried to wedge themselves.

"Frances will have to sit beside her mother, Little Bud," I said. "They're learning from a more advanced reader, since they've been here longer. But I'm sure you'll catch up in no time. Then you may sit beside each other."

Little Bud looked as if she might cry, but Frances kissed her on the cheek and told her to "Hurry up and learn, it's easy," before sitting at her desk.

Ruby, however, still stood rooted to the same spot by the door. And I realized, too late, that I should have let her know that the Ruffins would be here today.

"We've some new students today, Ruby," I said.

"I can see that," she said, raising her chin and leveling her eyes at the Ruffins. "I know Little Bud right well, but these others, well...I've seen you all around, you know. Here and there. I recall you, Louise. And Walter. You too, Jesse. You were just a babe when I left..."

"Hello to you," said Louise. "'Course I remember you, Ruby. And your mama. We sure did miss you all when you left."

"You can call me Mrs. Craft. And yes, I do believe you missed having us around."

Louise squeaked in surprise and turned around in her chair.

"We don't see you in church," said Walter. "Mama and Daddy always say, 'Now where's Ruby and poor Frannie at? Should be here in church.'"

"I'd say we're none of your family's concern, Mr. Walter."

Luella snickered. Ruby now seemed to be swaying gently, as if a wind was battering her back and forth. Frances hopped up and ran to her, and hugged Ruby around her skirts.

"Mama?" asked Frances, taking Ruby's hand. "Come on. Let's sit down."

Ruby blinked down at her daughter and roused herself to be led to her chair.

Memories of teaching in the Freedmen's School came rushing back to me, where white and black learned alongside one another. But it hadn't lasted. Not even the Peabody money could keep such a place from crumbling. Everywhere across the country, schools were mostly segregated by race, with Negroes getting the bare minimum of support, if they received it at all.

I placed a hand on Ruby's, where it rested on her reader, ready to open it. Her eyes met mine, and she gave a slight nod.

"We are all students here," I said. "Even me. My husband teaches us about science. Bert and Digby and Andy teach us about hunting and fishing. Ruby teaches us about cooking, and Jennie teaches us about drawing. We all have things to teach, and to learn. So we will treat one another with the respect we deserve."

Mr. Wharton appeared at the end of my speech, his eyes widening at the full classroom.

Ben stepped over and pulled out his chair for him.

"Thank you, Ben," he said skeptically, eyeing the chair as if something distasteful had been placed on it.

"Didn't want you to miss the science lesson," said Ben.

"Science lesson?" he asked. "I didn't know Abby was teaching science."

"She's not. I am."

"You? How are *you* qualified to teach science?"

Ben shrugged. "Mayhaps I'm not."

And in a few minutes, Ben began the science lesson, using Jennie's fulgurite to explain about the high temperature of lightning, so hot it melted sand sometimes deep below the land's surface.

To my surprise, Mr. Wharton followed along with interest, taking down notes and nodding along. Even Walter, who'd been throwing off black looks, seemed to forget his misery as he watched Ben break open the fulgurite to show the cooled glassy layer inside.

That night, as he lay on his tick below, he reached up his hand up and probed about under the coverings until he found mine.

"Aren't schoolmarms supposed to whack their students on their hands with rulers when they misbehave?" he asked, reachin' his other hand over to pat my hand.

"Walter needs more than a good smack on the hand with a ruler," I said. "I should have told Ruby about them coming today."

Ben grunted. "Ruby set them all straight, I reckon."

My guts squeezed, remembering the way Ruby had swayed, as if battered by her memories.

He looked thoughtfully at me. "I'll bet folks in Nashville didn't know what to do with you. A Southerner who acts like a Yankee. I used to try to picture you there, at that Normal School. Where you were teaching. Who you were talking to. Like to drive me crazy, some days."

He chuckled sadly, and was quiet for a moment.

"I wondered...were there other men?"

"No," I said at once. I squeezed his hand so hard my fingers lost their feeling. "They didn't hold my attention. They were all alike."

"So just Top Hat, then."

I leaned over the edge of the bed. "Top Hat? Is that what you call him?"

He started to laugh. "Most everybody does, but I don't. I've got another name for him. Do you think he liked the science lesson?"

"I do. You have a way of making everything seem...magical."

"Nature *is* magical. I'm just the one who's pointing it out."

I leaned back onto my pillow, my belly clenching at the thought of my next question. "And you? Any women?"

He sniffed. "Naw."

"Just Jennie, then."

He laughed softly. "You thought we were together."

I climbed out of my bed, onto Ben's tick and under his blankets. He cried out at my cold body and tried to push me away, but I clung tightly to him, hands behind his back. I was silent as his warmth stole over me, like sunlight moving across the cold water of the sound.

"All of the miles between us. All of the months, just gathering together like geese on the wing, flying away from me," I said, squeezing my arms tighter around him, remembering how lonely I was. "And yet I spoke to you every night as if you were in bed with me. Sometimes, I woke in the night and felt you to be next to me. As if I'd never left Nags Head."

He took a lock of my hair and twirled it tightly around his finger, raised it to his nose to sniff, then let it go. Over and over, he wound my hair, before speaking again.

"I'd let you go," he said softly. "Just last summer. 'Twas like pullin' anchor after years at bay and lettin' my skiff go where it would. It was the hardest thing I'd ever had to do. But I felt relief too. Thinkin' of you—gone so far—gave me too much pain."

My body had gone cold once again, though I was still pressed against him. I recalled how fearful he'd acted when he'd seen me in the schoolhouse the first time.

Ben pulled my face toward his with his finger, still wrapped in my hair. "I'm sorry, Abby. I held on a long time."

"And now?" I whispered.

He sighed. Our chests pressed harder into each other, our hearts reaching.

"Things do change," he said at last. "Bankers don't like change, but Darwin says we are all of us changing, every second of the day. Making ourselves better in tiny little ways. And we're passing along the best of our changes to our young'uns.

"Everything I see," he went on. "The red-shouldered hawk, the partridgeberry, the sweet gum. I see them all different than I used to. Now, I see their pasts, presents and futures, all togetherlike. All changin' and changin' and changin' again, right before my eyes."

I could feel his eyelashes stroking my cheek. "I think of you and me that way too."

"Just when you thought we'd gone extinct," I murmured.

By the end of the week, the Ruffins and I had gotten into a routine. The boys came later in the morning, when their fishing and farmwork were done, and the girls left early in the afternoon to help Alma in the kitchen and the gardens and with minding the baby.

Ben offered science lessons twice a day to accommodate all of the students' varying schedules, and I had concocted a new seating arrangement to divide the room by reading ability.

Just when we thought we'd figured it all out, the Weekes and the Moores at last arrived, adding ten more students to the schoolhouse. Alice and Ida followed their children into the schoolhouse, each of them carrying a basket.

"We brung you some sticks for your stove and some cuttings for the soup we heard about," said Ida. "Everything fresh."

"Roy butchered a beef yesterday, so we brung a few cuts of meat too. But don't think you're getting anything close to that next time," said Alice.

"Thank you," I said, taking the baskets from them. "We've never had beef for our soup. It will be a real treat."

Their eyes roamed about the classroom.

"Hello there, Benny," said Alice. "You the schoolmarm's assistant?"

A few of the students snickered, including Luella.

"And there's Mr. Top Hat, o' course," Alice continued. "I don't reckon he's ever gonna leave. Do you, Ida?"

Ida glared at Mr. Wharton and shook her head. "Not likely."

Alice stepped to the science table, where the aquarium and various jars and buckets stood. Ida, meanwhile, added the beef and vegetables to the herbs and broth already bubbling on the stove.

"I heard you been cutting up frogs and such," she said to Ben. "Showing everyone their insides."

"I have been. It's called dissection. We're learnin' about their reproductive and digestive systems."

"Their *what* systems? That sounds like Satan's work to me. My young'uns don't need to be cuttin' up any critters just for the lookin', you hear?"

"The frogs are already dead when I bring 'em here," said Ben.

"That don't matter a lick to me!" She turned to me. "Just stick to the alphybet, will you?"

"Don't worry, Alice," I said. "And if you and Ida ever want to stay, you'll both be welcome."

They glanced at each other, and Alice offered what I took to be a rare smile. "We may. Just to keep an eye on your assistant, there. He can be right wayward, can't he?"

As they stepped to the door, Alice said, "We'll see you both at church service, then. My house this Sunday morning."

After they'd gone, I helped the newest students get settled in, seating them near the Ruffins, who were only a few days ahead of them in the readers. I wrote their names on the blackboard, most of them nicknames, like Little Roy, Captain, Squirrel Tail, Sweet Pea and Jump.

When at last I turned, ten names later, I saw that all of the chairs and desks were finally full.

I smiled at them and said, "Welcome to the Nags Head School."

On Sunday morning, I dressed for church, but Ben didn't want to go. He kept trying to pull me down to his tick by the hem of my dress.

"You should go. To quell these rumors of devil worship."

"I'll allow, it's nice to stand around with a group of my fellows, singin' songs and listenin' to Bible stories. But I went just last week, and I couldn't get Darwin out of my head. Nothin' makes sense anymore."

"Well, you won't come to any conclusions by refusing to go to church," I said. "Men of science keep their minds open to new possibilities."

Ben huffed and tried to grab my dress again, but I stepped away from him just in time.

The early February day was unusually warm, the blue sky an upturned bowl full of sunlight.

The service was held in the front room of the house, which barely held the congregation; most of the Nags Head Woods families were in attendance in their best articles of clothing, hair tamed and faces washed. I spotted all of my students and their families scattered throughout the crowd; they eased my nerves with their smiles and waves.

Alice Weeks, severe in her dark homespun dress and tight knot of hair, nodded at us from her place at the front of the room, and her husband, Roy, waved to us above the crowd. And then I saw Mr. Wharton, standing with a handsome older woman whom I took to be Mrs. Keets. We nodded at each other, as the crowd watched us closely. Ben squeezed my hand hard.

Even during the Bible reading and sermon, their eyes constantly strayed from the preacher to Ben, to me, and to Mr. Wharton. Their inattention caused the preacher to keep raising his voice, but it didn't work.

When the service came to a close, we were the first ones out the door. Ben grabbed the basket, filled with food he'd made for our picnic, and I hurried along behind him.

"So he's comin' to church service now too?" fumed Ben. "He has a lot of gumption, spoilin' the service like that."

"I imagine he was accompanying Mrs. Keets," I said.

But Ben would not be settled. "He was lookin' for you."

The sound of an approaching horse and wagon interrupted his tirade. We turned and saw Alma and Erb Ruffin atop the seat of the wagon and the rest of the family behind them in a clump.

"What do we have here?" Erb pulled the horse to a stop. "The schoolmarm and schoolmaster, snuck off for a picnic?"

"The weather's so fine, we figured we'd head to Run Hill," said Ben. "And we didn't sneak off. We just didn't want the food to spoil in the sun is all."

"What did you think of the service, Miz Whimble?" asked Alma. "Not as highfalutin as the services you're used to, I'm sure."

"I liked it very much," I said.

Louise peered over at us from the back of the wagon. "Preacher McMillan's gonna bring all of us some Bibles next time he comes," she said. "So we can try to see what-all words are in it."

Alma clucked her tongue. "What she's tryin' to say is, she didn't find a Bible in that hoard of yourn," said Alma. "She'd like to practice with it, you know."

Erb sighed. "Only book in the house is my mama's Bible. Got her name on it, but I can't read the letters."

"Bible just sits on the dresser," said Alma. "Gatherin' the dust. But Erb won't let anybody touch it. 'Cept to dust it, o' course."

"I have my mama's as well," I said. "I know how he feels. But don't worry. I'll order some for the classroom. And I can help them learn to read it. It will take time though."

"I wasn't born yesterday. I know it'll take a grist of time," said Alma, but she was grinning. "That'll be fine, Miz Whimble. See you next Sunday."

As they ambled off down the road, Ben said, "I reckon you'll be the Sunday school teacher next."

I laughed. "Wouldn't that make us a pair?"

As we climbed the sand hills, our feet sank deep into the soft grains, and we were both breathless when we got to the top of Run Hill. Gone were the days when Ben could gallop to the top of a dune; the illness had taken all of his youthful strength.

"I haven't been up here," he breathed, "in years."

More breaths, and then, "Looks different."

We walked about, looking for the loblolly pine tree that had captured our interest so many years ago. She'd been slowly dying as her trunk became more and more engulfed by sand, and by the time I'd left for Nashville, her canopy had been just brittle sticks.

But now there was nothing there but a towering pile of sand. She had disappeared for good, joining the graveyard of trees beneath, and both of us fell silent at the realization, our ragged breaths quickly coming to a stop.

"That's a shame," said Ben. "She had a lot of gumption."

He pulled from the basket a thin cloth covering to spread over the spot where we thought the tree had stood. Then we sat down, looking out over the sloping sand and the canopy of trees to the sound.

Ben pulled out a tin of corn bread, two apples, and a plate of fried fish he'd cooked at the schoolhouse this morning. He handed me a fork, and we both took bites of the cold fish.

In the quiet, I heard the ocean waves landing on the opposite shore. A woodpecker drilled nearby, and a host of gray clouds moved over the sun, reminding us that it was still February. Soon, the food was gone, yet Ben stared off to the sound, deep in thought.

At last he turned to me, his soft blue eyes reaching. "What if God *is* evolution?"

"You mean...He's the cause of it?"

He shook his head slowly, and said, "That's not it, exactly."

He was silent again, but after a while, he sat up straight and pointed at an osprey, diving with a splash into the calm water of the sound.

"Take that osprey there," he said. "What if, this very second, a change is goin' on inside of her that will make her future young'uns better divers? A tiny switch in the very folding of her wings that could make 'em hit the water just a bit cleaner, so that the fish can't even see her 'til they're eye to eye in the sky and headin' for the trees..."

"Go on."

"Mayhaps that switch, that moment of the change," he said, and snapped his fingers, "is God himself. He's nothing we can ever see or know ourselves, but He is there, inside all living things, abidin' in the changes that make species better."

My mouth opened wide, and I looked at him in wonder. In Ben's view, God dwelled in the betterment of all: a change in a feather color, a tweak in the lid of an eye, a lengthening of a toe. All around us, God breathed.

"You *did* keep an open mind in church service, didn't you?"

He laughed at the intensity of my gaze. "They're just notions, that's all. I'm not saying I believe them."

I pulled his face to me and kissed him hard. Though he lacked the physical strength of a younger man, his mind had more than made up for the absence. It was a feature of human evolution that we took for granted—the fountain of youth inside our very own brains.

Pulling back for a breath, I asked, "But what if they're true?"

"Then I reckon I just made up the most newfangled religion in the world. Darwin and Jesus, brothers forever."

Just then, the osprey emerged from the sound with a dripping fish in its talons. Its wings pumped slow and steady until the osprey was out of sight.

"You should write down your science lessons in a journal," I said. "For a textbook to be used in classrooms like ours. Perhaps I could find a publisher for it."

He grinned. "I never thought of that. A book for young'uns to learn science! I'll start tomorrow. Dr. Brooks will be happy to help, I'll bet. And Jennie could draw the pictures!"

We both lay back, our heads on the soft sand and our hands holding tight. We concentrated on the sky above us, limitless and full of promise, while the dead forest beneath us lay silent, forgotten, at least for a time.

CHAPTER NINETEEN

Benjamin Whimble
April 10, 1882
Nags Head, North Carolina

To admit all this is...to enter into the realms of miracle, and...leave...Science.
— **Charles Darwin,** *On the Origin of Species*

Sleepin' on Abby's bed wasn't as easy as she made it look. I wanted to toss and turn, but Abby was always smack up against me, her head in the crook of my arm. And oftentimes, that arm would go to sleep, so that I feared it would never wake up again. I yearned for my simple tick on the hard floor, but I wasn't about to complain, on account I loved the feel of her soft hair, her slumberin' skull on my skin.

I'd dozed a few times during the night, and each time I woke, I believed myself to be caught in a dream. The water below, streamin' through the night visions. The springtime breeze through the open windows easing my lust, if only for a bit.

But now, the morning light was comin' through the windows, and I knew Luella and Jennie would soon be here for their learnin'.

I kissed her, soft as a butterfly wing, on her parted lips.

"You best wake afore the early birds come a-knockin'."

She grinned, and opened her big green eyes. "They're both progressing well, don't you think?"

Luella had soon picked up on Jennie's hell-bent pace and tried to match herself to it, usin' the tricks Abby had taught her. She talked to her boy Bo out loud as she wrote in her journal, which annoyed Jennie right much. But they now sat side by side, helpin' each other as they plowed through their work.

"Jennie'll be ready for that job any day now," I said. "I can't wait to show her off to Dr. Brooks."

Sighin', Abby ducked her head further into the crook of my arm. We'd been two-steppin' around my summer plans, but the fact was, I'd gotten a couple of letters from Dr. Brooks, makin' sure I was comin' to help guide in two months' time.

He'd also asked about Jennie, and if she'd for sure be comin'. 'Course, I told him she was. Abby saw me writin' back to him a couple times, for I'd used her teacher desk to do it, scribblin' along in my best inky script. But she'd never said a word.

Abby sat up to stretch at last, but when I tried to move my arm, it hung back like a stubborn hound.

"Got a dead soldier here," I said. I picked it up with my other hand and shook it a bit. Slowly, the blood came sneakin' back in. "Guess it's no surprise your head is so heavy, all the brains you keep in it."

"I suppose you could sleep on the floor again," she joked. "If you're uncomfortable. I myself like the current arrangement."

"'Course you do. Got you a real nice pillow." I rubbed my stingin' arm.

"And a stove."

She knew as good as I did that I'd brought the tick back to my own abode, where Luella cackled to see it.

"I believe we need some more space," I said. "Wouldn't you agree?"

She stopped pullin' up her stockings and eyed me. "What are you saying?"

"I guess I'm sayin'...we could use us a house."

"A house? For you and me?"

"Mayhaps some chickens and pigs too. We'll have to see."

"How? How could we pay for it?" she asked. "Luella won't be living in your cabin forever, you know. I'd be perfectly happy living there. It's so close to the schoolhouse."

"That old shanty?" he cried. "Naw, that place has served its purpose as a place of livin'. It's just a holder of memories now."

I took the stockings that she was still strugglin' to put her feet into and put them aside. "Listen, I still have some money saved from last summer. Seems guidin' for some scientists is right profitable. Who knew?"

I couldn't see her face, for she'd rushed to hug me tight. Her breath came fast against my chest.

"I'm still going to sleep on your arm, though," she warned. "No matter how big a bed we buy. You can't get rid of me that easy."

"So we're buying a bed now, are we? This contraption hurts my back."

She just laughed, and hugged me even tighter.

"I'm glad you like the notion," I said to her hair. "I already arranged for some wood from none other than Mr. Wells, back in Elizabeth City. His leftover lumber arrived yesterday, and construction starts next week."

She pulled away from me, her eyes sparkin' with light. "Next week? Who's going to teach the science lessons?"

"I won't be gone for too long. Everybody's pitchin' in to help, so it should go up right fast. The students can survive without science for a couple of weeks."

"I'm not so sure about that." She laughed. "But Ben, the whole village? How did you manage that?"

"They thought it was the right thing to do, you being the schoolmarm and all. Though they'll never understand why I chose to build by the ocean again."

"The ocean?"

"Same spot as before. Well, even a little closer to the sea."

My wife looked at me, not with fear, but with wild hope. "You're tempting fate."

"The beach is wide there. Won't be like that forever, but now, well, I think it suits us."

I grabbed her arms. "I'll build her strong. We can move her if we need to. But I'm hopin' for the best."

"Don't forget a porch."

"How could I?"

We pulled ourselves together once more, and I felt to be as close to her as I'd ever been. No light between our bodies, but no darkness neither.

Who knows how long we would have stayed that way, for Luella knocked her hard and fast knock on the door and up we jumped. Luella was inside by the time we came into the school room, brushin' our hair and tyin' laces, but she seemed not to care.

She was learnin' for herself, for Bo, for all of the folks who didn't yet get the chance.

The sun was swingin' down to the west when I hopped into my skiff and sailed south toward the widow's house, not far from the Blounts' house on the sound.

John Keets had been married to Nell for a time, but he'd passed when Nell was still right young. Nell had never wanted to get hitched again, though she'd had plenty of takers being as she was so fine-lookin', not to mention her skills as a cook and seamstress. After a while, folks started callin' her "the widow Nell," and then just "the widow." I reckoned that even if she did get hitched again, it wouldn't change a thing.

And now she stood before me at the door to the old abode, her long white hair piled high in a bun, her cheekbones fit to shave a peel from an apple. She wore a nice dress of light green cotton, which lit up her cat-like eyes.

"Hey there, Nell," I said. "You're lookin' fine this evening."

"Ben," she said with a nod.

"I need to speak a word with him."

"We're sittin' down to supper," she said, her fine face pinchin' into a glare. She called over her shoulder, "Graham, Ben Whimble's here to see you. I'll send him on his way, if'n you say so."

"It's quite all right, Nell," he called. "Send him on back."

Graham? Nell?

She shook her head, disgusted. "Come on, then."

I followed her back to the kitchen, where Mr. Warthog sat at a small table, a dish of steamin' baked fish, collards and fried potatoes with gravy before him. He wasn't surprised to see me. Fact, he smiled, lookin' quite the man of leisure.

His thin grayish hair was a tumbleweed atop his head, and what's more, he was in his shirtsleeves and a pair of worn britches I'd never in my life imagined him to wear. His bare white feet shone beneath the table. There were his books and papers, ink and pen, and even a typewriter piled on a table nearby, and his many hats and coats hung on hooks nailed into the wall.

I almost laughed, for it seemed he was now the man of the house, whether he knew it or not. I reckoned Nell had just bided her time, waitin' for the right one, or at least the one with the most to offer. She'd set her own plate across from him, but now she took it up and headed out the back screen door to eat.

"Please, sit down," he said.

I sat, but I did feel queer sittin' in the widow's chair. I wondered what they spoke of durin' their meals together. The missin' of spouses? The loneliness that followed?

"That's quite a spread," I said. "Gettin' your money's worth."

He shrugged. "She likes to cook."

He nodded and took a bite of the fish and chewed. "What can I help you with, Ben?"

"This business with Abby. Still comin' and goin' from the schoolhouse, checkin' up on her, scribblin' your notes," I said. "It's enough. You need to leave us be."

"You may not understand the concept of an investment," he said, wipin' his mouth with a checkered cloth. "I've put quite a bit of money into the schoolhouse, and I'd be foolish indeed to just leave it in the hands of a woman—however capable—and a crowd of Bankers, not until I was satisfied of its continued success."

My anger rose up fast, hot as baked fish in my mouth. "That's not why you're stayin' on," I said. "You're waitin' on Abby."

He sighed, and at once looked the old man that he was becomin'. "That was true, at first," he said, sittin' back on his chair. "For many years, I believed you both to be estranged. No mention of you at all. I'm sure you can understand how confused I was when she told me she wanted to come back here. I believed—and foolishly so, I see that now—but I believed that she and I could...well, could have a happy life together."

I snickered. "She came back out here to be with me again and you know it. You've always known it. And the truth is, we're no longer 'estranged.'"

"I've heard. And I've seen you teach the science lessons. Anyone can see that you're in love with each other. And now you're building her another house, in the approximate location as the original."

"That's right."

"You're sure this is what she wants? What you want? You may end up in the same spot as before. Abby told me how hard it was, living out here. How poor you were."

"It ain't a concern of yours. And Abby's a lot stronger than you know."

He shoveled a big bite of fish into his mouth and took his time chewin' and swallowin'.

"You're wasting your time here, Ben. My life has taken another turn."

I heard a squeak from Nell, just outside on the steps.

"I won't be around nearly as often, though I'll check in at the schoolhouse from time to time. To make sure everything is running as it should be. To help her with anything she may need."

I shook my head back and forth. "Hold out your hand."

I put the chunk of ambergris in his soft white palm. He looked askance at it.

"It's ambergris."

He displayed a look of witlessness, which I savored.

"You know, from the bowels of the whale? Aged in the sea for years and years, 'til it's something worth high dollars for certain men that make perfumes?"

He pulled his spectacles from his shirt pocket and looked at the ambergris up close, then far away. He sniffed it, and backed away like it was gonna bite him in the nose.

"How can it be? It smells like...the beach. Not here, but in Nantucket. Like...a picnic, of fine wine and oysters and cheese."

His eyes grew watery, and he gripped the ambergris hard in his hand. "It's very strange, but it reminds me of my wife. My late wife, Anna."

Eliza had left this chunk with Pap when she'd come to fetch the barrel from my house, but we never had cause to use it. Fact, I tried to give it back to her a few years ago, but she wouldn't take it. She told me that, to her, it smelled of newborn pups and old books.

"We all smell somethin' different in it."

I no longer wanted to smack his face left and right. All my fight had gone. 'Course he'd loved Abby. She was somethin' golden in his life, when, after his wife had passed, all he'd had was rusted iron.

"I'm givin' this to you now, all right? To pay you back for the schoolhouse, so that it's not yours any longer, but Abby's. As for helpin' her fix anything, or buy anything, we can take care of all that ourselves. Me, and Abby, and the folks of Nags Head who care about the school. That's what Abby wants. It's what she's always wanted."

He blinked at me, then down at the ambergris. "How much is it worth? Do you have any idea?"

"That there chunk is likely worth thousands. But you'd have to sell it to a dealer to find out for sure. As you can see, there ain't many fellers out here on the Banks that could turn ambergris into bank notes."

He looked down at it for a long while, and in the silence I heard the call of a newborn osprey, hungry for fish. Its mama must be close, searchin' for its sustenance.

"If you love her, you'll let her go. It's what I did, five years past, and now it's your turn."

"All right, Ben," he said, his words doubtful as sinkin' sand. But when he shook my hand, his grip was firm. "It's yours."

"I reckon I should thank you for taking such good care of Abby for all those years," I mumbled. "She's broke up, you know, about the way things turned out between you two. Her own pap was a son of bitch if there ever was one. He moved to Texas, and she never heard from him again. I reckon she took to you like a daughter to a daddy. That's all she ever wanted from you."

His face fell flatter than a beaver's tail. "I hope I can still be a...mentor to her."

I was full of scorn, but I said, "I reckon she's way past anything *you* can teach her. But it's up to her."

I got up to go, and we said our short goodbyes. Through the window, as I made my way to the skiff, I saw him sniff the ambergris, eyes closed.

I wondered, then, if he'd ever go through with sellin' it.

The thick planks of heart pine I'd bought from Mr. Wells back in Elizabeth City had come on a barge just yesterday, and just about all the Nags Head men helped me load 'em onto wagons and bring 'em to the ocean side. For some befuddled reason, they were eager to take part in a task they all bet would fail in the first year out.

I'd picked out a spot even closer to the sea than the first house, but near to our daughter's gravestone. Now, there were just a few stumps left over from the hurricane a few years back. No protection or shade, just sand and sea and takin' chances.

But I'd learned a few things about buildin' on the ocean side since the first time I'd done it. The first house had been more like a cooter, hunkerin' down in the mud. This one would raise its head and shoulders above the sand; this one would have some flair. Two stories, with wide porches and a high hip roof, plus cypress shingles, from trees that were accustomed to water and wouldn't rot.

And of course, I'd designed it to move, for the ocean wouldn't stop eatin' the land any time soon. It would need to be repaired, and refashioned, and likely rebuilt too—but most everything in life did, eventually.

The sun was just now warmin' the sky in the east, but a dozen men had met me at the site, ready to help with the construction. The handful of ocean-side houses that the mainland folks had put up to the north of us looked on, happy for the company. Safety in numbers, they'd say, but they'd be wrong.

There was no safety to be had, out here by the mighty Atlantic. But me and Abby—well, we were ready for the view.

CHAPTER TWENTY

Abigail Whimble
May 11, 1882
Nags Head, North Carolina

But natural selection, as we shall hereafter see, is a power incessantly ready for action, and is immeasurably superior to man's feeble efforts, as the works of nature are to those of art.

—**Charles Darwin,** *The Origin of Species*

The woods greened up day by day, and everywhere wildflowers sprouted and birds conversed. Frances and Little Bud presented me a bouquet of twayblades just yesterday, and Jennie painted a picture of a water violet, which now hung on the wall beside my desk.

Even so, I constantly yearned for the ocean.

Every afternoon after school, I rode to the construction site on a young Banker pony that Ben had bought for me. Her brown coat wasn't as striking as the coat of the red pony my daddy had bought all those years ago, but she was much tamer. She'd been tried out by the Weeks to pull a wagon but was declared too slow and meandering. I called her Patience.

It had grown so warm that I kept the windows of the schoolhouse open all of the time, thankful that the screens Ben had installed the week prior prevented the numerous mosquitoes and flies from finding us.

Today I watched from a window as most of the students sailed home on their boats, which included the smallest of rowboats to the Ruffins' large skiff.

I fastened a sunbonnet to my head and stepped from the schoolhouse, glad to at last be done with coats, scarves and gloves. I closed the door behind me and trotted down the steps to the sand, but startled. Mr. Wharton stood in the shade of the shed Ben had constructed for Patience.

I hadn't seen him in a month, and he appeared almost a stranger to me. He wore a slouch hat and common leather boots. Vestless, his shirt was unbuttoned at the neck, revealing curly white hairs on his chest. His face had grown brown, and his graying beard was untrimmed. He smiled at me the way he used to, back when we were just colleagues.

"Good afternoon, Abigail. You're looking happy," he said, doffing his hat. "It is lovely weather we're having."

"It is," I said, moving to stroke Patience's muzzle. "And I am. Happy. You look the same. I like your new fashion."

He chuckled, running a hand over his balding head. "I am happy as well. Content, one might say."

"Ben told me about the ambergris," I ventured.

"Yes," he said. "An intriguing substance, is it not?"

I nodded, remembering how Oscar's dog, Duffy, believed it to be some kind of food. "I thought it smelled of soil, and freshly fallen leaves. Of my uncle Jack's coat."

He stared out to the sound, his eyes glazed and unblinking. "The schoolhouse is yours now. I'll have my attorney in Nashville draw up the papers."

"Thank you."

I smacked a mosquito on my hand, too late. "When are you departing?"

"That's what I came to tell you. I won't be departing. I'm...staying here, on the island. With Nell."

I couldn't hide my surprise at this turn of events, although word had traveled around the village that the two had become more than housemates.

He fanned the air about his face with his top hat to discourage the swarming insects.

"I won't be coming around as much as I used to. There are things I need to attend to at the house, to earn my keep, as they say. You won't be seeing me much."

He looked down at our shoes in the sand and chuckled.

"You'll find this hard to believe, but I find myself walking about in bare feet half the day. And the attire you see here. The lack of a schedule suited me, I think. I suppose it's time for me to retire."

"Perhaps it is. More time to enjoy life with a partner," I teased.

Mr. Wharton dipped his head in embarrassment. "Nell took such good care of me, you see. We had lovely walks down the shore—she's quite an intriguing person, with many interests and abilities. But unfortunately, she's illiterate, so I suggested she attend the school. But she says she'd rather that *I* teach her. So I might give it a try. In fact, I've ordered some of the same readers and slates you use. Quite a lot of them, actually. For the future school of California."

I gasped. "That's very generous! Thank you, Mr. Wharton."

The residents of California had never left my thoughts, but keeping up with the demands at the Nags Head School occupied all of my time and energy. Mr. Wharton hadn't forgotten them either.

"Ben is building some desks and benches from the scraps of leftover wood. I believe he already has a dozen or so desks and two long benches. I even have someone in mind for a teacher."

"Who?"

"Luella."

"Luella?" he asked doubtfully. "Has she progressed as far as that?"

"She has," I said, with pride for all of our hard work. "She told me of her family's desperate circumstances in Jarvisburg. Lionel is a sharecropper, working for an unscrupulous landowner, and they reside in a former slave cabin with no windows but plenty of insects and rats. She believes their future is brighter on Roanoke Island."

"She may be right."

"I mentioned the possible opportunity for her to teach the people of California, and I must say, I've never seen her quite so happy. She left for the mainland a few days ago to tell Lionel and Bo and Ruth about her plan."

"I hope it works out for her," he said. "I can see why you're so fond of her. She has an indomitable spirit that's quite infectious. She would surely make a memorable teacher."

Patience stepped forward, nudging my neck, and I laughed. I fastened the saddle to her back, and Mr. Wharton helped me up as I hitched my skirts to sit astride her, instead of riding sidesaddle.

Mr. Wharton just laughed. "I'm happy for you, Abigail. It took me some time to see it, but this special place is your home. These people are your people. And this schoolhouse is undoubtedly your own."

He lowered his head. "Please forgive me...for the strain I must have caused you. And Ben. I see now how I jeopardized everything for you. I did—I do—believe in the promise of this school. And I do care for you still...but not as I once believed I did. I'm so sorry, Abigail."

I could have shamed him even more with the long strings of insults and accusations that I often worked up in my troubled mind in the evenings before sleep. But gazing up at the schoolhouse he'd fostered, I decided to err on the side of peace.

"I do forgive you, for I know the power of a grieving and lonely heart," I said. "And now, we must be off before the mosquitoes eat us alive. I'll see you and Mrs. Keets at church service. It's to be held in the schoolhouse from now on, you know."

He nodded, smiling. "It's a generous gesture, Abigail. Perhaps one we should have thought of sooner."

He tipped his head and donned his hat as he made his way to the packed sand of the sound. To my surprise, he removed his boots and socks and stood for a while in the wet sand, lifting one foot and then the other in a slow, sticky dance.

The unusual sight made me laugh out loud as I rode along through the woods, startling Patience into a slightly quicker pace.

The house was going up quickly, with so many men helping out. But as much as Ben hurried everyone along, it wouldn't be completed until after he'd left for Beaufort, set for two weeks from today.

I spotted Ben on the porch, gesturing to Walter Ruffin. Walter, it had been found, was not only good at building but also arithmetic;

he could measure with accuracy and quickly calculate complicated sums in his head. So, in a strange turn of events, he'd become indispensable to Ben.

When Ben saw me, he jumped down from the porch and pulled me off Patience into his embrace. He smelled of sweat and sawdust.

His eyes twinkled. "Come on," he said, taking my hand. "We made some good progress today."

Walter, strong arms flexing, was sanding down a plank when I stepped up to the porch.

"Hello, Walter. Straight from school to work, I see."

He glared at me, a normal reaction and one that I didn't take personally. "I don't mind hard work."

"Oh, I've learned that by now," I said. "As long as it's not sweeping."

He didn't laugh at my jest. Even so, I reached into the pocket of my dress and pulled out a bunch of fox grapes I'd picked on the way over here. "In case you get hungry."

He took them, and I couldn't be sure, but I believed I saw a little smile on his chapped lips. "Thank you, ma'am."

Ben led me about the skeleton of the house, a ritual he'd insisted on every day I visited. The parlor faced the ocean, and the bedroom was up a narrow staircase to a second floor. A kitchen house jutted from the rear.

In the makeshift work shed, he pointed out the new desks and benches for California, blocky little structures in unfinished wood. On top of one of the desks rested a rectangular board; stepping closer, I saw that it was a fine-looking placard with the words **Nags Head School** painted on it in black. Just like the one that Mama had made for the Elijah Africa Freedmen's School.

"Figured it was about time that school had one of these," he said, coming to stand next to me. "I wanted to paint it in script, just to see you laugh. But then I thought better of it."

"It's perfect," I said. "Thank you, Ben."

I ran my fingers over the dried letters, thinking of all that had come before and wishing that everyone—Elijah, and Asha, the students, even Mama—could see that the work of education carried on, even on the remote barrier islands of the Outer Banks of North Carolina.

The men departed one by one as the daylight faded, leaving Ben and me alone. We sat on the porch steps and gazed out at the silver sea.

The waves landed every few seconds, exhaling their final breaths as they made their way up the sand. *Boom,* and then *aaahhhhsssshhh.* Again and again. A little death, or perhaps a rebirth? It was the music of our lives.

He put his arm over my shoulder, and at times we rested our heads together. We didn't speak. Our words, our thoughts, took the form of a house by the sea. Our past, our present, our future, all within these pine planks.

"If you need me, I'll be back in two shakes of a cat's tail," he said.

"And if you should need me?"

He laughed. "The same thing, I reckon."

He turned to me. "I always need you, Abby. Even when you're right here with me. I can't make sense of it."

I got up from the step and held out my hand to pull him up. Then I led him inside to the bedroom upstairs, with a view of both the sea and the sound through the windows. By the light of the moon, we undressed. Naked, we looked at the sawdust-strewn floor.

"We'll get splinters in our backsides," he warned.

He took up his shirt and pants and placed them on the floor, so I lay down on top of them. Ben gently lowered himself to me, grunting in pain.

"Did you hear all those pops?" he exclaimed. "Like an old ship at sea."

I laughed, and kissed the salty skin of his forehead. "The most seaworthy, I've heard."

He propped his head on an elbow. "You know, Bishop told me Darwin's written other books too. Books that try to answer some of the questions we've had. He plans to lend 'em to me at the laboratory this summer. Mayhaps...you could get copies of 'em too. We could read 'em sort of togetherlike this summer."

"Hmmm, I don't know. I was planning on reading a novel by Henry James. *The Portrait of a Lady,* it's called. I have a copy to give you, if you're interested."

Ben moaned and buried his head in my neck. "That sounds awful tiresome, Abby. But for old times' sake, I'll read it. Only after I've had my fill of Darwin, now."

He tickled his fingers along my belly, making me squirm. "What kind of a lady are we talking of anyway?"

"One who desires her freedom and denies several marriage proposals, only to accept one that goes dreadfully awry."

"You may find that book right familiar," he mused. "Save the part about the bad marriage."

I laughed. "We're past our troubles, then?"

"Nobody can outrun trouble. But the good news is, you can't outfox love neither."

In no time at all, our bodies came together, moving in waves as steady as the breakers rolling to shore. Now and then, my eyes reached up through the open rafters to the swirling black, with thousands of stars caught in its current, and thousands more tossed to its infinite shores like treasure.

It was Jennie's last day before leaving for Beaufort with Ben, and the students were in a somber mood.

Andy especially moped around all day; even Walter had given her a bouquet of wildflowers.

I wasn't immune to the mood either. I looked about at the walls, where her sketches filled every square inch. Sea creatures, birds, shells, and portraits of everyone in the schoolhouse.

Ben had kept the one she'd sketched of me to bring with him to Beaufort.

As the day was drawing to a close, Jennie handed me a piece of paper on which she'd drawn her own likeness. She'd taken to pinning up her hair, which made her look older and, if possible, even more beautiful.

"My very first picture of myself," she said. "What do you think? Does it look like me?"

Sadness wrapped around my throat. I could only nod.

"Is it that bad?"

"You'll need some dresses for your job," I said in a rush. "Would you like some of mine?"

"Oh, no," she said. "I couldn't take your fine dresses. Ben says I'm just gonna be mucking about with the scientists."

I gathered up two dresses from the trunk in my apartment and piled them into her arms.

"This is a new start for you, Jennie. At least arrive wearing one of them. You'll make a fine impression. Oh, and do pack your reader and some books, especially your book of Latin. Don't forget to keep learning."

She laughed. "I don't know why everybody's in such a pucker. I'll be back at the end of August, if I even last that long."

"You're ready, Jennie." I squeezed her hand beneath the dresses. "Don't forget to write me."

She shook her head in wonder. "I've never written a letter afore. Never thought I'd need to neither."

"Make sure Ben writes too. He needs the practice in script."

We laughed together, recalling how far we'd come from the early days of teaching Fido new tricks.

"I'm coming back, Miz Whimble. It may not be our birthplace, but Nags Head is our home, ain't it?"

I reached out to embrace her, dresses and all. "Please, call me Abby."

Come July, Andy and I sailed to Roanoke Island with his uncle's bigger skiff packed high with the numerous benches and desks Ben had made, as well as the crates of books and slates that Mr. Wharton had ordered.

Not surprisingly, Luella had convinced Lionel and Ruth to move to the island, and were now renting a house and farming the land in the heart of California.

George had picked us up at the docks and ridden us and our cargo to the church there. And as we rode along down the rural pathway, I saw in the distance a large group of people gathered near the road.

The closer we got, I realized the entire population of California must have come out to meet us and help us set up. I made out the faces of Mercy and Leo, who called happily up to us.

Leo helped me down from the wagon and embraced me heartily. "I can't believe my eyes, Miz Whimble," he said. "But you ain't aged a day."

"On the contrary." I laughed.

Mercy stepped over, holding a tiny baby wrapped in a blanket. "You said you'd figure out a way to help us, and sure enough, you did. Just look at all you brought."

She held the baby out for me to hold, and my arms began to tremble. But one peek at the baby's curious eyes battled away my fears, and I snuggled the bundle to my body.

"Her name is Calafia. Named her after the queen of California in that old book you sent us. Leo's been reading it to me here and there—just the parts about California, you know. The rest of it ain't worth much."

I smiled at her, and Calafia smiled back. "She looks very intelligent."

"'Course she is," said Leo. "I'm her daddy, ain't I?" He held out his arms for his daughter, then cooed down at her.

"And now she's gonna have her own school to learn at," said Mercy.

"It ain't just for her, you know," said Leo. At least two dozen children had crowded around the wagon, looking at the school supplies.

In the crowd, I spotted Luella, making way to me, a boy dragging along by a hand behind her.

"What took you so long?" she cried. "We been standing around here all day, watching the grass grow."

"There were a lot of supplies to load." I laughed.

Luella smiled down at her son, all irritation vanished. "This here is Bo. Bo, this is Miz Whimble, my teacher."

The way she'd said "my teacher" made my heart ache with gladness.

I held out my hand to shake with him. "Hello, Bo. I'm happy to finally meet you."

"Hello, ma'am," he said, then turned to Luella. "You were right, Mama. She does have a lot of spots on her skin."

"I never said any such thing," she scolded. "And anyways, they're called freckles."

A man in overalls and a straw hat sidled up to them.

"I lost you back there," he said. "Figured you'd caught sight of Miz Whimble. This must be her."

"And you must be Lionel," I said.

He removed his hat and bowed his head. "I need to thank you for all you've done for us," he said. "This here is a place full of promise, and that's a hard thing for Negroes to come by these days."

"Thank you for moving your family here," I said. "Luella's going to make a wonderful teacher."

"She already taught me my letters!" cried Bo.

"Mine too," said Lionel.

"And your mama?" I asked. "Where is she?"

"She's poorly, lying abed back at the house," said Luella. "Her heart, you know. The move seemed to make it even worse. She was sad to miss you, but she figures she'll see you soon anyway."

The desks and benches and crates of supplies passed us by, carried by many hands into the open doors of the church.

"They want me to get started today," said Luella. "But I ain't quite ready, truth be told."

"You're ready, Mama," said Bo. "Come on."

As Bo pulled her toward the church, Luella turned back to me. "I *know* you want to spy on me for a bit. Come on, then."

"I wouldn't miss it."

The windows of the church gave a generous amount of light to the room, so that the pine of the desks and benches glowed as if just hewn. But the benches were rapidly being filled with people, both adults and children, all craning their necks to see Luella at the front. Soon, there was no place left for anyone to sit, so they contented themselves with standing along the sides of the room.

I located the readers, still packed in a crate, and passed them out, gently telling them to share with the person beside them as I moved along. I counted roughly fifty people, many more than I'd imagined would come.

At last the room quieted, and Luella stood very still, her hands gripping her dress and her eyes finding mine. I winked at her, which brought a small smile to her face. She took a deep breath.

"Lord knows I done lots of jobs afore. But this here is my first time being a schoolmarm. That there is my teacher, Miz Whimble," she said, nodding at me, "and she taught me how to read and write, in spite of the fact that I had a *problem* with learning that made reading about as hard as birthing that baby boy right there! I could never be as good as her. But I hope I can be what you all need."

Everyone in the room cheered and applauded and hollered out "thank-yous" and "amens."

Luella's confident voice led everyone through the alphabet then, as everyone followed along in the readers. I slipped out the door as Luella bent to show a young girl the proper letter in the reader and joined Andy and George for the ride back to the docks.

I could hear Luella, it seemed, from many miles away.

CHAPTER TWENTY-ONE

Benjamin Whimble
August 29, 1882
Roanoke Sound, near Nags Head, North Carolina

There is grandeur in this view of life, with its several powers, having been originally breathed into a few forms or into one; and that, whilst this planet has gone cycling on according to the fixed law of gravity, from so simple a beginning endless forms most beautiful and wonderful have been, and are being, evolved.
—Charles Darwin, The Origin of Species

Tessa groaned with every swell, so loaded down was she with the marine biology textbooks, specimens and old laboratory supplies Dr. Brooks gave me to use in the schoolhouse. He'd taken a great interest in the science schoolbook too, and had promised to help find a publisher for it.

In one of her letters, Abby had told me that she'd moved the chairs and desks about to better suit the different groups of students and, in doing so, had made the classroom laboratory space even bigger.

I'd written her back just last week, telling her I doubted everything I'd collected would fit in her special space. But I told her not to worry, that I'd find the wood to make that schoolhouse even bigger. Mayhaps I'd even make the laboratory bigger than the schoolhouse itself!

Seemed like these big thoughts of mine filled the skiff up even more. And yet, *Tessa* was still missin' something.

Dr. Brooks had grown to depend on Jennie so much that she traveled with him on every outing, both on water and by land. He cottoned to the fact that she was still learnin' how to read and write, but her sketches were so fast, and so good, that he at times helped her with her labelin' and notes.

She'd learned so fast this summer that he'd asked her to come back with him to Baltimore to work at the university. She'd be back in Nags Head at Christmas time, and then who knew where life would take her. There was talk of art school and a research trip to Bermuda.

Della and the boys and even Jimmy, home for a few weeks, had traveled down to Beaufort to see her a couple of weeks back, so they'd gotten to spend time with her afore she sailed to Maryland. Not a one could get over the new Jennie, livin' in her own room and workin' such a highfalutin job with a bunch of men who talked science as easy as fishermen talkin' fish.

They were a sad bunch when it came time to leave her, but I had to hand it to Jennie—she kept up a smile the whole time she was wavin' goodbye. Her tears had been happy ones, she'd told me, with thoughts of both a bright future and a loving family waitin' for her.

And just last week, Abby had written, tellin' me that Della had started comin' to the schoolhouse now and then, learnin' to read and write so she and Jennie could keep up proper.

It'd happened thusly: The last time Digby'd tried to read one of Jennie's letters to her, he'd spun a long and winding yarn about Jennie joining up with a pirate crew and sailing for the Caribbean islands. So Della had decided she'd had enough of that nonsense— she'd read her only daughter's letters by herself, and write to her in her own words too.

Facts—that's what everybody dealt in at the laboratory. What you wanted to get was proof of an idea before you could go spoutin' off about your theory. Darwin, he did a pretty decent job presentin' his facts. But in my view, there was something missin' *in between* all the facts, something akin to magic, or spirit, that tied the whole job together.

No lab equipment could prove its existence, at least not now, but who knew about the future? Things were movin' quick now, and we all had best hold tight to the tiller to keep up.

Not wantin' to wait a minute more to see Abby, I left everything I'd brought in the skiff and just about ran as fast as I could to the new house by the sea. With all of the summer work, my body had grown a bit stronger. But I knew that strength was owed to other things besides—the fillin' of my empty heart, and the growin' of my mind.

The sun was movin' toward the sound, bringin' around that golden, dusky time of day, and the summer folks were makin' the most of it, splashin' about in the breakers and playin' games in the sand. I passed the summer homes, squattin' happy on the sand, and ran by a couple holdin' hands, their sun-filled faces full of color, just like one of Jennie's pictures.

I soon came to the house, and there she was, sittin' in the rocker on the porch, readin' a book and pullin' me back to 1868, the first time I saw her and she'd been doin' just the same thing. She looked up when I got to the bottom of the steps, suckin' wind.

"You didn't have to run," she said, smilin' big. "I'm not going anywhere."

She stood, then, and that's when I saw her belly, round beneath her homespun. She put her hands atop it and rubbed, and met my eyes with hers.

In a daze, I stepped up to the landing and put my own hands atop hers, feelin' that belly so firm and full of promise. I leaned over the circle between us and kissed her hard.

"Loretta says it's a boy," she said softly. "The way I'm carrying. Due in two months' time."

"Well, she should know, I reckon." I was havin' trouble taking the air. "You could've written to me. What if something had happened to you?"

"It would have been just words on paper. You know that," she said, movin' her hands from her belly to cup my shaggy face. "I wanted to wait."

I nodded, and we pressed our foreheads together, sharin' the memories, both good and bad, of the young'uns we'd lost along the way. They ebbed and flowed, same as the ocean beside us, and slowly my early fear turned to nothing but sunblind joy.

Abby pulled away first. "Do you want to take a walk? Or are you tired from the journey?"

I sniffed. "I'm up for it, but how about you? You're the one with child."

She laughed. "As long as I walk barefoot. My shoes have been pinching my fat feet. I can hardly stand to teach!"

I moved her skirts aside to peek at her feet, and whistled out at the sight of her pale, puffed-up flesh.

"They're like two overfed flounders! They're set to burst!"

She swatted my shoulder and yanked her skirts back over her feet.

"Well, that's the last *you'll* see of them then."

"Even if I offer to rub them every night?"

She thought a bit. "You may rub them blindfolded."

I laughed and took her hand, and we began our walk, one of likely a hundred such already walked. But this one, so different than all that came before. I wanted to fly with the gulls that soared over our heads, quick down to the sand, then out to the boilin' waves, cryin' out with that queer mix of hunger, and doubt, and the pure joy of just bein' alive in this hard, hard world!

I tried to stay calm for Abby. "Have you been ill a-tall?"

"No." Every few steps I saw a shiny white foot peek out from her skirts. "It's different this time."

The scientist in me asked, "How so?"

"It seems my body is more...welcoming," she said, givin' a shrug. "I'm not afraid of what's to come anymore. Loretta comes here almost every day to check on me and bring me special broths and poultices. And a doctor stayed in one of the nearby cottages in July, who also called on me a few times. People are curious about the schoolmarm who lives by the sea."

I tripped over my own feet then, on account I couldn't walk, talk and look at her at the same time. Her face was brown and freckled from the sun, her hair streaked with gold. And now, her beautiful face fell a bit, a portent of bad news.

"The Crafts left for the mainland across from Pea Island a few days ago. I fear the schoolhouse won't be the same without Ruby and Frances."

"We can visit, and so can they."

She nodded. "Even Andy left. The boatbuilder we met on Roanoke Island knew about Andy's education and offered him an apprentice position. He says he'll be back in the winter, but I'm not sure...maybe if Jennie returns."

She smiled sadly at me, then pointed at a shell, shinin' forth from the wet sand. "Would you?"

I bent and picked it up for her, a large nautilus.

"A new home for Stinky and Smelly," she said, holding it to her eye to peer inside.

"Those old buggers still alive?"

"Everyone takes such good care of them. Restocking the water, cleaning the tank, bringing them morsels." She laughed. "They've gotten so big, they keep outgrowing their shells. I hope they don't fight over this one."

"Survival of the fittest," I said, showin' off some of my newfound Darwin knowledge. Abby nodded and grinned, for we'd already talked of that particular theory in our many letters.

We walked for a while more, and then turned back for the house. I could just see the tip of the roof winkin' at us. Every step I took, I felt to be walkin' toward something good. A rare and precious feeling, it was—that all the hard and lonely days of the past few years had been addin' up to something of worth.

The whole way back I peeked at her belly, our babe ridin' along with Abby. All of our evolution, the best of ourselves, passed on to someone brand-new.

ACKNOWLEDGEMENTS

My first novel, *The Outer Banks House*, was published in June of 2010. Its sequel, *Return to the Outer Banks House*, was published in December of 2014. Some would say that I waited too long to publish this third novel, but sometimes, as Ben and Abby know, time allows for the clouds to clear.

It was hard to put Ben and Abby aside, but I was unsure how their stories would unfold. Years later, as I was innocently walking my dog and minding my own business, Ben and Abby appeared out of nowhere and insisted on telling me their plans for themselves, and I hurried back to my office to write down their ideas. They were pretty tired of being kept waiting. I promised them I'd start the book.

But even then, life got in the way: my family moved to Phoenix, Arizona during what we didn't know then were the *very* early days of the pandemic. There was no time or energy for story-telling, or so I believed. Much to my surprise, Ben and Abby had come with me, and my longing for Virginia, and for the beaches of the Atlantic, and for family and friends, became Abby's longing for her seaside home and Ben's longing for his lost love. Writing from the trenches of a lonely and heart-breaking pandemic, their story poured out of me; a good reunion was what we all needed, I believe.

So first and foremost, I would like to thank the readers, who let me know that they were dissatisfied with the ending of *Return to the*

Outer Banks House, and as such, dearly expected a third novel in the series. This book is for you, and for all of its future readers who know that true love should never be set aside for too long.

Thank you to my Outer Banks bookstore buyers, who continue to peddle my books: Gee Gee Rosell at Buxton Village Books, Susan Sawin (and Bill Richardson) at Island Bookstores, and Jamie Anderson of Downtown Books and Duck's Cottage. Your support has meant everything to me.

During quarantine, it was, at times, nice to be able shut the office door and get back to work, but thank you to Sean, Dorsey, Katherine and Ellery for knowing that I needed to. Thank you to my friends and family who always ask "how is that book coming along?" in spite of the fact that books take a long time to write and ennui with the timeline must surely set in.

I wouldn't be a writer without the muse of music, so I must mention FKA twigs, Tennis, Brittany Howard, Kacey Musgraves, Nathaniel Rateliff, and Bon Iver.

Thank you also to my agent, Byrd Leavell, who continues to respond to my emails, though he has long outgrown my little love stories. It was because of his belief in the story of Ben and Abby that the first novel ever caught the eye of—shall we say—an exceedingly bright editor at Crown. Thanks always to Lindsay Orman.

AUTHOR'S NOTE

The quotes at the beginning of each chapter were excerpted from the following books:

Twain, Mark. The Adventures of Tom Sawyer. Hartford: American Publishing Company, 1876.

Darwin, Charles. On the Origin of Species by Means of Natural Selection, or the Preservation of Favoured Races in the Struggle for Life. London: John Murray, 1859.